"I am one of three, three who once became one when there was need: Kyllan the warrior, Kemoc the seer-warlock, Kaththea the witch. So my mother had named us at our single birthing; so we were."

Thus opens the final saga of Andre Norton's already classic WITCH WORLD novels. SORCERESS OF THE WITCH WORLD is the dramatic and fabulous novel of Kaththea, sister-witch-protectress, daughter of an Earthman and an Estcarp Wise Woman.

Kaththea's destiny had yet to be resolved—and in her efforts to regain her knowledge of the forbidden sciences of that strange world we are drawn into a series of adventures which put a fitting and breathtaking climax to this series. It is a full-length novel, complete in itself, of fantastic adventures among strange races and on alien worlds, of high magic and low, and of wizardry and super-science.

ANDRE NORTON

Sorceress of the Witch World

ACE BOOKS, INC.
1120 Avenue of the Americas
New York, N.Y. 10036

Novels in this series include:

WITCH WORLD (G-655)

WEB OF THE WITCH WORLD (G-716)

THREE AGAINST THE WITCH WORLD (F-332)

YEAR OF THE UNICORN (F-357)

WARLOCK OF THE WITCH WORLD (G-630)

SORCERESS OF THE WITCH WORLD (H-84)

Printed in U.S.A.

I

THE freezing breath of the Ice Dragon was strong and harsh over the heights, for it was midwinter, and the dregs of a year which had been far from kind to me and mine. Yes, it was in the time of the Ice Dragon that I took serious thought of the future and knew, past all sighing and regret, what I must do if those I valued above all, even my own life, were to be free from a shadow which might reach them through me. I am—I was—Kaththea of the House of Tregarth, once trained as a Wise Woman, though I never gave their oath, nor wore the jewel which lies so heavy on the breasts of those who take it to them. But such learning as was and is theirs was given me, though not by my choosing.

I am one of three, three who once became one when there was need: Kyllan the warrior, Kemoc the seer-warlock, Kaththea the witch. So my mother had named us at our single birthing; so we were. She was of the Wise Women of Estcarp also, and was disowned for wedding with Simon Tregarth. He was no ordinary man, though, being a stranger who had come through one of the other world gates. Not only was he one learned in the stern art of war (which was of vast use to Estcarp, for that torn and age-worn land was then locked in struggle with Karsten and Alizon, her neighbors), but he had that which the Wise Women could not countenance in a man, some of the Power for his own.

Thus, upon her wedding and bedding it proved that Jaelithe, my mother, was not summarily shorn of her witchery as all believed she would be, but rather found a new path to the same general end. This raised the ire of those who had turned their faces from her on her choice. However, though they would not openly acknowledge she had proved tradition naught, they had to lean upon her support when there was great need, as there was.

Together, my father and mother went up against the remnants of the Kolder, those outland devils who had so long menaced Estcarp. They found the source of that spreading evil and closed it. For the Kolder, like my father, were not from our time and space, but had set up a gate of their own through which to spill their poison into Estcarp.

After that great deed the Wise Women dared not openly move against the House of Tregarth, though they neither forgot nor forgave what my mother had done. Not that she wed—for they would have accepted that, feeling only contempt for one who allowed emotion to beckon her from their austere path—but because she remained one with them in spite of her choice.

As I have said we were born at a single birthing, my brothers and I, I being the last to enter the world. And for a long time thereafter my mother ailed. We were put into the care of Anghart, a woman of the Falconers whom fate had used hardly, but who gave us the loving care my mother could not. As for my father, he was so enveloped in my mother's sufferings that he scarcely knew during those months whether we lived or died. And I think he could never, in his innermost heart, warm to us because of the hurt she took to bring us forth.

When we were children we saw little of our parents, for

their combined duties in that ever-present war kept them at the South Keep. My father rode the borders there as Warden, and my mother as his seeress-in-the-field and more. We lived at a quiet manor where the Lady Loyse, who had been a comrade-of-war of my parents, kept a small circle of peace.

Early did the three of us learn that we had in us that which set us apart: we could link minds so that three became as one when there was need. And, while we used this Power then for only small matters, we were unconsciously strengthening it with each use. We also instinctively knew this was a thing to be kept secret.

My mother's break with the Council had kept me from the tests given all girl children for the selection of novices. And she and my father, whether they guessed our inheritance or not, set about us such guards against absorption into the Estcarp pattern as they could.

Then it was that my father disappeared. In one of the lulls of active raiding he had taken ship with the Sulcar, those close allies of Estcarp and his old battle friends, to explore certain islands rumored to have suspicious activity sighted on them. Neither he nor his ship were thereafter sighted nor heard from.

My mother rode into our sanctuary and for the first time she summoned Kyllan, Kemoc, and me to a real trial of power. With our strength united to hers, she sent forth a searching and saw our father. With so slender a clue, she went forth again to seek him; we remained behind.

When Kyllan and Kemoc joined the Borderers and I was left, the Wise Women moved as they had long prepared. They sent to the hold and had me taken to their Place of Silence. And for some years I was cut off from the world I knew and my brothers. But other worlds was I shown and there is a kind of hunger for such knowledge born in those of my blood which feasts and grows, until at times it fills one to the loss of all else. I fought, how I fought, during those years not to yield to the temptation of full eating, to keep part of myself free. So well did I succeed that at last I was able to reach Kemoc. Thus, before they could force the final vow upon me, he and Kyllan came to bring me out.

We could not have broken the Council's bond had it not been that all the Power was gathered up for a day and night as one pulls into one hand all the threads of a weaving. They hoarded their strength that they might deal a single blow to Karsten and put an end to their most powerful enemy. They took all their force and aimed it at the mountain lands, churning the heights, twisting the very stuff of the earth by their united will.

So they had none we could not break to spare elsewhere. And we rode eastward into the unknown. Kemoc had discovered a new mystery, that those of the Old Race of Estcarp had been mind-locked in some very ancient time, and therefore the direct east to them did not exist. This had been done when they had come from that direction into Estcarp.

Thus we went over mountain to find Escore. And there, to save us and to learn what we must know, I worked certain spells, almost to the undoing of the whole land. For this was a place where in the past mighty powers and forces had been unlocked by adepts, very ancient, but of my mother's people. And they had blasted the land in their strivings for mastery. At last those who had founded Estcarp had fled, roiling the mountains into a supposedly eternal barrier behind them.

But when I wrought my spells (small compared to what had been done in Escore in the past), forces were awakened, a delicate, hard-won balance was destroyed, and struggle between good and ill once more awoke.

We came into the Green Valley, which was held by those older even than the Old Race, though they had a measure of our blood too. But they were not of the Shadow. As we stood comradely to arms, and sent forth a warn sword to summon all of good will for a combat against the Dark, there came one they accepted as of their kind.

He was of the Old Race, a hill lord who had had for a tutor one of the last of the adepts to choose to stay in Escore and not meddle. But Dinzil was ambitious and he was a

8

seeker. Nor was he corrupted by the love of domination when he first began that seeking. He was long known to the Green People and they met him with honor and good will. He was a man with much in him to draw one's liking—yes, and more than liking, as I can testify.

To me, who had known only my brothers and the guardsmen my father had set about us, he was a new kind of friend. And there was that which stirred in me for the first time when I looked upon his dark face. Also, he set himself to woo me, and that he did very well.

Kyllan had found his Dahaun, she who is the Lady of Green Silences, and Kemoc was as yet unheart-touched. Kyllan did not set hand to sword when I smiled upon Dinzil, and Kemoc's frowns I took, may I be forgiven, for jealousy because our three might be broken.

When Kemoc vanished, lost to us, I yielded to Dinzil's promise for aid in finding him, as well as to the wishes of my heart. The end being that I went secretly with him to the Dark Tower.

Now when I try to remember what was done there, I cannot. It is as if someone had taken water and a strong soap to wash away all the days I was Dinzil's aid in magic. Though I try to force myself to recall it, I have only pain and more pain within me.

But Kemoc, together with the Krogan maid Orsya, came seeking me, as he tells in his part of this chronicle. And he wrought with more than human endurance and strength to bring me forth from what had become an abiding place of the Shadow. By that time I was so tainted with what Dinzil and my own folly had plunged me into, that I stood at the end with Dinzil to do hurt to those I loved best. And Kemoc, daring to see me dead before I fell so low, struck me down with half learned magic.

From that hour I was as one newborn, for that stroke rift from me my learning. At first I was as a little child, doing as I was bid, without will or desires of my own. For a little I was content to be so.

9

Until the dreams began. I could not remember them wholly when I awoke; it was well I did not, for they were such as no sane mind could hold. And even the faint memory of some portions left me sick and cold, so that I lay upon my bed in Dahaun's feather-roofed hall and could not eat, and dared not sleep. All the protection I had learned against such ills in my days among the Wise Women had been stripped from me, so that I was as one body bare to the winter's blast. Save that what I stood naked before was worse than any sleet-laden wind, for what buffeted me was of the Shadow and very foul.

Dahaun wrought as she could, and she was a healer. But her healing was of the mind and body, and this was a matter of spirit. Kyllan and Kemoc sat by me and strove to keep the Shadow at bay. All the knowledge of those within the Valley was shaped to the end of saving me. But in those moments when I knew what they did, I understood the evil of this. For the Valley needed full protection, not only the protection of visible weapons, but also of the mind and spirit. To fight my battle weakened their defenses.

My child's clinging to the small safety and comfort they offered I must put away. So did I grow older and no longer only an unthinking child. I also knew that the dreams were only the beginning of what might attack me, and through me others. For when my own knowledge had been taken an emptiness had been left, and into that something alien was striving to pour itself.

So, even though I no longer thought as Dinzil had made me, I was still enemy to those I loved best. And I could prove a gate set in their midst through which ill could reach them, breaching their defenses.

I waited until there was an hour when Kyllan and Kemoc went into council of war. And I sent a message to Dahaun and Orsya. To them I spoke frankly, saying what must be done for the good of all, perhaps even for me also.

"There is no rest here for me." I did not ask that, I stated it as a truth. And in their eyes I read agreement. "This is also true: I am fast becoming a door to that which waits

10

only for an entrance to be shaped for it. I am a worse enemy than any monster prowling beyond your safeguards. Strong are you in ancient magic, Dahaun, for you are the Lady of Green Silences, and all which grows must pay heed to you, all animals and birds. And you, Orsya, also have your own magic, and I can testify that it is not to be lightly thought on. But I swear to you that this struggling to enter through me now is greater than you two joined together.

"I am empty—I can be filled, and with that which we would not like to think on."

Slowly Dahaun nodded. There was a sharp stab of pain within me then. For, though I knew I spoke the truth, yet some small, weak part of me had held a dying hope that I could be wrong and that she, who in her way was so much the superior of anyone I had once been, would tell me so. But rather she agreed with the verdict I had to face.

"What would you do?" Orsya asked. She had come from the stream to my side and her hair was drying, forming a luminous silvery cloud in the air, but there were still droplets of water on her pearly skin, and those she did not wipe nor shake away, for to the Krogan water was life itself.

"I must go forth from here—"

But to that Dahaun shook her head. "Beyond our safeguards what you fear will surely come, and soon. And Kyllan and Kemoc would not allow it."

"Yes, and yes," I answered. "But there is something else. I can return whence I came and find aid. You have heard that the churning of the mountains broke the power of the Council. Many of them died then because they could not contain so long the force they had to store until they aimed it. The Wise Women's rule is done in Estcarp. Our good friend Koris of Gorm is now the one who says this is done or that. But if even two or three of the great Wise Ones still live they can raise this from me and Koris will order them to do that speedily. Let me return to Estcarp and I shall be healed and you will be free to carry on battle here as you must."

Dahaun did not answer at once. It is part of her magic that

she is never the same in one's eyes, but always changing, so that sometimes she seems of the Old Race, dark of hair, white of skin, while at other times her hair is ruddy, her cheeks golden. Whether this is done by her will or not, I do not know. Now it seemed she was of my own race as she absently smoothed a strand of black hair, her teeth showing a fraction upon her lower lip.

At last she nodded. "I can set a spell, a spell which may carry you safely as far as the mountains, if your travel is swift, so you need not fear invasion. But you must aid it with all your strength of will."

"As you know I shall," I told her. "But now you must give me aid in another way, the two of you, standing with me when I tell this to Kyllan and Kemoc. They know that I will not be in danger once I reach Koris. . . . We have learned from those coming to join us that he is seeking us. But they may try to hold me here even so. Our tie is as old as our years. So we must be three set firm for this, saying even that I shall return once I am given a new inner shield."

"And this will be the truth?" asked Orsya. I did not know if she thought of me with any charity. When I was Dinzil's I had been an enemy to her, even seeking her life by my brother's hands, so she had no reason to wish me well. But if she were as one with Kemoc as I suspected, then perhaps she might, for his sake, do me this service.

"I do not think so. I might be cleansed. But to return here would be a chance I would not dare." I told her frankly.

"And you believe you can make this journey?"

"I must."

"It is well," she said. "I shall stand beside you."

"And I," promised Dahaun. "But they will want to ride with you—"

"Set your own spells, the two of you. Let them seek the border with me; I do not think we can keep them from that. But thereafter make them return. There is nothing in Estcarp for them, and they have now given their hearts to this land."

"That also can we do, I think." Dahaun replied. "When will you ride?"

"As soon as can be. If I grow too worn with this battle, I shall lose before you are rid of me."

"It is the month of the Ice Dragon; the mountains will be ill going." But again Dahaun spoke as if she were not forbidding the effort, but rather searching in her mind for ways to overcome difficulties. "There is Valmund, who has ridden those trails many miles, and we can call upon the keen eyes of Vorlong and his Vrangs to scout before you, that no great ill may lie in wait. But it will be a cruel, cold trail you take, my sister. Be not overconfident."

"I am not," I assured her. "Only the sooner I am out of Escore, the sooner will what we hold dear be the safer!"

So it was settled among us, and having set our minds firmly upon the matter how could those others stand against us? Hard and fierce arguments they raised, but we showed them the logic of what we would do, even until they were in agreement against their wills. I swore and swore again that once healed I would return, with one of the parties from overmountain. Now and again there came those to join us, their coming always made known in good time by sentinels the Green People maintained where there were passes. The sentinels were of many kinds, some scouts from the Valley, a few former Borderers who had come to serve under my brothers, others the winged Flannan, or Dahaun's green birds, whose messages only she could understand, or once in a while a fighting Vrang, wide-winged hunter from the high clouds.

It was one of those who broke our first plan into bits when he reported that the direct route to the pass over which we had first come into Escore was now closed. Some messenger or liege thing to the Shadow had wrought a sealing there which would be better avoided than assaulted—with me as one of the party facing it. I think Kyllan and Kemoc rejoiced to hear that, deeming that we would now abandon the project altogether.

Only I sweated and shrieked under the dreams more and

more, and perhaps they knew that I could not long continue to stand against that which sought to occupy me. Death would have to be my portion then, and I had sworn them to that by an oath they could not break.

Summoned, Vorlong himself came to the Valley. He perched on a rock already well worn by the scraping of his talons and those of his tribe before him, his red lizard head in bright contrast to his blue-gray feathers, his long neck twisting as he turned his eyes from one of us to another while Dahaun made mind talk with him.

At first he would not give us any hope, until, at last, with continued pressure, she brought out of him an admittance that by swinging farther east and north, it might be possible to avoid the pass we knew for a higher, more difficult passage. And he would send us a flying scout. From the Green People volunteered their best mountaineer, Valmund.

In the Green Valley the Ice Dragon was kept at bay. The season there was no cooler ever than late fall in Estcarp. As we rode past those symbols of power which kept that small pocket inviolate, the full blast of winter met us.

There were five of us who rode the sure-footed renthan—those four-footed beings who were not animals, but comrades of battle as they had proved many times, and who were the equal of all in wit, perhaps superior in courage and resource. Kyllan took the fore, Kemoc rode to my right, Valmund for a space at the left, and behind was Raknar out of Estcarp, who had chosen to go overmountain with me to my final goal, since he sought to find certain liegemen of his and bring them back to swell the host in Escore. He was a man of more years than the rest of us and one my brothers trusted highly.

Beyond the boundaries of the Valley, as the renthan beat down snowdrifts with their hooves, a shape dove from the sky to become clear in our sight as a Vrang, Vorlung's promised guide.

We traveled by day, since those of the Shadow are more used to the ways of night. Perhaps the severity of the weather

14

had immured them in their lairs, for, though we once heard afar the hunting cries of a pack of wolf-men, the Gray Ones, we did not sight them or any other of the Dark ones. We wove a way with many curves and small detours to avoid places which Valmund and the Vrang found dangerous. Some were only groves, or places of standing stones. But once we looked upon a somber building which seemed not in the least gnawed by time. In those walls were no windows, so it was like a giant block pitched from some huge hand to lie heavily on the earth. Around it the snow was not banked, though elsewhere it lay in white drifts from which a weak winter sun awoke sparkles of diamond. It was as if the ground was too warm there, so that a square of steaming earth enclosed that ominous masonry.

At night we sheltered in a place of blue stones, such ones as were to be found here and there as islands of security in the general evil of the land. When it grew quite dark pale light shone from these; that light beamed outward rather than toward us, as if to dazzle anything prowling beyond, to blind them from seeing our small party.

I tried not to sleep, lest those crowding dreams bring disaster, but I could not fight the fatigue of body, and, against my will, I did. Perhaps those blue stones had some remedy even greater than the power Dahaun had brought to my succor. For my sleep was dreamless and I awoke from it refreshed as I had not been for a long time. I ate with an appetite, and I took heart that my choice was right and perhaps our trip might be without ill incidents.

The second night we were not so lucky in finding a protected camp site. Had I still the learning I had once made my own, I might have woven a spell to cover us. But now I was the most helpless. Vrang and Valmund between them had brought us into the foothills of the mountains we must cross, but we were still heading north, rather farther to the east than would serve us.

We had rested in a place where stunted trees made a thick canopy, in spite of the fact they had lost their last

15

year's leaves. And in that half shelter the renthan knelt, giving us their bodies to lean against wearily as we chewed journey cake and drank sparingly from our saddle bottle. It was Green Valley wine, mixed with water from the springs there, a well known restorative.

The Vrang winged off to a crag of his own choosing and the men settled the watch hours among them. Again I fought sleep, sure that with no safeguard I would be vulnerable to whatever the Shadow sent after us.

I did not think beyond our piercing of the mountains and the coming to Estcarp. Only too well did my imagination create for me what might happen between this hour and that when I was again in the land of my birth . . . though I knew that in the marshaling of such ills I was harming myself.

Valmund sat to my left, his green cloak about him. Even in the gloom, for we dared not light a fire, I could see his head was turned to look toward the mountains, though before him now was such a screen of brush and tree limb that he might not see through. There was something in his stance which made me ask in a half-whisper: "There is trouble ahead?"

He looked now to me. "There is always trouble in the mountains at this time."

"Hunters?" What kind? I wondered. There had been fearsome surprises enough in the lowlands. What foul monsters might seek us out in the heights?

"No, the land itself." He did not try to hide his fears from me and for that I was glad. For what he spoke of seemed less to me than things my dreams brought. "There are many snowslides now and they are very dangerous."

Avalanches—I had not thought of those.

"This is a dangerous way? More so than the other?" I asked.

"I do not know. This is new country for me. But we must go with double care."

I dozed that night and again my apprehensions were not

16

realized. I might not have slept in a protected place, but I did not dream.

In the morning, when the light was strong enough for us to move on, the Vrang came to us. He had been scouting across the heights above since first light and what he had to report was none too good. There was a pass leading west, but we must reach it on foot, and would need a mountaineer's skill to do so.

With a great curved talon the Vrang drew a line map in the snow, went over each point of probable danger for us. Then he rose again, once more to seek the heights and so scout even farther ahead than the distance we could cover in the hours of this day. Thus did we begin our mountain journey.

II

AT first our way was no worse than any mountain trail I had yet seen, but by the time the pale sun was up we had reached that portion the Vrang had foretold where we must say farewell to the renthans and go thereafter on our own two feet. What had been a path, though steep and to be followed warily, now became a kind of rough staircase fit for two feet but not four.

The men packed our scant supplies and brought out the ropes and steel-pointed staffs which Valmund among us knew best how to use, and he now took the lead. We started up a way which was to be a test of endurance.

I could almost believe that we did indeed tread a stairway, one fashioned not by the whim of wind and weather, but by the need of some intelligence. I could not believe that the maker, or makers, had been men like us, however, for the steps were far too steep and shallow, sometimes giving

17

only room for the toe of one's boot, very seldom wide enough to set the full length of a foot upon them.

Yet there was no other indication that we trode a way which had once been a road. And the constant climb made one's legs and lower back ache. At least the wind had scoured the snow and ice from these narrow fingers of ledge so that we had bare rock to tread and need not fear the additional hazard of slippery footing.

That stairway seemed endless. It did not go straight up the slope, although it began that way, but rather turned to our left after the first steep rise, to angle along the cliff face, which led me even more to surmise that it was not natural but contrived. It brought us at last to the top of a plateau.

The sunlight which had been with us during that climb vanished, and dark clouds lowered. Valmund stood, his face to the wind, his nostrils expanded, as if he could sniff in its blowing some evil promise. Now he began to uncoil the rope which had belted him, shaking it out in loops, so that the hooks which glinted in it at intervals could be seen.

"We rope up," he said. "If a storm catches us here . . ." Now he pivoted, looking toward what lay ahead, seeking, I believed, for some hint that we might find shelter from a coming blast.

I shivered. In spite of the clothing which made me move clumsily, the wind found a way to probe at me with icy fingers which wounded.

We made haste to obey his orders, snapping the rope hooks to the front of the belts we wore. Valmund led the line, and after him Kyllan, then Kemoc, and I, and, bringing up the rear, Raknar. I was the least handy. During the border war my brothers and Raknar had had duty in mountain places, and, while they did not have Valmund's long training, they knew enough to be less awkward.

Staff in hand, Valmund moved out, we suiting our pace to his, to keep some slack in the line linking us, but not too much. The clouds were thickening fast, and while as yet no snow had fallen, it was hard to see the far end of the plateau.

Nor had the Vrang returned to give us any idea of what might await us there.

Valmund took to sounding the path before him with his staff as if he thought some trap might await under seemingly innocent footing; he did not go as fast as I wanted to, with the wind striking colder and colder.

Just as the climb up the stair had seemed to be a journey without end, so did this become a matter of trudging toward a goal which was hours, days before us. Time had no longer any true meaning. If it was not snowing, the wind raised the drifts already fallen to encircle us with bewildering veils. I feared that Valmund was indeed a blind man leading the blind, and we were as well able to blunder over some cliff as to walk a path to safety.

But we won at last to a place of shelter where the wind-driven snow was kept from us by an overhang of rock. There my companions held council as to the matter of going on or trying to wait out what Valmund feared to be a storm. I leaned back against the rock wall, breathing in great gasps. The cold I drew into my laboring lungs seemed to sear, as if I inhaled fire. And my whole body trembled, until I was afraid that if Valmund did give the signal to return to that battle outside I could not answer with so much as a single step.

I was so occupied with the failure of my own strength that I was not really aware of the return of the Vrang until a harsh croaking call aroused me. The Vrang waddled in under the overhang, an awkward creature out of its element of the upper air. It shook itself vigorously, sending bits of snow and moisture flying in all directions, and then it squatted down before Valmund in the stance of one come to settle in for some time. So I gathered that perhaps our travel for this day was over, and I slid thankfully down the wall which supported me, to sit with my legs out, my back still resting against the mountain rock.

We could not have a fire, for there was no wood to feed it. And I wondered numbly if we would freeze here under

19

the lash of the wind which now and again reached in to flick us. But Valmund had an answer to that also. He produced from his pack a square of stuff which seemed no larger than my hand when I first pulled it forth. In the air, though, as he began to unfold it, it spread larger and larger, fluffing up, until he had a great downy blanket under which we crept and lay together. From this heat spread to thaw my shivering body as it served my companions also, even the Vrang taking refuge beneath one end, its bulk making a hump.

The covering had the soft consistency of massed feathers where it touched my cheek, but it looked more like moss. When I ventured to ask Valmund explained that it was indeed made from vegetation but via insect handling, since a small worm found in the Valley feasted upon a local moss and then spun this in turn, meant to make a weather protection shell. The Green People had long since, in a manner, domesticated these worms, kept them housed and fed, using the tiny bits of substance each produced to fashion such blankets. Unfortunately, as it took hundreds of worms to make a single blanket, each one was the work of many years; there were few of them, those in existence being among the treasures of the Valley.

I heard my companions talking, but their words became only a lulling drone in my ears as I drowsed, because of the fatigue of my aching body no longer trying to fight sleep. It seemed that here all my fears faded, and I was no longer Kaththea who must be constantly alert lest I fall prey to the enemy, but rather a mindless body which needed rest so sorely that lack of it was pain.

I dreamed, but it was not one of those nightmares from which I roused crying out with dread horror, though it was as vivid, or more so, as one of those. It seemed that I lay with the others under that soothing blanket and watched, with a kind of lazy content, the roar of the gathering storm outside, secure and safe with my protectors around me.

From that storm there spun out a questing line, silvery,

alive, and this beamed over us, hovering just above our
huddled bodies. In my dream I knew that this was a questing
from another mind, one which controlled Power. Yet I did not
think it evil, only different. And the end of that silvery beam
or cord swung back and forth until it came to hold steady
over me for a space. Then I seemed to rouse for the first time
to a feeling of vague danger. But when I summoned what
small defenses that I had, the line was gone and I blinked,
knowing that I was now awake, though all was just as it had
been in my dream, and we lay together with the storm beyond.

I did not tell my brothers, for my dreams must not be used,
I made certain in my own mind, to flog them into dangerous
efforts in the mountains. At that moment I decided that, if I
did feel the touch of true evil any time as we climbed these
perilous ways, I would loosen my fastening on the life rope
and plunge, to end my problems, rather than draw them after
me.

We spent the rest of the day and the next night in our
hiding place. With the coming of the second dawn there was
light and no clouds. The Vrang took wing, to soar high, coming
back with news that the storm was gone and all was clear.
So we broke our fast and went on.

There were no more stairways. We climbed and crept, up
cliffs, along ledges. And all the time Valmund studied the
heights above us with such intent survey that his uneasiness
spread to us, or at least to me, though I could not be sure
what he feared, unless it was an avalanche.

At midday we found a place on a wider ledge than we had
heretofore traversed, and crouched there to eat and drink.
Valmund reported that we were now within a short distance
of the pass and that perhaps two hours would see us through
the worst of the journey ahead and on the down slope, where
once more we could angle east. So it was with some relaxation that we munched our blocks of journey bread and sipped
from flasks filled with the Valley brew.

We had crossed the pass well within the time Valmund

had set and were on a downward trail which did not seem so bad compared to the way we had come, when our mountaineer leader called a halt. He tested the rope ties and signaled he must reset them. So we waited while he shucked his pack to begin that precaution. It was then that the danger he had foreseen struck.

I was only aware of a roaring. Instinctively I jerked back, trying to flee—what I knew not. Then I was swept away, buried, and knew nothing at all.

It was very dark and cold and a weight lay on and about me. I could not move my arms nor legs as I tried to reach out in a half-conscious fight against that punishing burden. Only my head, neck and half of one shoulder were free and I lay face up. But all was dark. What had happened? One moment we had been standing on the mountainside a little below the pass, the next, so had time passed for me, I was caught here. My dazed mind could not fit that together.

I tried again to move the arm of the free shoulder and found with great effort I could do so. Then with my mittened hand I explored the space about my head. My half numbed fingers struck painfully against a solid surface I thought was rock, slipped over that. I could not see in this gloom, only feel, and touch told me so little—that I now lay buried in snow save for my hand, shoulder, arm, head resting within a pocket of rock. That chance alone had saved me from being smothered by the weight which imprisoned the rest of me. I could not accept that imprisonment, and began, in a frenzy of awaking fear, to push at the snow with my free hand. The handfuls I scooped up flew back in my face, bringing me to understand I might thus bring upon myself the very fate from which the rock pocket had saved me.

So I began to work more slowly, striving to push away the burden over me, only to discover I was too well buried; I could make no impression on that weight.

At last, exhausted, sweating, I lay panting, and for the first time tried to discipline the fear which had set me to such useless labor. There must have been an avalanche, sweeping us downslope with it, burying us—me. The others could be digging now to find me! Or they might all be . . . Resolutely I tried to blank out that thought. I dared not believe that a chance rock pocket had saved me alone. I must think the others lived.

More bitterly than I ever had since I had fallen in that last struggle at Dinzil's side I regretted my lost communication with my brothers. With my magic that had been rift from me also, my punishment for being drawn into the underfolds of the Shadow. Perhaps . . . I shut my eyes against the dark in which my head lay, tried to rule my mind as once I had, to seek Kyllan and Kemoc—to be one with my brothers as had been our blessing.

It was as if I faced some roll of manuscript on which I could see words, clearly writ, but in a language I could not read, though I knew that reading might mean life or death for me. Life or death—suppose Kyllan, Kemoc, the rest of our company had survived; suppose that it would be better for them now if they did not find me . . . . Only there is that stubborn spark of life in us which will not allow one to tamely surrender being. I had thought I might throw myself into nothingness in their service if the need arose. Now I wondered if I could have done that. I tried to concentrate only on my brothers, on the need that I now speak with them mind to mind. Kemoc—if I had to narrow that beaming to one, I would select Kemoc, for always had he been the closer. In my mind I pictured Kemoc's dear face, aimed every scrap of energy toward touching him—to no avail.

A cold which was not from the snow imprisoning me spread through my body. Kemoc—it might be that I tried to reach one already gone! Kyllan then, and my elder brother's face became my picture, his mind that I sought, again to reach nothing.

It was the failure of my power, I told myself, not that they were dead! I would prove that—I had to prove it!—so I thought of Valmund with what I hoped was the same intensity, and then of Raknar. Nothing.

The Vrang! Surely the Vrang had not been included in our disaster! For the first time a small spark of hope flashed in me. Why had I not tried the Vrang? But that creature had a different form of brain channel: could I succeed with him where I had failed with men? I began to seek the Vrang as I had the others.

There was the picture in my mind of the red head swinging above the gray-blue feathered body. Then—I had touched! I had found a thought band which was not that of a man! The Vrang—it must be the Vrang! I cried aloud then and the sound of my own voice in that small pocket was deafening.

Vrang!

But I could not hold that band long enough to aim a definite message along it. It wavered in and out so I could only touch it now and then. Only it was growing stronger, of that I was sure. The Vrang must be seeking us somewhere near, and I doubled my efforts to send an intelligible message. The wavering of that communication band was first irking, and then raised the beginning of panic in me. Surely when I touched that intelligent creature would try to pinpoint me in turn. Yet as far as I could sense it did not. Was the consciousness of that touch mine only, so that the Vrang could *not* be guided to where I lay?

And how much longer could I fight to hold my small sense of communication? I was gasping. For the first time I became aware that it was difficult to breathe. Had I pulled too much of the snow back on me when I made those first ill-directed attempts to free myself? Or was it that this pocket of rock held only a limited supply of air and that was becoming exhausted?

Vrang! The picture in my mind slipped away. Another took its place. And I was so startled at the single glimpse of a creature I did not expect that I lost contact.

No lizard-bird. No, this was furred, long of muzzle, pricked of ear, white or gray, like the snow about me, but with amber eyes narrowed into slits. The Gray Ones—a wolf-man! I had brought upon me a worse fate than being smothered by snow. Far better to gasp out my life in this pocket than be broken loose by the thing or things now questing for me.

I willed myself into a kind of mind sleep, trying with all my strength of will to be nothing, not to think, not to call— to hide to my death from discovery. And so well did I succeed, or else so bad had become the air about me, that I did lapse into a dark I welcomed.

But I was not to end so. I felt air blow upon my face. My body, playing me traitor, responded. But I would not open my eyes. If they had dug me free there was a small chance they might believe they had brought into the day a dead body and leave me. So small a chance, but it was all I had left to me now with my power gone and no weapons.

Then my ears rang as a baying began from far too close. It was not quite a howl, nor as sharp as a bark, but somewhat between the two. There followed a sniffing; I felt the puff of a strong breath across my face. My body jerked, not in answer to my own muscles, but because there was a grasp on my jacket close to my throat and I was being dragged along. I willed myself to lie limp, to seem dead.

The dragging stopped. There was another energetic sniffing of my face. Could the creature tell I was not dead? I feared so. I thought I heard movement away. Dared I hope—could I escape.

I raised my heavy lids and light was a pain for a moment or two, I had been so long in the dark. It was bright, sunshine. And for a space I could not adjust to it. Then a shape stood well in my line of vision.

So sure had I been that one of the Gray Ones had dug me out that it took me a long instant to see that one of the man-wolves did not crouch there. Wolf it looked, yes, but wholly animal. Its hide was not the gray of the Shadow's pack, but rather a creamy white; its prick ears, a long stripe down its backbone which included the full length of its tail, and its four well-muscled legs were light brown.

Most striking of all, it wore a collar, wide band which gave off small flashes of bright, sparkling color as if set with gems. As I watched it, my eyes now fully open in startlement, it sat on its haunches, its head turned a little from me as if it waited the coming of another. Its well-fanged jaws opened slightly and I could see the bright red of its tongue.

It was an animal, not a half-beast. And it was one who obeyed man or it would not wear that collar. So much did my survey satisfy me. But in Escore one never accepts the unusual as harmless; one is wary if one wants to hold to life or more than life. I did not stir, only slowly I turned my head a fraction at a time, to see what lay about me.

There was a mighty churning of snow, not only of the slide, but also where the animal had apparently dug to free me. It was day, though whether the same day we had come through the pass, I could not tell. Somehow I guessed it was not. The sun was very bright, enough to hurt my eyes, and involuntarily I closed them.

In that glimpse about I had seen no indication that any of our party, save myself, had been dug free. And now, as I braced myself to look again, I heard the animal once more voice its summons (for I was certain it was a summons) to master or companion.

This time a shrill whistle answered, to which the hound, if hound it was, replied with a series of sharp and urgent barks. Its head was turned fully from me as it gave tongue and I used my remaining rags of strength to push myself up. I had the feeling I wanted to face the whistler on my feet, if I could do so.

The hound did not appear to notice my struggles. It was on its feet now, running away from me, throwing up the loose snow in its going. I got to my knees with what haste I could, then to my feet, where I stood weaving dizzily back and forth, afraid to take a step in the snow lest I tumble again. The hound still floundered away, not looking back.

Now! Balancing with care lest I fall, I turned slowly, striving to discover some small shred of proof that I was not the single survivor of the slide. I swayed and stumbled eagerly to it, falling there to my knees, brushing and digging with my hands to uncover the pack Valmund had shucked moments before the catastrophe had struck.

I think I wept then, my eyes blurred, and I stayed where I was on my knees, lacking the strength to pull up. My hands rested on the pack as if it were an anchor, the only sure anchor left, in a world gone wrong.

So it was that the hound and its master found me. The animal snarled, but I would not have had the energy to raise a weapon even if I had one to hand. I stared blearily up at the man wading through knee-high snow.

He was human as to body. At least I had not been found by one of the nightmare things which roamed the dark places of Escore. But his face was not that of the Old Race. He was dressed in garments of fur unlike any I had seen before, a wide gem-set belt pulling in the loose tunic of bulky fluff about him. A hood, beruffed about the face with a band of long greenish hair like a tattered fringe, had slid back on his head to show his own hair, which was red-yellow, though his brows and lashes were black, and his skin dark brown. So wrong in shade did that hair tint seem that I could believe it a wig colored so in purpose.

His face was broad instead of long and narrow as those of the Old Race, with a flat nose having very large nostrils, and his mouth was thick-lipped to match. He spoke now, a series of slurred words, only a few of which bore slight resemblance to the common speech of the Valley, which in turn was different from what we used in Estcarp.

"Others"—I leaned forward, bearing my weight on my arms braced against the pack—"help—find—others—" I used simple words, spaced them, hoping he would understand. But he stood with one hand reaching to the hound as if to restrain that animal. Measured beside the man I could mark the huge size of the beast.

"Others!" I tried to make him understand. If I had survived that fall, surely the others might. Then I remembered the

27

rope which had linked us together and fumbled to find it. Surely that could be a guide to Kemoc, who had been before me. . . .

But there was nothing, save a tear which had cut into my jacket where the hook must have been pulled out with great force.

"Others!" My voice spiraled up into a scream. I crawled back to the tumbled snow where rocks showed here and there, ripped loose by its sweep. I began to dig, without guide or purpose, hoping that if the stranger did not understand my words, though I used the intonation common in the Valley, he would follow my actions.

His first answer was a quick jerk which nearly brought me over on my back again. The hound had set its teeth into the fabric of my jacket near the shoulder. With those fangs locked it was exerting its strength to pull me back to its master. And at that moment the animal had more strength than I could resist.

But the man made no move to approach me, nor to aid the hound in its efforts. Nor did he speak again, merely stood watching as if this was no affair demanding his interference.

The hound growled in its throat as it pulled me back. And my position was such that I could not have beaten it off, even if I had had a weapon. A final sharp jerk and I sprawled on my side, sliding down and away from where I had tried to dig into the debris of the avalanche.

There was a shrill whistle again. This was answered, not by the hound which stood over me still growling, but by a barking in the distance. Then the man waded down to me, though he did not try to touch me, only waited.

What he waited came: a sled which was a skeleton framework, drawn by two more hounds, their collars made fast to thongs. The hound which had found me stopped growling and wallowed through the snow to the sled, where he took a position slightly to the fore of his fellows as if waiting to be hitched in turn. Then his master reached down and put a firm grasp on my shoulder, pulling me up with surprising ease. I tried to struggle out of his hold.

"No! The—others—" I mouthed straight into his expressionless face. "Find—others—"

I saw his other hand lift, but I was still astounded as it flashed at my jaw. There was a moment of shattering pain as it met flesh and bone and then nothing.

III

THERE was an ache running through my whole body. Now and then I was shaken so that the sullen, constant pain became a twinge of real agony. I lay upon something which swayed, dipped, was never still, but which added to my misery by movement. I opened my eyes. Before me, across ground where the sun made a blaze to set tears gathering under lids, ran the three hounds, straps from their collars fastened to the sled on which I now lay. I tried to sit up, to discover that, not only were my wrists and ankles trussed tightly together, but over me was an imprisoning fur robe made fast to the framework of the sled.

Perhaps that was meant for warmth as well as a safeguard, but at that moment of realizing my helplessness, I saw it as another barrier between me and freedom.

The sleds I had known in Estcarp had always been more cumbersome, horse-drawn. But at the pull of the huge hounds this one moved at what seemed to me a fantastic speed. And we traveled more silently. There was no jingle of harness, no chime of bells which it was customary in the west to hang on both harness and sled frame. There was something frightening in this silent flight.

Slowly I began to think more clearly. The pain was centered in my head and that, added to the shock which had come

29

with the avalanche, made any planning now a task almost too great. My fight against the bonds was more instinctive than reasoned.

Now I ceased to struggle, slitting my eyes against the too bright sunlight, enduring the misery of my aches and pains, as I set myself to the needful task of piecing together what had happened.

I could remember rationally now up to the blow the stranger had dealt me. And it was apparent I was not rescued, but his prisoner, on my way to his dwelling or camp. Also all I knew of Escore, which I was ready to admit was very little (even the Green People did not stray far from their Valley stronghold), mostly came from rumor and legend. Yet never had I heard of such a man and such hounds.

I could not see my captor now, but thought his place must be behind the sled. Or had he sent me on alone in the care of his four-footed servants, to be made sure of before he turned his attention to other survivors?

Other survivors! I drew a deep breath, which also hurt.

Kyllan . . . Kemoc . . .

There was this, which I clung to with all that was within me, as a mountain climber might cling to an anchoring rope when his feet slipped from some precarious niche: so deeply were we united, we three, that I do not think one of us could go from this world without the others knowing instantly that a fatal blow had been dealt. Though I had lost my power, yet there was still such a need and hold that I could not believe my brothers dead. And if not dead—

Once more I fought against the cords holding me, to no avail, thumping my head against the frame of the sled behind me, the answering stab of agony was so intense that I nearly lost my senses again. Now—now I must override fear, bring to what lay before me such coolness and mind alertness as I could summon.

Among the Wise Women I had learned such discipline as perhaps even warriors need not bend to. And I called upon what was left to be my armor and support now. One thing at a time. I could not hope to aid, if aid they needed, those who were the most in the world to me, unless I won my own freedom. And to present myself as a captive who needed constant watching was to defeat any chance I might have.

I knew so little about my captor, what role I must play to outwit him. My best chance at present was to be what he had thought to make me, a cowed female whom he had beaten into submission. Though this would be difficult for one of the Old Race, especially from Estcarp, where the Wise Women had been considered the superiors of males for so long that it was bred into them to take the lead without question. I must indeed seem worse than I was, weak and easily overborne.

So I lay motionless in the sled, watching the bobbing of the hounds pulling it, trying to marshal my thoughts. Had I been able to tap the Power as once I did, I would have been free from the moment I roused, for I had no doubt that I could have brought both hounds and master under my domination. It was as if someone who had always depended upon her legs now found herself a cripple, and yet was faced with the necessity of walking a long and perilous road.

Twice the hounds came to a halt and sat panting in the snow, their long tongues lolling from between their fangs. The second time they did so their master came up beside me to look down. I had had warning enough from the crunch of his feet on the snow to shut my eyes, presenting, I trusted, a most deceptive picture of unconsciousness. I dared not look about again until the hounds were once more running.

When I did, cautiously, I saw that the surface over which we sped was no longer unbroken ahead, but that there were signs that other sled runners had here beaten down the snow. We must be nearing our goal. Now more than ever I must fix my mind on the part to be played—that of a broken captive. But as long as I could I would sham unconsciousness, that I might learn more of these people, for, by the number of tracks, I thought I could assume that my captor was not alone, but had companions in plenty ahead.

The hounds ran downslope into a valley where trees showed dark fingers against the snow, stark and clear, though the sun was now down, leaving only a few lighter streaks in the sky. The trees sheltered those we sought, but I saw the leap of flames marking more than one fire. And there arose a chorus of howling, which the hounds pulling me answered in full throat.

It was a camp, I noted between almost closed lids, not a place of permanent dwellings such as the Green People had. Though it was already dusk among the trees I could make out tents, ingeniously set to make use of the trees as part of their structures. I was reminded of Kemoc's tale of his stay among the Mosswives, whose dwellings were walled with moss hanging from the branches of age-old trees.

But these were not moss walls, rather sheets of woven hide, cut into strips and then remade in large sections, supple and easy to handle, draped and staked to form irregular rooms, each about some tree, the fire set before the door and not inside.

At each there stood, barking furiously at our coming, two, three, four of the hounds. Men came out to see the cause of their clamor. As far as I could detect in the limited light, they were all of the same general cast of feature and coloring as my captor, so much so that one could believe them not of just one tribe or clan but from a single inbred family. As the sled slowed to a stop on the fringe of the wood, they gathered close about it, which was my warning to counterfeit as best I could one who had never regained her senses.

The cover which had been part of my bonds was thrown off and I was picked up, carried to where odors of cooking fought with those of fresh hides, hounds, and strange bodies. I was dropped on a pile of stuff which yielded under me enough to cushion my aching body, yet not enough to spare me an additional throb of pain.

I heard talk I could understand, was pulled around, felt warmth, and saw light even through my closed lids as some torch must have been held close to my face. I had lost my cap somewhere during my journeying and my hair hung free. Now fingers laced in it, pulled my head even farther to one side and I heard excited exclamations as if they found my appearance surprising.

But at last they left me and I lay, not daring to move yet, listening with all the concentration I could summon to learn if I was still in company. If I was not, I wanted very much to look about.

I began to count in in my mind. At fifty—no, one hundred—I would risk opening my eyes, though I would not turn my head or otherwise stir. Perhaps even such a limited field of view would give me aid in assessing my captors.

When I reached that hundred further caution kept me still for another. Then I took the chance. Luckily the last inspection of the tribesmen had left me lying with my head turned toward the open flap of the tent and I could see a small measure of what lay beyond.

Under me was a pile of furred hides tucked over fresh cut branches which were still springy enough to give an illusion of some comfort. To my right I had a quarter view of some boxes covered also with hide from which the hair had been scraped, the resulting leather painted with bold designs, though that paint was now faded and flaking. I did not recognize any symbols that I knew.

Against the other side of the doorway was a shelved rack, made of uprights notched to have the narrow shelves set sloping toward the back. These were crowded with bags, wooden boxes, and unpainted pottery which was well-shaped but bore no decorative patterns. There also hung two hunting spears.

The light by which all this could be viewed caused me the greatest amazement. From a center pole stretched two cords running from one side of the tent to the other. Along these were draped strips of filmy stuff which was like the finest of the silken strips Sulcar raiders sometimes brought from overseas. Entangled in this netting of gauze were myriads of small insects, not dead as one might see them in a spider's larder,

33

but alive, crawling about. And each insect was a glowing spark of light, so that the numbers together gave to the tent a luminance, dimmer, yes, than that familiar to me, but enough to see by.

I was staring at these in surprise, which betrayed me when the stranger came in and caught me open-eyed and plainly aware. Angry at my own foolishness, I tried to play my chosen role, assuming an expression I hoped he would read as fear, wriggling back on the bedding as one who would flee but could not.

He knelt by the side of the bed and stared down at me critically, appraisingly. Then he suddenly thrust his hand inside my jacket with brutal force, in a manner I could not mistake. Now I did not have to play at fear; I knew it, and what he would do, as well as if I could still read minds clearly.

I could no longer hold to my role of cowed female. It was not in me to allow without a struggle what he would do. I bent my head vainly, trying to snap my teeth into the hand which was now joined by his other, ripping loose my jacket and the tunic beneath. And I brought my knees up, not only to ward him off, in an effort but to battle as best I could.

It would seem that this was a game he had played before and he took delight in it. He sat back on his heels and there was such a grin on his face as promised evil of another kind than I had known. Perhaps drawing out and prolonging my degradation was also pleasing to him, for he did not proceed as I thought he would. Instead he sat watching me as if he would think out each step of what he would do, savoring it in fantasy before taking action.

But he was never to have his chance. There was a sharp call and the head and shoulders of another appeared under the tent flap, letting me view my first tribeswoman.

She had the same broad features as my captor, but her hair was coiled and pinned into an elaborate tower on her head, the pins being gem-set so that they glinted in the light. Her fur coat was not tightly belted, but swung loose to show that under it, in spite of the chill of the weather, she wore nothing above the waist but a series of necklaces and collars of jeweled work. Her breasts were heavy and the nipples were painted yellow with petals radiating from them as if to simulate flowers.

While she spoke to my captor she stared at me with a kind of contemptuous amusement, and her air was one of authority such as would set on a minor rank Wise Woman. Somehow, I had not expected to find this among these people, though why I had deemed it a male-dominated society I did not know, except for the way the stranger had served me.

Their words were oddly accented and they spoke very fast. I thought that here and there I caught a part of speech I did dimly recognize, yet I could make no sense of it at all. Again I yearned for my lost power, even a small measure of it. Only one who has held such and lost it can understand what I felt then, as if a goodly half of me had been emptied, to my great and growing loss.

Although I could not understand their words, it was plain that they speedily grew to be ones of anger, and that the woman was ordering my captor to do something he was loath to do. Once she half turned to the door behind her and made a gesture which I read as suggesting that she call upon someone else to back her commands.

The leering grin had long since vanished from his fat-lipped mouth. There was such a sullen lowering there now as I might have feared to see had I been the woman. But her contempt and impatience only grew the stronger and she swung again as if to call that help she had indicated stood outside. Before she could do so, if that was her intent, she was interrupted by a low, brazen booming which rang in one's ears as if the air reechoed it.

And, hearing that, I for a short instant of time forgot where I lay and what ordeals might yet be before me. For that sonorous sound awoke in me something I thought I had lost forever—not only a bit of memory but instantaneous response which was for me so startling I wondered that I did not cry out as one suffering a sore wound.

Though my Power had seemingly been rift from me, memory had not. I could call to mind the skills, spells, domination of will and thought which had been taught me, even if I could not put them to use. And memory told me that what had sounded through this barbaric camp was a spirit gong. Who might use that tool of sorcery in such a place I could not guess.

The woman's triumph was plainly visible, my captor's scowl uneasy. He drew from his wide belt a long bladed knife, stooped over me to saw through those twisted cords which held my ankles tightly together. When I was free he hoisted me to my feet, his hands moving viciously over my body in a way which promised ill for the future if he could not have his way now.

Placed on my two feet by his strength as if I had no will of my own, he gave me a push forward which would have sent me helplessly on into the wall had not the woman, with muscles to match his, not caught me by the shoulder.

Her nails dug in in a grip which was cruel. Holding me, she propelled me out of the tent into a night which was alight with fires. Those about the flames did not look up as we passed, and I had the feeling they were deliberately avoiding sighting either of us for some reason. There still hung a trembling in the air, a vibration born of the gong, which had not died with the sound.

I stumbled along, both upheld and forced forward by the woman, past the fires, other tents, deeper into the woods, by a winding way which the trees gave us. With the fires well behind us now it seemed very dark and our path completely hidden. But my guard—guide—never faltered, walking confidently as if she could either see better in the dark than I, or had come this way so many times that her feet knew it by heart.

Then there was the wink of another fire, low, with flames which burned blue instead of crimson. And from it rose an aromatic smoke. That, too, I knew of old, though then it had spiraled from braziers and not from sticks set in the open. Had

36

I been brought to a true Wise Woman, perhaps some exile out of Estcarp come overmountain even as we in search of the ancient homeland?

The fire burned before another tent and this was larger, almost filling the small glade wherein it had been pitched. A cloaked and hooded figure did sentry duty at its door, stretching forth a hand now and then to toss into the flames herbs which burned sweetly. Sniffing those, knowing them well for what they were, I was heartened by this much: this was no power from the Shadow. What was fed, or could be summoned to such feeding, was not of the dark but the light.

Magic stands in two houses. The witch is one born to her craft, and her power is of the earth, of growing things and what is of nature. If she makes a pact with the Shadow then she turns to those things of evil which abide on earth—there are growing things to harm as well as heal.

The sorceress may be a born witch who strives to climb higher in her craft, or she may be one without the gift who painfully learns to use the Power. And again she chooses between light and dark.

Our Wise Women of Estcarp were born to their craft and I had been one of them, though I had not vowed their vows, nor taken on my breast the jewel as one of their sisterhood. Perhaps I could once have been deemed sorceress, since my learning went far beyond the simple witchcraft I could have wrought without struggle and preparation.

Which did I front now, I wondered as my guide bore me on toward the tent doorway? Was this a witch, or a learned sorceress? And I thought perhaps I should be prepared for the latter, judging by the evidence of that gong.

While the tent in which my captor had put me had been wanly lit by his entrapped insects, this was brighter. There were the strips of gauze with their prisoned, crawling things, but there also was, on a low table meant for one who knelt or sat crosslegged rather than in a chair, a ball of glimmering crystal. I was impelled to enter and that light which seemed to swirl fluidly within the container flared to sun brightness.

"Welcome, daughter." The accent was archaic by Estcarpian standards, but the words were not the gabble I had heard used elsewhere in this camp. I went to my knees before the globe, not compelled by my guide, but the better to see who spoke.

The Old Race do not show signs of age, though their span of years is long, until they are close to the end. And I had seen few—one or two among the Wise Women—who ever showed it so plainly. I thought that she who huddled, bent and withered, beyond the table of the crystal must indeed be very close to death.

Her hair was white and scanty, and there had been no attempt to twist and pin it into the style favored by the tribeswoman. Instead it was netted close to her skull, and that I knew, too, for it was common to the Wise Women. But she was not lengthily robed as was their fashion. Around her shoulders was the bulk of a fur coat and that hung open showing a necklace with a single large jewel as a pendant lying on her bared body where her ancient breasts were now unsightly flaps of leathery skin. Her face was not the broad, thick-lipped one of the tribe, but was narrow, with the cleanly cut features I had seen all my life, though very deeply wrinkled, the eyes far sunken in the head.

"Welcome, daughter," she repeated (or did the words just continue to ring in my head?). She reached forth her hands, but when I would have completed that old, old greeting and put mine palm to palm with hers I could not for the bindings on me. She turned to my guard, spitting words which made that woman cringe hastily down beside me, slitting at the cords with a knife.

My hands rose clumsily, the returning circulating prickling in their numbness, but I touched her skin, which was hot and dry against my own. For a moment we sat so, and I tried not to flinch from the mind which probed mine, learned my memories, my past as if all had been clearly written on an oft read roll.

"So that is the way of it!" She spoke in my head and for so

38

little I was cheered, that I had received her thought so clearly, as I had not been able to do, even with Kyllan and Kemoc.

"It need not remain so for you," she was continuing. "I felt your presence, my daughter, when you were still afar. I put into Sokfor's mind, not openly, but as if he had thought it for himself, to go seeking you—"

"But my brothers—" I broke upon her sharply. With her power could she tell me now the truth? Did they still live?

"They are males, what matters it concerning them?" she returned with an arrogance I knew of old. "If you would know read the crystal."

She dropped my hands abruptly to indicate the glowing globe between us.

"I have no longer the power," I told her. But that she must already know.

"Sleep is not death," she answered my thought obliquely. "And that which sleeps can be awakened."

Thus did she echo that faint hope I had held when I had started for Estcarp. I had not only feared that my emptiness might be filled by some evil, but I wanted, I needed, to regain at least a small part of what had been so rift from me.

"You can do this?" I demanded of her, not truly believing she would say yes, or that it could be so.

I sensed in her amusement, pride, and some other emotion so far hidden and so fleeting that I could not read it. But of them all pride was the greatest and it was out of that she answered me now.

"I do not know. There is time, but it is fast being counted bead by bead between the fingers." Her left hand moved to her waist and she dangled into my sight one of those circlets of beads which, each strung some distance from the other, are smooth and cool and somehow soothing to the touch. Wise Women use them to govern the emotions, or for some private form of memory control. "I am old, daughter, and the hours are told for me swiftly. But what I have is yours."

And so overjoyed was I by this offer of help, never thinking then that I might be enspelled by her power, or that no bargain benefits but one alone, that I relaxed, and could have wept with joy and relief, for she promised me what I wanted most. Perhaps some of Dinzil's taint remained within me, that I was too easily won to what I desired, and had not the caution I should have held to.

Thus I met Utta and became one of her household, her pupil and "daughter." It was a household, or tenthold of women such as was fit for a Wise Woman. I do not know Utta's history, save that, of course, that was not her true name. An adept gives that to no one, since knowing the true name gives one power over its owner. Nor did I ever learn how she came to be one with this band of roving hunters, only that she had been with them for generations of their own shorter lives. She was a legend and goddess among them.

From time to time she had chosen "daughters" to serve her, but in this tribe there was no inborn gift to foster and she had never succeeded in finding another to share her duties even in the smallest part, or one who could comprehend her need for companionship. And she was very lonely.

I told her my tale, not aloud, but as she read my thoughts. She was not interested in the struggle for Escore, light against dark; long, long ago she had narrowed her world to this one small tribe and now she could not nor would not break the boundaries she had so set. I accepted that when I found she might help me regain what I had lost. And I think that the challenge I represented gave her a new reason to hold to life. She clung to that fiercely as she set about trying to make of me again at least a ghostly copy of what I once had been.

IV

THE Vupsall, for so these rovers named themselves, had only vague legends for their history. Nothing that I overheard while dwelling among them suggested that they had once had fixed abodes, even when Escore was an untroubled land. They had an instinct for trade and Utta, in answer to my questions, suggested that they may have been wandering traders as well as herdsmen or something of the sort, before they turned to the more barbaric life of hunters.

Their normal range was not this far to the west. They had come here this time because of the raids of a stronger people who had broken up their larger bands, reducing most to fleeing clans. And I also learned from Utta and her handmaids that to the east, many days' travel by tribal standards, there was another sea, or leastwise a very large body of water from which these enemies had come. As the Sulcar of the west they made their homes on ships.

I tried to get more exact information, a drawing of a map. Whether they were honestly ignorant of such records, or whether they were, out of some inborn caution, deliberately vague, I never knew, but all I learned was hazy as to details.

They were restless and unhappy here in the west, and they could not settle down, but wandered almost aimlessly among the foothills of the mountains, camping no longer in any one place than the number of days to be told on the fingers of both hands, for so primitive were they in some things that was how they reckoned.

On the other hand they were wonder-workers with metal and their jewels and weapons were equal to the finest I had seen in Estcarp, save the designs were more barbaric.

A smith was held in high esteem among them, taking on the role of priest among such tribes as had not an Utta. And I gathered that few were provided with a seeress.

While Utta might rule their imaginations and fears, she was not the chieftainess. They had a chief, one Ifeng, a man in early middle years who possessed all the virtues they deemed necessary for leadership. He was courageous, yet not to the point of recklessness; he had a sense for trail seeking, and the ability to think clearly. He was also thoughtlessly cruel, and, I guessed, envious of Utta, though not to the point of daring to challenge her authority.

41

It had been his sister's eldest son who had found me via his hound's aid. And early the morning after Utta had appropriated me to her service, he came to her tent together with my late captor to urge the latter's rights, by long custom, over my person.

His nephew stood a little behind, well content to let the chief argue in his favor, even as I sat crosslegged the length of a sword behind my new mistress, the dispute being left to our elders. He watched me greedily and I thanked what Powers beyond Powers that there are walking the far winds of the world that Utta was here for my shield.

Ifeng stated his case, which by custom was clear and could not be gainsaid. I could not follow his speech, but I knew well the purport of it from the frequent glances in my direction, the gestures at me and in the direction of the mountains.

Utta heard him out and then with a single sharp-voiced sentence broke his arguments to bits. Her thought at the same time rang in my mind:

"Girl use your power. Look upon yonder cup, raise it up and bear it to Ifeng by your will."

A feat easy to do in the old days but beyond me now. But such was the strength of her order that I obediently raised my hand and pointed to one of the cups wrought of silver, focusing my will on the task she demanded of me.

I shall always think that it was her will working through me which brought results. But the cup did rise and travel through the air, to come to rest at Ifeng's right hand. He gave an exclamation and his fingers jerked from proximity to it, as if it were molten hot.

Then he swung to his nephew and his voice arose in what could only be berating before he turned again to Utta, touched his hand to his forehead in salute, and went from us, urging the younger man before him.

"I did not do that," I slowly said when they were safe gone.

"Be still!" Her order rang in my head. "You shall do far more if they will be patient. Or wish you to lie under Sokfor's body for his pleasure?" She smiled, and all the thousand wrinkles of her face creased as she read my instant reaction of disgust and horror. "It is well. I have served the tribe for long, and neither Ifeng, nor Sokfor, nor anyone else will rise to cross me. But remember this, girl, and get you to our work together, I alone am your buttress against that bed-service until you relearn such skills as shall protect you on your own."

Such logic gave me even more reason to plunge into the training she devised, which began almost at once.

There were two other members of her tenthold. One was a crone almost as old as Utta in appearance, though much younger in years for she was of the tribe. She was, however, far stronger than she looked, and her bone-thin arms, her crooked fingers, accomplished a vast amount of labor in the general work of the tent. It was she, cloaked and hooded, whom I had seen feeding the herb fire on my first night in camp. Her name was Atorthi and I seldom heard her speak. She was totally devoted to Utta, and I think the rest of us did not exist for her except as shadows of her mistress.

The woman who had brought me to Utta was also of the Vupsall, but not of this clan. She was, I learned, the widow of a chief of another tribe the Vupsall had overrun in one of the fierce feuds which kept them from becoming a united people. As spoils of war she had been claimed by Ifeng as a matter of course, only Ifeng already had two wives under his tent and one of them was very jealous.

After two or three tempestuous days of domestic altercation he had made a ceremony of presenting this human battle spoil to Utta as a servant. Within the seeress' establishment Visma had found a place which suited her as perhaps Ifeng's would not, even if she had been the first or only female there. She was a woman of natural dominating qualities, and her new position as liaison between Utta, who was seldom seen outside her tent except well muffled in furs on a sled during a march, and the rest of the clan, gave her just what she wanted. As a guard and overseer she was perfectly placed.

I think at first she resented me bitterly, but when she saw

I was not in any way a threat to her own sphere of authority she accepted me. And finally she used reports of my growing power as a new accent to her standing in the tribe.

There was a duality within the nomadic community. Utta and her tenthold reproduced a way of life I had known, a community of women using the Power to bolster their rule. Under Ifeng the rest of the encampment followed an opposite pattern of a male-dominated society.

I soon saw that Utta was right that I must make haste in learning or relearning what I could, for she could not be far from death. The wandering life of the clan was not good for her in this cold, though she was surrounded and tended by every possible comfort that Atorthi and the rest of us could offer.

At last Visma went directly to Ifeng and stated firmly that he must soon locate a more permanent campsite and there settle for a lengthy period or she could not say how long Utta would yet live. That suggestion so frightened him that he straightaway sent out his best scouts to find such a place. For Utta's service had for generations kept this clan "lucky," as they termed it, far beyond the general lot of their kind.

They had been traveling eastward again for a space of some ten days since my taking. I had no way of telling how many leagues we had put between us and the mountains, which still loomed high behind. I had begged many times of Utta a reading in her seeing globe for some news of my brothers, but she said repeatedly she was no longer able to waste her strength on such a search. Until I learned enough to lend my winging thought to hers it was a useless exhaustion for her which might even bring about her death. So it was to my self-interest, if I wished to use the globe, to protect her from such a drain and obey her commands to learn, cramming into me all she could give. I grimly noted, though, that when she was following her own desires in any matter she was far more strong and able than when I pushed for my own wishes.

I saw that I must humor her if I would gain what I had lost. And not to have her as a buffer between me and the men of the clan, especially Sokfor, who continued to follow me with his eyes whenever we were in sight of one another, was a danger indeed. Could I relearn certain parts of my Power I would be free of that peril at least: a true witch cannot easily be forced against her will—as my mother once proved in the Hold of Verlaine when one of the arrogant nobles of Karsten would have claimed the role of bedfellow.

So I bent my will to Utta's. And she was not only content but triumphant in an almost feverish fashion, working me for long hours with a hectic need, it would seem, to make me as much her equal as she could. I thought at that time it was because all these years she had sought for an apprentice and found her not, so that all the frustrations which had so long haunted her were now fastened on me.

She had few of the techniques of the Wise Women; her talents were more akin to witchcraft than sorcery, so perhaps the easier for me to assimilate now. I soon found it irking that her mind seemed to skip erratically from one piece of knowledge to another which appeared to be no kin to the first, so that what I accumulated (at the best rate I could) was a vast mass of odds and ends I never seemed to have a chance to unravel and put into any order. I began to fear that I would be left like this, an aide to her when she needed, but without enough straight knowledge in any direction to serve myself. Which was very well what she might intend.

Twice after those first days of traveling we established longer camps, one to the extent of ten days, while the hunters were out to replenish our supplies. Before each of these hunts Utta worked her magic, drawing me in to lend my strength to hers. The results of her sorcery were detailed descriptions to be set in the minds of the hunters, not only for the locating of game, but listing those places under the influence of the Shadow which must be avoided.

Such sessions left her exhausted, and we would not work together for a day or so thereafter. But I could understand how valuable was her gift for these people, and what dangers and losses lay in wait for any clan who had no such guardian.

45

I had kept track of the days since my awakening under the fringe of the avalanche. And it was on the thirtieth thereafter that our sleds swept into the mouth of a narrow valley between two ridges of very rough cliff seamed here and there by frozen runnels of water. As we descended farther into a narrow end of a funnel-shaped area, that water thawed and dripped. And the snow which had been heavy and thick-crusted became slushy and light, so that those who had ridden the sleds, save for Utta, now walked, that the struggling dogs would have lighter loads.

Finally the snow disappeared altogether. Two of the younger men trotted closer to add their strength to the pull lines of Utta's sled. The brown earth showed bits of green life, first a coarse moss, then tufts of grass and small bushes. It was as if coming down that way we had advanced from one season to another, all in a few steps.

It was warm, so much so that we must first open our outer coats, toss back their hoods, and then take them off; the men and women of the tribe both went bare to the waist and I found my under tunic sticky with sweat, clinging dankly to my body.

We came to a stream and had I not been warned by the steam which hung above it I might have tried to drink, since my throat was dry and the damp heat made me very thirsty. But this was hot water, not cool, and must arise from some boiling spring. It was its breath which made the core of the valley into near summer.

Our traveling pace had grown slower, not just because of the lack of snow for the smooth passing of the sleds, but we also paused for intervals while Ifeng conferred with Utta. That this was a place the clan longed to enter was plain, but that it might hold some great danger for them I also guessed. At last Utta gave the signal that they might advance without fear, and so we came into what had manifestly been a favored camping site—if not for this clan, then for others, and for a long time.

There were the scars of many old fires, and lengths of

46

bleached wood had been set upright to form posts for tents. Walls of loosely piled rocks were also ready to be used as additional security. And the Vupsalls speedily set about making a more permanent settlement than I had seen.

The hide walls of the tents were fortified from the outside by new walls of stone until finally the hide was only visible as a roof. In the steamy mildness of this place, however, there appeared to be less need for such protection than there had been in the snow waste through which we had come.

Pools and eddies of the hot steam provided us with water that needed no heating. And in the privacy of our hut-tent we washed our bodies thoroughly, which to me was a great comfort and joy.

Visma brought fresh garments out of those painted chests and saw that I was clad as a tribeswoman in breeches with painted symbols, a wide jeweled belt and many necklaces. She wanted to paint my breasts, having so redecorated her own, but I shook my head. I later learned from Utta that my instinct had been right, for a virgin did not so adorn herself until she chose to accept some warrior, and I might have unwittingly given an invitation I was not prepared to follow in a way acceptable to a proud clansman.

But I did not have much time to consider the formalities of daily living for once more Utta plunged me into learning, hardly giving me time to eat or sleep. I grew thin and strained, and had I not earlier known the discipline of the Wise Women I might have cracked and broken. Yet it seemed to me that Utta throve, not suffered as I did.

What she taught me was the same knowledge she used for the welfare of the clan. And more than once in the following days she put me to service answering some need of those who sought her out, sitting by to watch, but allowing me to follow through the spell by myself. To my surprise the clanspeople did not resent this as I well believed they might, asking for mistress instead of student. Perhaps it was her sitting by which led them to trust me more.

47

Healing spells I learned, and those for hunting. But as yet she had not brought me into direct foreseeing as she used when Ifeng needed it. And I began to suspect that she did this of a purpose, not wanting to give me the chance to contact any beyond this camp as I might well do, since the method of such foreseeing and the long-looking of straight mind search was largely the same.

My struggles on my own behalf seemed to be hampered in that direction; the haze which had covered my last days with Dinzil lifted enough to let me know that this was the portion of the Power which I had truly misused, and so perhaps I might never regain it. I remembered with a shiver and a feeling of hot guilt what Kemoc had told me, that, fully in the grip of the Shadow, I had used the calling to try to summon Kyllan for the betrayal of the Valley. No wonder it was now forbidden me. It is of the very nature of the Power that once misused, or used only for a selfish purpose, it can recoil or be drained past recovery.

And all my pleas to Utta to let me know whether my brothers lived or died went unanswered, save for some enigmatic statements which could be interpreted many ways. I could only cling to my belief that so strong was our birth tie I would have known it if they were dead.

My toll of days, marked on the innerside of my jacket by pinprick, reached forty and I reckoned up what I had accomplished during that time. Save for the forereading-mind search, I had as much now at my service as I had had in my second year of schooling among the Wise Women, though what I had learned was more witchcraft, less sorcery. And there were still gaps Utta could not, or would not, bridge.

Although the surroundings of our camp were much easier for the clan than the harsh necessity of travel had been, they were not idle. Now they turned to craftsmanship. Furs were tanned and made into garments, and the smiths set about the mysteries of their calling, attended by their chosen apprentices.

Hunting parties ranged out from the valley of the warm springs in greater numbers, always assured by Utta that they had naught to fear. I gathered that though the raiders were many in autumn, the winter months were not good for seafaring. Free of that danger, as well as encroachment from other clans, who had been earlier exterminated by the raiders or also driven west, the Vupsalls had an empty land to themselves.

Here it was almost possible to forget one was in Escore: we saw no ruins; there were no near places of ill repute where the Shadow taint lingered. In fact, there were no traces of the Escore I had known. And the tribesmen were so unlike the Old Race or those mutants who were allies of the Valley that I sometimes speculated as to whether they were native to this world at all, or had come through one of those Gates which the adepts had opened to make passage from one world to another possible.

We had a healing session, a child brought by its mother. A fall among the rocks had injured it beyond the knowledge of the people. I used the inner seeing and made right what was wrong, plunging the little boy into the deep sleep of healing so that he could not undo with movement what had been done. And Utta had in no wise given any aid, but had left it all to me.

When the mother had gone carrying the child, the seeress sighed, leaning back against the padded rest she now used all the time to support her skeletal frame.

"It is well. You are worthy to be called 'daughter.' "

At that moment her approval meant much to me, for I respected her knowledge. We were neither friends nor unfriends, but more like two chips hewn from the same tree whirling together in a pool to float side by side; there was too wide a span of years, experience, strange knowledge separating us for there to be more than need, respect, and agreement to bind us.

"I am old," she continued. "If I looked into that"—she gestured at the globe which ever sat at her right hand, and which she now never used. "If I looked into that I would see naught but the final curtain." She fell silent but I was held to her side by a strong feeling that there was more she must say and that it was of great importance to me. Then she raised her hand a little, signing with her fingers toward the doorway of our hut, and even that slight effort seemed to exhaust her.

"Look—beneath the mat—"

It was a dark mat, not fashioned of woven strips of hide and fur as were the others in the hut, but rather of some fiber. And it was very old. Now at her bidding I went to lift it, to look upon the underside, which I did not remember having seen before.

"Your—hand—above—it—" Her mind words were as whispers, fading.

I turned it all the way over and held my hand above its surface. Straightaway there was a glowing of lines there and runes came into being. Then I knew what bonds she had laid upon me, not by my will, but by hers. For this was a spell which would only affect those in tune to such mysteries. It would tie me to her and this way of life. And in me resentment was then born.

She hitched herself higher on the rest; her hands lay on the ground on either side of her body.

"My people—they need—" Was that an explanation, even the beginning of a plea? I thought so. But they were not *my* people; I had not accepted them ever. I had not tried to escape because she had offered me the regaining of my lost knowledge. But let her indeed pass behind the final curtain and I would be gone.

She read my thoughts easily. In our relationship I could not shut her out. Now she shook her head in a slow, wavering movement.

"No," she denied my plan, elusive as it was. "They need you—"

"I am not their seeress," I countered quickly.

"You—will—be—"

I could not argue with her then, she was so shrunken, so

50

fallen in upon her wisp of body, as if even that slight clash of wills between us had drained her almost to death.

I was suddenly alarmed and called Atorthi. We gave her what restoratives there were, but there comes a time when such can no longer keep a struggling spirit within worn-out clothing of flesh and bone.

She lived yet, but only as an anchor to her spirit, which pulled impatiently at this useless tie with the world, eager to be free and gone.

And through all the rest of that day and the next so did she lie. There was naught Atorthi and Visma could do to arouse her. Nor could I reach her via the power any more to know that she still had a faint tie with earth and us. And when I looked outside the tent-hut I saw that all the clan was sitting in silence, their eyes fixed upon the door.

At the midnight hour there was a sudden surge of life, as a high tide might flood a bay. I felt once more her command in my head as her eyes opened and she looked at us with intelligence and the need to bend us to her desires.

"Ifeng!"

I went to the doorway to signal to the chieftain who sat between two of the fires they had built as men erect defenses against that which prowls the dark. If not eagerly he came, neither did he linger.

Visma and Atorthi had braced her higher on the backrest so she almost sat upright with some of her old vigor. Now her right hand gestured me to come to her—Visma withdrawing to give me room. I knelt beside her and took her cold claw, the fingers closing about mine in a tight and painful spasm, but her mind no longer touched mine. She held to me but she looked to Ifeng.

He had knelt, a respectful distance from her. Then she began to speak aloud, and her voice, too, was strong as it might once have been when she yet kept age and eventual dissolution at a goodly distance.

"Ifeng, son of Tren, son of Kain, son of Jupa, son of Iweret, son of Stoll, son of Kjol, whose father Uppon was my first

51

consort, the time has come that I step behind the final curtain and go from you."

He gave a low cry, but her hand raised, as the grip of the other on mine tightened yet more, and she held out both to him, drawing my hand with hers.

Now he put forth both his hands to her and I saw there was not so much personal sorrow to read on his face, but fear such as might be felt by a child threatened with desertion by an adult whose presence means security against the terrors of the dark and unknown.

Under Utta's grip my hand was brought to his and she dropped it between his palms where he closed upon it with a hold harsh enough to make me cry out, had I not steeled myself against such a display.

"I have done for you the best I might," she said and the gutturals of this language I had learned were as harsh in my ears as his grip. "I have raised up one to serve you as I have"—she made a mighty struggle to complete that, the effort bringing her forward from the rest, wavering weakly from side to side—"done!" She got the last word out in a cry of triumph as if it were a war shout to be uttered into the very face of death. And then she fell back, and that last thin thread holding her to us was broken forever.

V

UTTA'S burial was a matter of high ceremony for the Vupsalls. I had never witnessed such before and I was astounded by their preparations: there was such ritual as one would not associate with a wandering clan of barbarians, but rather a civilization very old and pattern-set by years. Perhaps it was the last vestige of some age-old act which was all they had brought with them from a beginning now so hidden in the foggy past they could not remember it.

She was dressed by Atorthi and Visma in the best her traveling boxes had to offer, and then her wisp of body was bound round and round with strips of dampened hide which were allowed to shrink and encase her withered flesh and small bones for eternity. Meanwhile the men of the tribe went south for almost a day's journey and there set about digging a pit which was fully as large when they had done as the interior of the tent in which she had spent her last days. To that pit the tent was taken, along with sleds full of loose rocks, all to be set up again.

I tried to watch for my chance of escape during all this, but the magic Utta had laid upon me held and I had not enough power to defeat the runes I had so' unknowingly set foot on when I crossed into her tent. Let me try to venture beyond the boundaries of the camp alone and there came upon me such a compulsion to return as I could not fight, not unless I gave my full will and purpose to it, which a fugitive could not do.

During the four days of preparation I was left to myself in a new tent set a little apart. Perhaps the tribe expected me to make some magic beneficial to their purpose, for they did not urge me to help with the labors for Utta, for which I was thankful.

On the second day two of the traveling cases were brought by women and left just within my tent. When I explored these I found that one contained bundles and bags of herbs, most of which I identified as those used for healing, or to induce hallucinatory dreams. In the other was Utta's crystal, her brazier, a wand of polished white bone, and two book rolls encased in tubes of metal, pitted and eroded by time.

The latter I seized upon eagerly, but at first I could not master their opening. They were carved with symbols, some of which I knew, though they had slight differences from the ones I had seen many times before. On the ends of each were deeply set a single design or pattern. The markings seemed to have been less affected by time than the cases. There were fine twists of rune lettering—but I could not read it—

surrounding as a border a small but very distinct picture of a sword crossed by a rod of power. Hitherto I had never seen two such symbols in close combination, for among the Wise Women the rod was the sign of the sorceress, the sword that of the warrior, and such were considered unseemly in contact, one female, the other male.

By very close study I finally found the faint cleavage mark which was the opening of the cases, and by much labor sprung their very stiff catches. But my disappointment was great to discover, though the rolls inside were intact, that I could read neither. Their runes might be the personal jotting of some adept who had devised a code for the better keeping of secrets.

At the beginning and end of each roll the crossed sword and rod were clearly drawn in colors: the sword red, the rod green touched with gold. This at least reassured me that what I held was not of the Shadow, for green and gold were of the light, not the dark.

The drawing surprised me, for here, as was not so apparent in the pattern on the cases, the sword was laid over the rod, as if suggesting that action was the first interest of the user, to be backed, not led, by the Power. And printed with a broad pen beneath it were letters which did make sense—or at least they formed themselves into a readable name, though whether of a people, a place, or a person, I did not know. I repeated it aloud several times to see if by such sounding I could awake a spark of memory.

"Hilarion."

It meant nothing, and I had never heard Utta mention it. But then she had told me very little of her past; she had concentrated instead on my learning what she had to teach. Baffled, I rewound the rolls, slipped them once more into the cases.

For a space I sat with my two hands pressed to the surface of the crystal, hoping against hope that I would feel it warm beneath my palms, glow, become a mirror to show me what I would know. But it did not, and that, too, I returned to the chest with the wand which I knew better than to touch, since such rods of power answer only she who fashioned it for service.

On the fifth day two women came to my tent; not waiting for permission, they boldly entered. Between them they bore a heavy jug of steaming water, together with a bathing basin. A third followed them, garments laid across her arm, a tray with several small pots and boxes on it in her hands.

While the two who carried the basin and jug were commoners, she with the robes and tray of cosmetics was Ifeng's newest wife, Ayllia. She was very young, hardly more than out of childhood, but she carried herself with stiff arrogance, thrusting forward her small breasts thickly coated with paint. She had chosen so to depict two scarlet blooms, her nipples at their centers glistening as if tiny shards of gemstone were mixed with the pigment. It was a very garish display, more barbaric than those worn by the others.

Her glance at me was sharp, surely more unfriendly than any I had met since Utta had taken me as her pupil and companion. Ayllia's lips pushed forward in what was close to a pout as she swept me with a long, measuring stare which was wholly hostile.

"It is time." She broke the silence first and I think she liked me even the less that she must do that and that I had asked no questions. "We take the old one to her time house; we do her honor—"

Since I did not know their customs, I judged it best to follow their lead. So I allowed them to bathe me in the water, to which they added a handful of moss which expanded in the moisture to be used as a sponge. It gave off a faint odor, not unpleasant but strange.

For the first time I was not given the breeches of hide and fur which were the common wear, but the garments Ayllia brought, a long and wide skirt of a material very old, I thought, but preserved by metal threads woven into it in a pattern of fronds or lacy leaves. These threads were tarnished so that the design was now a very faint shadow, to be seen only by looking carefully. In color it was dark blue, which and it had a border of the same metal thread, a palm's width deep, which weighed it down, swinging about my ankles.

Under Ayllia's orders they painted my breasts, not with flowers, but with radiations of glitter pigment. They did not add to my clothing any of the necklaces which she and the other women wore; instead a veil was draped from the crown of my head, a netting of the tarnished metal thread. Once I was so clad Ayllia waved me out of the hut, taking her place behind me.

The tribe was drawn up in a procession headed by a sled. This was not drawn by dogs—the four which had served Utta walked on leashes held by tribesmen—but carried shoulder high. And in that lay, covered with choice skin robes, the body of their seeress. Directly behind that was a gap into which Ifeng's gestures urged me. Once I had obeyed, Visma and Atorthi fell in, one to my right, one to my left. They were newly clad and painted, but when I looked from one to the other, thinking to say some small word, not of comfort, perhaps—who could comfort their loss?—but of fellowship, they did not answer my glances, for each had her eyes fixed upon the sled and its burden. And each carried in her two hands, held high against her breast, a stone cup which I had not seen before. Dark liquid frothed and bubbled in the cups as if troubled by internal fire.

Behind us came Ifeng and the more important hunters and warriors. Then the women and children, so that we moved out and toward the grave in a line of the whole tribe. Once beyond the steaming pools and river of the valley it was cold and there was snow underfoot. I shivered within my ancient robe, but those walking beside me, half naked as in their tents, gave no sign of discomfort.

We came at last to the side of the excavation. And those bearing the sled went down a side ramp of earth to the tent set up below, coming from that empty-handed. Once they had returned Visma and Atorthi raised their bubbling cups and drank as women who thirsted for a long time and were

56

now given the sweetest of water. Still carrying the now empty cups they went hand in hand down to the tent and we saw them no more.

I did not realize the significance of what they had done at once, not until I saw those who held the sled dogs use their knives to kill quickly and painlessly. Then those furred servants were taken to join the human ones below. I started forward—perhaps it was still not too late . . . Visma, Atorthi—they must not—

Ifeng caught my shoulder and his strength was such that he held me helpless as the warriors laid the dogs outside the tent in the pit and fastened their leashes to stakes, as if they slept and did not darken the earth with seeping blood. And, though I wanted to run into that hole and bring out those two who had been Utta's women, I knew there was no use in trying. They had already followed their mistress beyond that last curtain from which there is no return.

I no longer struggled against Ifeng, but stood quiet in his grip, though I shivered now and then with the cold of this barren place. So I watched the members of the tribe, men, women, children, to the youngest baby at a painted breast, walk or be carried past the pit. And into it each threw some token, even the baby's hand being guided by his mother to do so. Weapons fell from men's grasps, the glint of gold from women. Small treasured boxes of scented ointment, dried delicacies of food, each gave a treasure, their greatest personal possession, I believed. I knew then the full of their regard for Utta. It must have seemed to them that a whole way of life had died with her, since she had dwelt among them for generations and was a legend while still in their midst.

The men drew then to one side and they had with them the bark shovels, the ropes for pulling stones, all they had used to dig this place and would now need to cover it from the light of day. But the women gathered around me and they took me back with them to the camp. However, they did not leave me alone in my tent.

Ayllia came with me, and several of the older women, though among them was not the chief's first wife, Ausu. When I had seated myself on one of the cushions sewn of hide and stuffed with sweet grass, Ayllia boldly pulled up another equal with it. At her move I saw several of the others frown uneasily. While I did not understand what lay in the future, I thought it well then to assert myself. Utta had named me seeress before Ifeng; I had no intent, however, of binding my future to the Vupsalls as she had done. Once I broke the rune ties on the mat I would be away.

But to achieve that desire I must have quiet and leisure to study with what power I had regained. And it looked as if that was about to be denied me.

At any rate, for a Wise Woman to accept Ayllia as an equal, chief's wife though she was, would be a grave error. I must make certain from the start that they held me in awe, or else lose the small advantage I did have.

So I turned swiftly to look full at the girl, and my voice was sharp as I asked, though perhaps my grasp of their tongue was halting: "What would you, girl?" I copied such a tone as I had heard Utta use upon occasion, which was such as the Wise Women brought to their command in the Place of Silence when a novice strove to be more than she was.

"I be she who places hand to hand." She did not quite meet my gaze; in that she showed uneasiness. But her answer was pert and had a defiant note in it: "So I am beside you."

If I knew more of her meaning I might have been prepared. As it was I could only move by instinct and that told me that I must preserve my superiority before any of the tribe.

"To One Who Sees Before do you so speak, girl?" I demanded coldly.

By ignoring her name and speaking as one who knew it not because such small matters were of no concern, I put upon her the shame of lessening in the eyes of the others. Perhaps I was doing wrong in making an enemy, but she was already my unfriend, as I sensed when we first came face to face, and I might lose more by a try for conciliation.

"To one who needs me to place hand to hand I speak," she began, when someone else entered the tent.

She walked with difficulty, leaning on the arm of a young girl with unpainted breasts and a plain face marred by a red brand down one cheek. The newcomer was an older woman, her towering pile of hair streaked with gray which silvered the bold red coloring. Her broad face was additionally swollen, as her ungainly body was fat, her breasts great puffy pillows. It was not a natural stoutness but a bloat, and she carried other signs of ill health which made me wonder why she had not been among those who sought out Utta's aid during the weeks I had trailed with them.

Two of the women by the door made haste to rise and draw forward the cushions on which they had been sitting, piling one upon the other to give greater height for the stranger, it being manifest that she would find it difficult to get to her feet otherwise.

To this seat she was lowered by her attendant and she sat there for a long moment breathing heavily, both hands pressed to her huge breasts as if to ease some pain there. At the sight of her Ayllia came to her feet, moving back to the wall of the tent, her sullen pout more pronounced, yet that slight uneasiness with which she had faced me had become almost fear.

The maidservant went on her knees to one side so that she could look from her mistress to me.

"This be"—her voice was barely to be heard above the harsh breathing of her mistress—"Ausu of the Chief Tent."

I raised my hands and made a gesture of one tossing or sowing, which I had learned from Utta. So I acknowledged the introduction.

"Ausu, mother of men, ruler of the Chief Tent, be blessings and more good than can be held in the two hands of all, on you!"

Her panting breath seemed to ease somewhat and I remembered now that alone of the tribe she had not been among those who had ushered Utta to her last resting place. It was plain to see why: her great bulk, her poor state of health would have made such an effort impossible. Now she parted her blubber lips to speak for herself.

"Utta spoke to Ifeng; she left you behind to smooth our paths." She paused as if expecting some answer or confirmation from me. I gave her what I could.

"So Utta said." Which was true but did not admit that I agreed with the seeress's high-handed ordering of my future.

"As with Utta then you come under Ifeng's hand," Ausu continued, her voice wheezing sometimes so it was difficult to understand her words, each of which whistled from her with visible effort. "I come to place hand for you. And you, being what you are, will now be head in Ifeng's tent."

Her head turned a fraction on her ponderous shoulders, just enough to allow her to favor Ayllia with a glance so cold and menacing that I was startled. Ayllia did not drop her eyes.

But it was no time to mark any byplay between these two wives of the chief. For, if I understood them aright—marriage! I was to wed with Ifeng! But did they not know that as a Wise Woman I would forfeit the power they needed by coming under any man's hand? Or would I? My mother had not. Perhaps that was superstition only, enlarged upon and nurtured by the Wise Women to keep themselves and their rule invulnerable. It was unknown in Escore. I knew that Dahaun did not anticipate any lessening of her gifts when she gave her final word to my brother and became the core of his house as well as his heart. And Utta herself had spoken of being the consort of Ifeng's long ago predecessor in the chieftainship.

Whether or not such a union was in truth a threat to my partly regained power, it was a threat to myself and one which I would not yield to unless this barbarian overlord took me by force. And there lay within close distance of my hand now such measures as would render me cold meat in his bed should the worst come. But before that last extremity there were other ways of escape, and at least one came to my mind now. None of these women could read my thoughts and I might prepare—if I had the time—such an answer as would satisfy all concerned for a space.

So did I trust I had not betrayed my surprise, which I might have well anticipated had I been only a little quicker of wit. But rather I again made a gesture of good will toward Ausu and said, "The Mother of Many does me honor as is meet between two who are as sisters," making a claim of equality as I would not do with Ayllia. "Though we have not shared the same cup as becomes those born of one mother, yet there shall be no forewalker or aftergoer between us."

I heard a murmur from the women about us as that refusal of her offer of headship over Ifeng's household was spoken, and I knew they would accept my words as binding.

She continued to eye me for a space, those eyes, half buried in her cheek and nose, on mine. Then she sighed, and the stiff erectness of her shoulders sagged a little. I was able to understand the iron will which had brought her to me, the determination which had led her to do what she believed right.

I hastened to make sure that what I needed most, my privacy would be allowed me.

"I am not as Ausu," I told her. I leaned forward and dared to take her puffy hands gently into mine. "As Utta I talk with spirits and so must have a tent to offer them room when they would visit me."

"That is so," she agreed. "Yet a wife comes to her master. And Utta abode part of the night with Ifeng when there was need."

"As is the custom," I agreed in return, my mind busy with my own answer for that. "Yet do I live 'apart. And, sister, is there not something which I can do for you? Your body ails, perhaps the spirits can find a cure—"

The oily rolls of fat making her face twisted. "It is the evil from the north. You have not been long enough with us,

61

sister, to know. This is a sending upon me for foolishness I wrought. Ah—" She broke my hold and put her hands once more to her breasts as she cried out in sudden pain. And her handmaid hurried to bring forth a capped cup made of horn, unstoppering it quickly and giving her to drink. Some of the colorless liquid dribbled from her lips to leave sticky trails across her wealth of chins. "A sending," she repeated in a whisper. "There is no answer save to bear it to my grave pit."

I had heard of such curses—illness of spirit attacking those who wittingly or unwittingly intruded upon some one of the pools of old evil, reflecting in the body the ill of soul. It would require very great power to defeat such. But this was the first time among the Vupsall I had come across any sign of some brush with the ancient ills of Escore.

There was a sudden clashing from without a loud, metallic clatter which startled me. From the women arose in answer a crooning song. Ifeng? Had my bridegroom come to claim me? But not yet! I had not had time to prepare. What might I do? And I lost most of my sureness in that moment.

"Ifeng comes." Ayllia pushed closer, though I noticed she did not go too near her superior in the household. "He seeks his bride."

"Let him enter." There was dignity in Ausu in spite of her grotesque body.

The other women drew back against the wall, with them Ausu's maidservant. When Ayllia did not follow them Ausu turned on her once more that glare which had force enough to move her.

Then the head wife raised her voice in a call. The flap was raised and Ifeng bowed his head beneath it, coming to Ausu's right. Her puffy hand groped out and he held his hard brown one where she might take it, though neither of them looked to the other, but rather to me.

I did not read in his face what I had seen earlier in his nephew's—that which promised me shame. Rather he was impassive, as one who went through a task set upon him by

62

custom and which was part of the dignity and responsibility of chieftainship. But over his shoulder I saw Ayllia's face clearly and there was no mistaking her expression: jealous rage which burned with a fierce flame.

Ifeng knelt beside the vast bulk of his first wife and now she held her left hand to me and I set mine within it, so that she brought my palm against his as earlier Utta had done. Her wheezing breath formed words I did not understand, perhaps in some archaic speech. Then her hands dropped away leaving us joined in our own grasp. Ifeng leaned farther forward and with his other hand pulled aside the metallic veil which I had draped as closely about my shoulders as I could striving to gain from it some small measure of protection against the cold. Then his fingers came down on my breasts, stripping away the paint there as one would strip away clothing. At that moment the women about the sides of the hut gave a cry which had a queer ring—not unlike that Utta had given at her death, so might they have marked some victory.

How far Ifeng proposed to go now was my growing concern. I had had no chance to take the precautions I had planned. But it seemed that the ceremony was now at an end. And, perhaps because she knew I did not know their customs well, Ausu courteously gave me the clue I needed as to the next step, and one which would carry out my own desires.

"The plate and cup now to be shared, sister. And to this tent blessing . . . ."

The maid and women swooped forward and hoisted her to her feet. I arose also to do her honor, bowing her out of the tent. Ayllia had already vanished, probably so angered by my new tie with her lord that she had no wish to witness more.

Ifeng was seated on one of the cushions when I returned and I went straightaway to Utta's chest of herbs. From it I took some dried leaves which could turn one of their ordinary brews into a fine feast-drink. These I added to the goblets which were brought on a tray to the door of the tent and shoved under the flap as if no one would now disturb us.

When he saw what I did Ifeng's eyes lighted, for Utta's stores were relished. And he waited with greedy eagerness while I dropped a few more leaves into his goblet, stirred them well with a rod.

It is not always necessary to say a spell aloud; the will being directed toward the needed result is what matters most. And my will was firm that night, the firmer for my need. I added nothing Ifeng could see except an herb he knew well, but what I added by thought was the first step in my plan of salvation.

At least Utta had not tied me in this as she had with the mat runes. Ifeng drank; he ate from the plate we shared. Then he nodded and slept. And from Utta's chest I took a long thorn of bright red. About that I wrapped two hairs pulled living from my head, and I spat upon it, saying certain words against which Ifeng's ears were now safely closed.

When it was prepared I thrust it deep into the hide cushion which supported his head, then I began weaving a dream. It was not easy to imagine that which one has never experienced, and I dared not let myself doubt that I was succeeding. But as Ifeng turned and muttered in his sleep he dreamed as well as I could set in his mind that in truth he had taken a wife and set his hand and body upon her.

Had it been so with Utta? I wondered when I was done and sat exhausted, watching him sleep in the thin glow of the netted insects. Was this how she had been wife to chiefs and yet still a Wise Woman? it would be tested when he awoke, the sureness of dream weaving.

VI

THE night was long and I had much time for thinking, also to foresee some of the perils which might now lie in wait. Utta had taught, or retaught me much, that I knew. But she had left, either by design or because we were not originally of the same order of Wise Women, blanks in my knowledge which could make me as a wounded warrior striving to defend a stretch of wall where he could only use one arm, and that the left, when the right was natural to him.

She had not given me back my foreseeing. And of all the talents the Vupsall might call upon me to display, that was perhaps the most important. I wondered more and more concerning that lack of preparation on Utta's part. Had she feared I might use the mind touch which was a part of it to bring aid from the Valley? Yet she had made no seeress of her people, bereft of the gift which would mean the most to them.

Ifeng slept on. I crept across the tent, reversed the rune mat, to read again the lines set there which bound me to those people. At the same time I searched my memory for all which pertained to such spells, their making and breaking.

There are many ways for a Wise Woman of Power to bind one (especially one who has lesser talent than herself, or who may be ignorant of such matters altogether). Such as to present something of value to the victim. If he accepts, then he is yours until you see fit to release him. But for the lesser dabbler in power that has one side danger—if he chances to refuse the gift the spell recoils upon the sender. There is a kind of overlooking with the proper spells, a weaving of dreams to drive someone from his body and make two entities slave to the witch, the soulless body and, in another world, the bodiless soul.

But mainly these were matters of the Shadow, and I knew that Utta, one-minded as she had been for the welfare of her adopted people, had not depended upon the light, nor the dark for her powers. No, if I were to break these runes to escape (and that I must do speedily) then it must be by some of Utta's own learning.

And I doubted whether my newly awakened skills could do that—yet. As in all arts practice is an aid; one advances in skill by the use of it. I crept back to Ifeng, listened closely to his breathing. He no longer dreamed the dreams I had sent him; rather was he now in a deep sleep which would hold him yet awhile. Moving with what care I could, I put off the bridal robe, folding it carefully. Now I stood with none of their making on my chilled body, scraping the remains of the paint from my breasts, putting aside all that was of the tribe. I must have nothing about me to tie me to these people, for I would try a piece of magic which I feared too great for my limping skill, but which was my only chance to foresee even a little.

There is this: any object which has been used by a human being takes to itself some impression of that owner. Though most of Utta's personal belongings had gone with her into the tomb pit, yet I had what lay in the two chests, which were part of her magic.

Shivering in the cold, I knelt by the box where I had found those scrolls with the unreadable runes. At least in handling all from the chest I had learned this much, that of all Utta had left there was the greatest concentration of Power in those.

I brought them forth, and sat, holding one in each hand, trying to make my mind an empty pool, a mirror, waiting to be filled, to bear some reflection which could come from these things.

There was a stir—slow, reluctant, thin—as if so long a time had passed between that day and this that only a shadow of a shadow of a shadow could be summoned, despite all striving to bring it into clear focus.

I was not a mirror, rather did I look upon a mirror which

66

was befogged by mist. Yet in that things moved dimly; dusty, dusky figures came and went. It was no use! I could not make them clear.

The containers in my hands grew heavier, dragging down my arms. Against the uncovered skin of my body they were icy cold, so that I shuddered.

If not the encased rolls, then what of the rolls themselves? One I laid aside, the other I opened, brought forth the scroll. This I took in both hands, lowered my head that I might press my forehead to a surface which felt like a long dried leaf.

Now—

I might almost have cried out at the sharp picture leaping into my mind had not long discipline warned me. It was a filling right enough, but such a filling, whirling about wildly, scenes which flashed so fast I could not grasp their significance. Lines of formulas, columns of runes came and went before I could guess their meaning. There was no reason, logic, nor sequence to this. It was as if someone had emptied a vast amount of poorly related material into an empty bin, and stirred it vigorously about.

I dropped the roll, thrust it back into its container. Then I put my hands to my head where that whirling of ill-timed, ill-sorted odds and ends of learning started such a pain as I had felt upon my first coming to the Vupsall camp. Nor could I at that moment advance further in my trial and error searching for Utta's secrets. I was suddenly so tired that I could not keep my eyes open. Almost, I thought with a small surge of unease, as if I had drunk such a cup as I had put in Ifeng's hands and was now about to follow him into a dream world.

I pulled myself together long enough to dress in the clothing I had laid aside when they had given me the marriage robe, though I moved sluggishly. Drawing one of the hooded cloaks about me, I fell back rather than laid me down, to sleep. And I had been right: I dreamed.

There was a castle, a keep as great, or so it seemed, as

that citadel which centered Es City. It was the largest work of men's hands I had ever seen. In parts it was as solid as the stones of Es, yet other parts shimmered, came and went, as if they had substance in this world, yet in another also. Though I knew that, I did not understand the why or how of it.

And there was one who wrought all this, both by the work of the hands of those he commanded, and by Power. The master here was no Wise Woman, but an adept who was far more than warlock or wizard. And the castle was only the outer casing of something which was strange and of greater power than the walls about it.

I saw him, sometimes as only a shadow thing, as I had seen when I held the tube to me, and again as clear as if he stepped at intervals from behind some veil held about him by spells. He was of the Old Race, and yet there was that about him which argued that he was partly of another time and place.

He was working with Power, and I saw him do things as if he gathered up the raw strings of force to weave them and shape them this way and that into a pattern obeying his desires. He moved confidently, as one who well knows what he would do and has no fear that it shall not follow his desire. Watching him I knew a bitter envy. So once had I almost known the same sureness, before I had become one to creep blindly where I would have run.

Under his feet runes burst in lines of fire, and the very air about him was troubled by the words he uttered, or the strength of his thought sendings. This was greater than aught I had ever seen, though it had been given me once or twice to watch the most powerful of the Wise Women at their spelling.

Now that I saw all his weaving and building was centered in the hall in which he worked, the lines of the runes, the troubling and stirring of the air gathered into one place. Finally there was to be seen there, standing straight, an arch-way of light. And I knew that what my dream showed me was the creation of one of those gateways to another world which are to be found in this ancient, sorcery steeped land. That they existed was well known, but that they were created by adepts, that we had learned only after we had come into Escore. Now I had witnessed the opening of one.

He stood there, his feet planted a little apart, his arms suddenly flung up and back in a gesture which was wholly human, one of triumph. The calm concentration on his face became fierce exultation. But, having his gate, he did not hurry to enter it.

Rather did he retreat from it step by step, though I saw no sign that his confidence ebbed. I believe that he felt then some unease which kept him from any rash leap into the unknown. So he seated himself on a chair and sat there, looking at the gate, his hands folded palm to palm, raised so that his steepled fingers touched his pointed chin, his look of one deep in thought or planning.

While he sat so considering his creation, I continued to watch him, as if the man himself and not the sorcery in which he had been engaged had drawn my dreaming. As I have said, he was of the Old Race, or was at least a hybrid of that breeding. Was he young—old? No age touched him. He had the body of a man of action, a warrior, though he wore no sword. His robe was gray and belted tightly about his narrow middle with a sash of scarlet along which rippled lines of gold and silver. If one fastened attention on them long enough, these lines seemed to take the form of runes, yet they glowed quickly and faded before one could read them.

He appeared to come to some decision, for he arose and held up his hands a little apart. As he brought them together with a sharp clap I saw his lips move. And in answer that gateway disappeared and he was in a steadily darkening hall. But it was in my mind that having so wrought once he could do it again, that his triumph remained.

But it would seem that my dream had only this much to show within that hall. Then I was outside, going down a passage, and between great towering gates on which crouched creatures out of nightmares; they turned their heads to look solemnly upon me as I passed, yet I knew they were bound against harming such as I.

That journey was in such detail that I thought, should I, waking, come upon that same place I would know it instantly and be able to find my way again into that hall, as if I had been born within those walls and lived there through my childhood.

The reason for my dream I did not know, though such dreaming is always sent for a purpose. I could only believe, when I awakened, that it had sprung from my attempt to "read" the scroll. My head still ached with a pain which made the morning light a torment to my eyes. But I sat up with a jerk and looked to where Ifeng slept. He was stirring and I lurched quickly to him, drew forth the thorn, hiding it in the hem of my cloak, and then sank back as he opened his eyes.

He blinked, and, as intelligence came back into his face, he smiled oddly with a kind of shyness which sat oddly on such a man.

"Fair morning . . ."

"Fair morning, leader of men." I gave him formal greeting in return.

He sat up on the cushions and looked about him as if he were not quite sure of where he had rested that night. For a moment or two I was wary, wondering if the dream I had spun for him had been so badly woven that he would know it for a dream. But it would seem that I need not have feared, for now he bowed his head in my direction and said, "Strength grows strength, Farseeing One. I have taken your gift to me and we shall be great always, even as it was under Utta's hand." Then he made a gesture with two fingers crossed which was common to his people when they spoke of the dead, so warding off any ill from naming those gone before. He went from me as a man well satisfied in the doing of some duty.

But if the dream satisfied Ifeng and those of the tribe he must have reassured with his account of that night, it also made me an enemy—this I was not long in discovering. For, after the custom, I was visited during the morning by the senior and chief women of the tribe, all bringing gifts. Ausu did not come to me since I had made it clear that we were equal in Ifeng's family, but Ayllia was the last to visit my tent.

She came alone, and when I was alone, as if she had waited until there was none to witness our meeting. And when she entered, her hostility was like a dark cloud about her. So much had my powers advanced that I could so read danger when I met it face to face.

Alone among her people she seemed in no awe of my sorcery. It was almost as if she could herself look into my mind and know how little I really knew. Now she did not sit, nor did she give me any formal greeting. But she flung with force, so that it struck the ground before me and burst open, spilling forth its contents, a small box cunningly and beautifully fashioned. And the necklace it had held was a great work of art.

"Bride price, elder one." Her mouth twisted as if the words she spoke tasted bitter. "With Ausu's welcome—"

I dared not allow her this insolence. "And yours, younger sister?" I asked coldly.

"No!" She dared that denial, though I noted she held her voice prudently low. For some reason she was wrought to strong anger, but she still had prudence in that she did not want those who might listen to know ill feeling lay so nakedly between us.

"You hate me," I put the matter bluntly; "why?"

Now she did come to her knees so that her face was nearer on a level to mine. She thrust her head forward so that I could see the congestion of fury darkening it, the small flecks of spittle at the corners of her wide mouth.

"Ausu is old; she is ruler in Ifeng's tent only in small things. She is sick—she no longer cares." The words came forth in a rush bringing mouth moisture with it to touch my cheek. "I"—her fist beat against her gaudily painted breast—"I am chief in Ifeng's sight, or was. Until your witchery stole his mind. Aye, dealer in spells, blast me, turn me into a worm

71

to be crushed beneath the boot, to a hound to draw a sled, to a stone to lie unheeding—better would that be to me than what I am now in the tent of Ifeng."

And I knew she spoke the truth. In her rage of jealousy she would rather have me enchant her as she believed I could rather than take her place and leave her to watch what she believed to be my triumph over her. It was the courage of complete despair and envy past bearing which led her to defy the person she thought I was.

"I want not Ifeng," I said steadily. Once I might have taken over her mind, her will, made her believe what I said was so. Now I strove to impress her with the truth, but I feared with small success.

At least she sat silent, as if she were thinking upon my answer. And I hastened to use any small advantage I might have gained.

"I am a dealer in spells, as you have said," I told her. "I do not depend upon the good will of any man, be he chief or warrior only. It is within me—me—do you understand that, girl?" I brought my hands to my breasts, took upon me with what I hoped was good effect a semblance of the arrogance the Wise Women wore as easily as their robes and jewels.

"You lay with Ifeng," she said sullenly, but her eyes dropped, seemed to study the open box and tumbled necklace which lay between us.

"For the good of the tribe. Is it not the custom?" I might—just might—have disarmed her completely with the true version of the night, yet I decided against it. To keep one's secrets well is the first lesson of any seeker after knowledge.

"He—he will come again! He is a man who had tasted a feast and goes hungry until he eats so again!" she cried out.

"No, he will not come again," I told her, and hoped I spoke the truth. "For this is true of those of us who walk the path of Power: we cannot lie with a man and use still our learning. Once—to make sure our strength passes to the chief in part as it should—but not again."

She met my eyes and this time her anger was dulled, but her stubbornness did not yield. "What cares a hungry man for words? They but sound in his ears and do not fill him. You have one mind, yes, but I tell you Ifeng is of another. He is as one who dreams—"

I tensed. Had she hit upon the truth of this without my telling? If so, what harm could come in her resentment?

"Tell me,"—she leaned still closer, until her breath mingled with mine—"what sorcery do you Wise Ones use to ensnare a man who has always thought clearly and was not bemused by such things?

"None of my making." But was it so? I had dealt quickly, and perhaps not with clear thought when I had laid Ifeng under my spell. If that was what mattered I had the answer now. My hands pressed on that part of the cape I had pulled about me, and through the fabric I felt the prick of the thorn I had concealed there. "Be assured, Ayllia, that if he was bespelled by chance, then shall I break it, and speedily. I want this no more than you do!"

"I shall believe you when Ifeng goes with clear eyes and comes to my bed place as eagerly as he did two nights agone," she told me bleakly. But perhaps she did believe in me a little.

Now she got to her feet. "Show me, Wise Woman, show me that you are not unfriend to me—perhaps to all of us!"

She had turned on her heel and went from me. When I was sure she was gone, I dropped the tent flap and made it fast to the inner stake set as a kind of lock to insure privacy. With the flap down, no one by custom would enter.

I had no servants such as had waited upon Utta, nor any novice learning my mysteries. Yet I moved with caution, still fearing that I might be in some way overlooked.

One of the braziers still held a coal not yet completely dead and I blew on that, fed it some bits of shaved wood, then some of the dried herbs. As the fragrant smoke puffed out I dropped my thorn into the heart of that handful of fire. A pity, since I would have to make another if the need arose.

But Ayllia was right; if Ifeng held me so firmly in mind I wanted the dream tie broken quickly.

It worked, for the chief did not approach me, nor was I troubled with any visitors for a space. It seemed that another move was in their minds. Though I had believed them well settled, perhaps for the rest of the winter, amid the warmth of the hot streams. This was not to last. It was a matter of game, which had become more and more sparse in the general vicinity. In addition I think some restlessness was a part of the spirit of these people, that they were not long happy nor content in any one place even though that promised an easier life.

Left to myself, save that they brought food and firewood to my door each morning, I spent hours in striving to recall with the aid of Utta's things more which could help me. Sooner or later, probably sooner, Ifeng and his men were going to demand a casting of foreknowledge of me. I could pretend such, but that was a piece of deceit which I dared not enter upon. It was a betrayal of the Power to claim what I had not. And in the present I wanted no more misuse to cancel the small gains I had made.

For all my desperate trying foreknowledge continued to elude me. Mind search efforts came to nothing at all. Perhaps had there been another learned in the Power to aid me, I might have made contact. But at last I came across another of Utta's tools, well wrapped and at the very bottom of her second chest as if it were something long forgotten or overlooked. I sat with it in my hands studying it.

This was a thing such as the novices in the Place of Silence use. It was a child's toy in comparison with more complex and better ordered aids, but I was certainly a child again in such matters and it would be better than nothing . . . I must be humble and use what I could.

It was a board of wood, runes carved on it in three rows. Traces of red paint, hardly to be detected now, were in the deep cracks of the first row, gold in small tarnished lines in the second, while the third was deep shadowed and must once have been painted a dire black.

Providing I could make this work, even a little, I would have an answer for Ifeng's asking and yet not practice deceit. I could no more than try it now. What of my own question, to which I so yearned to have an answer? What better beginning than that?

Kyllan, Kemoc! I closed my eyes, pictured those two nearest to my heart, my other selves, and under my breath I began a chant of words so old they had no meaning, were only sound to summon certain energies.

Laying the board on my knee, steadying it with my right hand, I touched its graven surface with the fingers of my left and began sweeping them from top to bottom, first the red row, then the gold, and then, though I had to force them to that task, the black. Once, twice, I made that sweep, then a third time—

So did my answer come. For suddenly my fingers were as fast to the uneven surface as if they had sunk into it, had become one with the wood. I opened my eyes to read the message.

Gold! If I could believe it, gold—life, and not only life but well-being for those I had so tried to reach. Straightaway, when I allowed myself to believe that, my touch on the board loosed and I could withdraw my fingers.

A burden I had not measured as I carried it was lifted from me. And I did not in the least disbelieve that I had read aright.

So . . . now for my own future. Escape—how, when?

This was more complex. I could not draw a sharp picture in my mind as I had of my brothers' faces. I could only try to build a strong desire of being elsewhere and wait for an answer.

Again my fingers adhered, but this time close to the foot of the red column. So escape was possible but it would come through peril and not in the immediate future.

There was a scratching at the flap of my tent.

"Seeress, we seek." Ifeng's voice. Had my countermagic failed? But surely as a husband he would not wait outside with such a call.

"They who seek may enter." I used Utta's formula, slipped the flap cord from its peg.

He was not alone; the three warriors who were the senior members of the tribe and acted as an informal advisory council were at his back. At my gesture of welcome they knelt and then settled back on their heels, Ifeng acting as spokesman.

"We must go hence; there is need for meat," he began.

"This is so," I agreed. And again I kept to Utta's formula. "Whither would the people go?"

"That we ask of you, Seeress. In us it is to go east again, down river to the sea where was our home before the slayers came over water. But will that bring evil upon us?"

Here it was, a demand for foreseeking. All I had was my tool of board and my finger. But I would do what I could and hope for a good ending.

I brought out the board and saw that they looked at it in a puzzled way as if it were something new to them.

"Do you not look into the ball of light?" Ifeng asked. "Such was the way of Utta—"

"Do you," I countered, "carry the same spear, wear the same sword as Toan, who sits at your right hand? I am not Utta, I use not the same weapons she did."

Perhaps that seemed logical to him, for he only gestured and did not question me again. I closed my eyes and considered the matter of journeying as clearly as I could arrange my thoughts. Again it was a question that was hard to form as a mind picture. At last I believed my best results were to fix upon myself, on such a journey. And in that choice lay my mistake.

I ran my fingers and they were caught and held swiftly. I opened to see them but halfway down the first column.

"Such a journey lies before us," I told him. "In it is some danger but not the greatest. The warning is not strong."

He nodded with satisfaction. "So be it. All life holds dangers of one kind or another. But we are not men to walk without eyes to see, ears to hear, and we have scouts who know better than most to use both. East it is then, Seeress, and we shall travel with the sun two days from now."

VII

I HAD no wish to travel eastward, farther and yet farther away from that portion of Escore which meant the most to me. Even should I now manage to break the rune bonds and be able to escape, leagues of unknown country would lie between me and the Valley, a country full of traps—many sly and clever traps. But Utta's magic left me no choice and when the Vupsalls marched so did I. My only resource was to memorize our path so that I might have some guides on my return. That I would break the rune spell and be free I did not doubt; it was only when I did not know.

We—or I—had forgotten the bite which winter held while we camped in the place of hot springs. Going out from there was stepping from early summer into midwinter.

Utta's sled and dogs had gone with her into the burial pit, but Ifeng, according to custom, furnished me with a new sled and two well-trained hounds, and sent me Ausu's maid to help in packing. As yet I had no servant from the tribe, nor had I asked for one, since I wanted no spying eyes when I strove to remaster my former skills. However I could see now that Visma and Atorthi between them had saved much labor during our travels. And since work with tents was new to me, I would have to ask for such an addition to my tenthold.

There were castes among the tribe, small as it was, and they had been set long ago. Some tentholds were always free from demands from Ifeng or the other leaders; others obeyed naturally. And I learned that the latter, as Visma, had been war captives, or the descendants of such.

77

SORCERESS OF THE WITCH WORLD

I watched those particular families with new attentions as we moved out, striving to see one of the younger women among them whom I might bring into my own tent. And my choice was undecided between two. One was a widow who lived with her son and his tenthold. She had a dull, time- and circumstance-beaten face, and moved among the family almost as did the Kolder slaves of my mother's long ago tales. I did not think that curiosity was still alive in her or that she would be a spy menace, but perhaps would learn loyalty to me if taken from the tent where she was a cowed drudge.

The other was a young girl who seemed biddable enough. She had a clubbed foot which did not appear to interfere with her work, but put her outside the hope of marriage unless she went as a second or third wife, more servant than mate. But perhaps she was too alert of mind to serve my purpose.

I had already learned to guide the dogs with the called commands to which they were trained from puppyhood. And, once all was laden on the sled, I took my place in line, just behind the sleds of Ifeng's household.

The men ranged out, flanking us through this stream country, busy at keeping the heavily loaded sleds going, lending their own strength, pushing and pulling. But we were not long in that place of sand, stones and warmth, moving up-slope into the snow and ice of the outer world. When our runners struck the easier going of the snow, our escort fanned out and away on either side of the main body of travelers, setting a protective screen between us and attack.

Once more we moved through a deserted country in which I saw no signs of old occupancy such as one marked easily in the western part of Escore. I wondered anew at his. For the country, even hidden under the burden of winter storms, gave the appearance of being one able to support garths and farms, to nourish a goodly population. Yet there were no marks of ancient fields, no ruins to say that the Old Ones had ever had their manors and lands here.

It was on the second day of travel that we came to the river. An icy crust lay along each bank, extending out over

78

the stream save for a wide dark band marking the center. There I saw the first signs that this had not been a totally forsaken wilderness. A bridge spanned that way, its pillared supports still standing except at midpoint of the stream.

Guarding either end of that broken span was a set of twin towers, looped for defense, large enough perhaps to provide garrison housing. One was intact; the other three had suffered and were crumbling, their upper stories roofless and only partially walled now.

But midpoint between these two guarding our side of the river was a stone arch which was so deeply carved that its pattern could still be read. And the symbol it bore was one I had seen before—on Utta's rune rolls—a sword and rod crossed.

On the other side of the bridge a smoothness in the sweep of snow suggested that a pavement or roadway extended on. But it was certainly not the choice of the tribe to make use of its convenience. Though I did not detect any taint of the Shadow about the ruins, we made a wide arc out and away, avoiding any close contact with those crumbling walls.

Perhaps the Vupsalls had long ago learned that such could be traps for the unwary and avoided all remnants of the past on principle. But I kept my eyes on the bridge and that suggestion of road, and wondered where it led, or had once led, and the meaning of those symbols above the gate. To my seeress' knowledge they had no rune significance, but must once have been a heraldic device for some nation or family.

The use of such identifying markings had long since vanished from Estcarp. But some of the Old Race who had managed to escape the Kolder-inspired massacres in Karsten and had fled for refuge over the border still used them.

We did not cross the river and on this side appeared no vestige of roadway. We paralleled the stream, once more heading due east, whereas we had angled northward out of the warm valley. I thought that this river must feed into the eastern sea my new companions sought.

I finally made my choice of tent aid and asked Ifeng at our second night's halt if I might have the aid of the widow Bahayi, which request he speedily granted. I believe the first wife of Bahayi's son was none too pleased, for Bahayi, in spite of her dull-witted appearance, was a worker of excellence. When she took charge of my tent all went with some of the old ease that had surrounded us when Utta's women had organized our travels. Nor did she show in the least any interest in my magical researches, rolling herself in her coverings to snore away the night. And I learned to ignore her as I sought a key to my prison.

With a growing intensity of need I made that search. There was almost a foreshadowing of danger to come. Each time that warning hung over me I would consult the answer board and always that reassured me. However, again I made the grave mistake of asking for myself alone—mistake I have since paid for with much regret.

Our course along the river did bring us to the sea; under the wintery sky that was a bleak and bitter place where winds searched out with fingers of ice any opening in one's cloak or tunic. Yet this seemed to be the place the tribe sought and under the winds they walked as people who had been in exile but are now returned to their own place.

It was along that shore that the ruins I had missed inland were to be seen. The major pile lay on a point which thrust like the narrow blade of a sword into the sullen and metal gray sea. What it had been—a single castle of fortification, a small walled town, a keep such as the Sulcar sea rovers had once built on Estcarp's coast—I could not tell from a distance.

And distance was what the Vupsalls kept between themselves and it. Their camp lay about midpoint of the bay into which the river emptied, and that pile of rocks was on the north cape protecting the inner curve, leagues away, so that sometime it was veiled from us by mists.

For the first time the Vupsalls made use of the remains of other structures. These were waist-high walls of well-set masonry. We may have been camping in the last vestiges of a town where men of the Old Race had once met shipping from overseas.

Our tents were incorporated with those walls for hybrid dwellings which gave us better shelter and such warmth as I, for one, welcomed. I noted that the tribe must have known this spot well and used it many times before, since each team and sled made its way to a certain walled foundation as if coming home. Bahayi, not waiting any direction from me, sent our own hounds to one of the foundations a little apart, the last intact one to the north of those chosen for dwellings. Perhaps this one was Utta's when she had been here. I accepted Bahayi's selction, for it served my purpose well, being away from the rest.

I helped her rather ineptly to use the tent walls plus those of a good-sized roofless room. Then she made an improvised broom of a branch, sweeping out sand and other debris, leaving us underfoot a smooth flooring of squared blocks. She brought in armloads of branches with small aromatic green leaves. Some of these she built into beds along the wall, others she shredded into bits and strewed on the floor, so that the scent of their crushing arose pleasantly to mask the odor the stone cell had had at our coming.

At one end was a fireplace which we put to good use. And when we were settled in I found this to be more comfortable than any abode I had been in since leaving the Valley. I sat warming my hands at the fire while Bahayi prepared our supper. I wondered what manner of man had built this house whose shell now sheltered us, and how long it had been since the builders had left the village to sand, wind, rain, snow and the seasonal visits of the nomads.

There had never been any way of reckoning the ages since Escore fell into chaos and the remnant of the Old Race had fled west to Estcarp, sealing the mountains behind them. Once I had, with the aid of my brothers, given birth to a familiar and had sent it forth questing into the past that we might learn what had happened to turn a fair land into a lacework of pitfalls set by the Shadow. We had seen through the eyes of that child of my spirit the history of what had passed, how a pleasant and seemly life had been broken and ravaged through man's greediness and reckless seeking for forbidden knowledge. The toll of years, of centuries, had not been counted in our seeing, and age beyond telling must now lie between our fire this night and the first ever lit on that same hearth place.

"This is an old place, Bahayi," I said as she knelt beside me putting forth into the heat of the flames one of those long-handled cooking pots which served at camp fires. "Have you come here many times?"

She turned her head slowly; her forehead was a little wrinkled as if she were trying to think, or count—though the counting system of her people was a most primitive one.

"When I was a child . . . I remember," she said in her low voice, which came with a hesitation as if she spoke so seldom she had to stop and search for each word. "And my mother—she remembered, too. It is a long time we have come here. But it is a good place—there is much meat." She pointed southward with her chin. "And in the sea, fish which are sweet and fat. Also there is fruit which can be dried and that we pick in the time of the first cold. It is much good, this place, when there are no raiders."

"There is a place of many stones there—" I pointed north. "Have you been there?"

She drew in her breath with an audible sucking sound, and her attention was suddenly all for the pan she held. But in spite of her manifest uneasiness I pursued the matter, for there was something about that wind and water assaulted cape which stayed in my mind.

"What is that place, Bahayi?"

Her right shoulder raised a little, she averted her head even more, as one who fears a blow.

"Bahayi!" I did not know why I insisted upon an answer; I only know that somehow I must have it.

"It is . . . a strange place—" Her hesitation was so marked

82

I did not know whether it was born of fear, or if her dull mind could not find words to describe what lay there. "Utta—once she went there—when I was a small child. She came back saying it was a place of Power, not for any who were not of the Wise Ones."

"A place of Power," I repeated thoughtfully. But of which Power? Just as there were pools of evil left by the passing or abiding of the Shadow in some places of this ill-treated land, so there were bastions from which one such as I could drawn sustenance and aid. And if the ruin on the far headland was like one of those refuges of blue stones, could a visit there be a strengthening of what I had regained?

Only it stood so far from us that I thought the rune spell would not permit me a visit. I had experimented from time to time, trying to discover how far I could travel from the tribe, and the distance was small indeed.

Suppose I could persuade some of them to accompany me, at least to the boundaries of the place, if they held the interior in too great awe or fear to go all the way? Would that lengthen my invisible leash to the point that I could go exploring?

But if it were a dwelling place of the Shadow, then the last thing I must do would be venture there in my present poorly defended state. If only Utta had left some record of her days with the tribe. By all reckoning she had been with them for generations. Perhaps if she had begun any such account the dust of many years had long since buried it. Living among a people who recorded only by some event she had doubtlessly lost her own measurement of time.

I thought of those two enigmatic scrolls in Utta's chest. Perhaps they had come from this cape citadel. And if that pile was the one shown in my dream . . .

There were two scrolls—I had used only one when I saw the adept and his open gateway. Suppose the other held some secret to give me what I now wanted, my freedom? With that thought I experienced a vast surge of impatience to get at such an experiment, to try to dream again and wrest from such dreaming the learning I needed.

I had to call upon hard-learned discipline before Bahayi. For though I was almost certain she was what she appeared to be, incurious and slow of wit, such dreaming could carry one out of one's body for a space. And so defenseless I wanted no witnesses.

Thus I called upon the same device I had used with Ifeng and brought out Utta's herb to turn our water-wine into a pleasant drink. Bahayi was so surprised that I offered her such a luxury that I reproached myself for not having done so before. And I set in my mind that I must do something for her. What better time than now?

Thus when she slept I wove a dream spell for her—one which would give her the pleasure she would enjoy the most, leaving it to her own mind and memory to set up the fantasy once I had turned the key to unlock the door for it. Then I set a lock spell on our door and stripped myself. I held the second scroll against the warmth of my breast, bent forward to lay my forehead to its upper end, opening my mind to what might enter.

Again there was a flow into my mind, so much of it incomprehensible, too obtuse for my unlocking; had I the time to puzzle it out, though, I might have gained very much. But I was in the position of one placed at a table on which there lay a vast heaping of gems, under orders to sort out those of one kind in a short time, so my fingers must quest for all the emeralds, pushing aside rubies, sapphires and pearls, beautiful and rare as those might be, and as much as I coveted them.

My "emeralds" I did pick here, there, and again here. Those bits and scraps were more to me as I awoke than any real gem. I returned the scroll to its container and looked to Bahayi. She lay upon her back, and on her face was the curve of a smile such as I had never seen before on that dull face.

As I drew my cloak about my shivering body and reached

out to lay more wood on the fire, I though again of what I might do for my tent fellow. A small spell might give her for the rest of her life this ability to enter happy dreams each night. To one who wanted more of life than sleep and dreaming it would be a curse rather than a gift. But I thought that for Bahayi it would be a boon. So I brought out what would best reinforce my thought commands and I wrought that spell before I turned to what else I must do that night.

For my "emeralds" had proved treasure indeed. As I had known from the first Utta's magic was more nature allied than the learning of Estcarp. And her rune ties were a matter of blood. But blood can cancel blood under certain circumstances. Though it would be painful and perhaps dangerous for me, I was willing to try that road.

I unfolded the mat with the runes, passing my hand across the dull surface so they blazed. Then I took one of the long tribal knives. Its point I put to a vein upon my arm and I cut so that the blood flowed red and strong. From Utta's hoard I had that rod I had discovered on my first delving. This I dipped into the blood and with care and my own red life, I repainted each rune, its blaze being smothered and darkened by what I had laid upon it. Often I had to stop to press the knife deeper, increase the flow by so much.

When I had done I bound a healing paste of herbs about my wound as quickly as I might, so that I could be about the rest of the spell. I did not know just which of the forces Utta might have called upon in the setting of those bounds, but I had for rebuttal those the Wise Women had known. And now I named them one by one as I watched the blood congeal, the runes hidden by those splotches. When I believed it was ready, I wadded it into a mass and thrust it into the fire.

This was my moment of testing. Had I not wrought aright my life might answer for such destruction. In any event it would not be easy.

Nor was it, for as the flames licked and ate at the mat, so did my body writhe and I bit my lips against screams of agony searing me. Blood trickled down my chin as well as my arm as my teeth met through my own flesh. But I endured without an outcry which might have awoken Bahayi. I endured and watched the mat until it was utterly consumed. Then I crawled to Utta's chest and brought out a small pot of thick grease which I smeared, with trembling fingers and many catches of breath, at the hurt, up and down my body, which was reddened and sore as if I and not the mat had lain unprotected in the heart of the coals.

So was the spell broken, yet the breaking left me in so sad a state that it would not be that day which was now dawning, nor even the one to follow, which could see me on my way. Also there were other precautions I must take, for any hound in the camp put to my trail could nose out my way and run me down were I to be found missing.

Bahayi roused with the daylight, but she was as one who moved in the afterglow of a dream, going about her duties with her usual competence but taking very little note of me save when it was necessary to bring food. And we were further aided in our solitude by a blizzard which made such a cloud about our ruins that those of each tenthold kept to themselves and there was no coming nor going.

By late afternoon my hurts were healed to the point I could move about, if stiffly and with some pain. And I set about my own preparations for flight. The thought of the cape ruins held steady in my mind. Utta had visited there and had said it was a place of Power, warning off the tribe. But she had not said of evil Power. And if I took refuge in such a place I might escape pursuit.

Were I to vanish there they might well take it to be an act of magic and be too frightened to come seeking me with hound and tracker. I could shelter therein and wait for better weather to start west again.

It seemed to me as I sorted through all of Utta's belongings, packet by packet, box by box, jar by jar, that all was very much for the best and that I was coming out of this venture very well. While I had certainly not regained all I had lost through my companionship with Dinzil, still I knew enough now not to be a menace to those I loved. And I might return safely to the Valley.

I made up a small pack of healing herbs and those I needed for such spells as I could use for defense during a journey. And, after Bahayi went to sleep again, I put aside a store of food choosing those things which would last longest and give the greatest strength and energy in the least bulk.

If I went openly, with the knowledge of the clan, to visit the ruins, I could have a sled for the first lap of my journey. However, after that it might well be a matter of carrying only what I could pack on my back. All the more reason to be sure I was fully cured of my ill taken in destroying the rune mat.

The storm came from the north and it held steady for two days and the night between. The howl of the wind overhead was sometimes strangely like voices calling aloud and Bahayi and I looked uneasily at each other, drawing closer together before the fire, which I fed with some of the herbs as well as from our fast dwindling pile of wood.

But at dusk on the second day the wind died and soon after there came a scratching at our door flap. Ifeng stamped in at my call, shaking snow from his heavy furs. He had brought with him a pile of driftwood gathered from along the shore and dumped it by our hearth place, together with a silver scaled fish Bahayi welcomed with a grunt of pleasure.

Having so delivered supplies he looked to me. "Seeress," he began, and then hesitated, as if not knowing quite how to put his request into words. "Seeress, look into the days to come for us. Such storms sometimes drive the raiders to shore—"

So I brought out my board and he squatted on his heels to watch. I questioned him as to the form of ship to be feared and his halting description gave me a mental picture not unlike those of the Sulcar ships of my childhood. I wondered if these other sea rovers were not of the same breed.

Holding that picture in mind I closed my eyes and read

with my fingers. Down the red line they slid rapidly, and down the gold. But on the third ominous black column they caught fast, as if the tips were clotted with pitch. I looked—they were fastened so close to the top I cried out in alarm.

"Danger—great danger—and soon!" I gave warning.

He was gone, leaving the door flap open behind him. I threw aside the answer board to follow, to see him in the dusk of early twilight floundering along the drifts between the ruined walls. Now and again he stopped at some downed flap to yell a warning, so he left all stirring behind him.

Too late! He wavered suddenly, as if he had trod on a treacherous bit of icy footing, falling back against a wall. He had drawn his sword but he never had a chance to use it. I saw in the half gloom the hand ax which had struck him between neck and shoulder, biting out his life. A thrown ax—another Sulcar trick.

Before he had more than fallen to the ground there was a flitting of gathering shadows racing between the low crumbling walls; I heard screaming from the other side of the settlement, where the raiders must have already forced their way into some of the shelters.

I turned on Bahayi, catching up the pack I had prepared. "Come! The raiders—"

But she stood staring at me in her most stupid way, and I had to throw her cloak about her, pull her to the door, push her ahead of me. The sled dogs had been loosed from their common kennel in the center of the settlement and were at grim work, buying time for their masters. I pulled and dragged at Bahayi, trying to urge her along with me northward.

For some moments she came. And then suddenly, with a sharp cry, as if she were awakening from a dream, she struck out at me, freeing herself. Before I could catch her again she was out of reach, on her way back to the very heart of the melee.

I looked back. Had I been such a one as Utta, with natural forces at my command, I might have been able to aid the tribesmen. Now I was the least in any defense they might summon.

So I turned resolutely north, struggling from one patch of cover to the next, leaving the fighting behind me, just as snow began to fall again.

VIII

THE swirling of the snow not only hid what was happening now in the village, but the rising of a savage wind also drowned out the cries. Within minutes I thought I had chosen the worse of two evils in my flight, for I was completely lost. But I kept blundering on, until I staggered into a half seen brush from which I recoiled. That told me that I was out of the ruins and into the beginning of the growth which masked my distant goal.

This brush was tall and thick enough to shelter me once I had fought a little way into it, and I half fell through a slit in it, which must mark a trail. The way was so narrow that I deemed it a game path. It ran with so many twists and curves that it certainly did not follow any ancient road, since mankind has a way of imposing his will on nature in the building of roads not yielding to her quirks.

Some of the taller spikes of brush, which were close to the stature of trees, held off the fury of the storm, and I was able to stumble along at a goodly pace. I believed that my sense of direction had not altogether deserted me and I was heading for the mysterious pile of timeworn masonry on the point.

Perhaps it would be better to strike directly away from the sea westward—but not in such a storm and with perhaps raiders on my trail. I believed that the building on the cape would be an excellent hiding place.

So far I had kept my mind on my own escape and the immediate future, trying to shut from my thoughts the probable fate of the tribe. It was the custom, as I had learned during my short time among them, for them to live in a continual round of blood feuds and raids. But the sea rovers were the worst of their enemies. The males of a defeated people faced certain death, the women, if they were pleasing enough, would be taken as minor wives; if uncomely they would be slaves. It was a hard life at best, but one they were bred to.

In my short life I had lived constantly with war, being born into the midst of Estcarp's death struggle with Karsten, my mother and father both serving on the border from which the greatest of threats came. I had seen my brothers ride off to battle before they had more than a faint shadow of beard on their cheeks. And I had been impressed thereafter to fighting of a different sort. Since we had fled into Escore, fleeing the wrath of the Wise Women, struggle had been ever sitting on our left hand, sword striking in our right. We had hung arm shields in childhood and we had never been allowed to put them off.

Therefore such a raid now did not come to me as a blow. Had my power been as great as it once had been, I would have used it to encircle the tribe against this ill before I left. I would have brought Bahayi with me had she allowed it. And I thought of Ausu with some regret. But there were no others among the tribe to whom I owed any allegience, nor whom I would have drawn steel to defend.

My wandering trail came out suddenly under an arch of leafless growth into a wider path, crossing that at an angle. I guessed that under the drifted snow was a road leading to the point and I turned into it. They might run me down with hounds, the Vupsalls, always providing they won the battle in the village. But if the hounds did lead them here, would they be bold enough to push in after me? I thought not, at least until they had built up their courage somewhat.

90

And since I had proved a poor seeress, they might follow me in revenge, but not for wish of more of my company.

The storm was growing worse and now such winds buffeted me, such veils of snow closed me around, that I grew alarmed. I would have to find some shelter and soon, or else I might fall and be covered with that white harvest, and so end ignominiously.

Brush grew on either side and among it, scarcely to be seen, were dark outcrops. I staggered to one of the nearest and found it to be a pile of rubble, debris of some structure. There was a hollow in it which my searching hands rather than my snow-blinded eyes discovered, and into that I pushed my way.

What I had found was a cave-like space between the tumble of several walls. It gave me the feeling of safety and, as I faced around to explore, the curtain of snow sealed me in. I knew I had done the best that I could for my protection.

Time and wind had deposited dried leaves here. I made good use of them, hollowing out a nest of sorts, pulling them over me when I settled into it. Then I practiced the small art which was part of my inheritance from Utta. I chewed a palmful of herbs and lulled my mind by will.

It was not a true trance—I would not have dared to enter one under such circumstances—but akin to it. In this state the cold meant little to my body; I would not slip into that icy induced sleep from which there was no waking.

I was aware of where I lay, of the dark and storm, but it was as if all that had no meaning, as if I had withdrawn into a small portion of my body, leaving the rest lulled into tranquil waiting for an end to outer discord.

There were no dreams. I willed myself to no mental activity such as planning ahead or speculating as to what the next hour, the next morning might bring, for that would break the spell I was using as a buffer between me and the ills of exposure. This was endurance only, and one who had lived long in the Place of Silence knew how to hold steady in that state.

Toward morning the wind slackened. Snow had drifted against the door of my pocket, so that I had view of only a small slice outside. It was enough to tell me that the storm was past, or else in lull.

I pulled out of my nest and took out some of the dried meat that was pounded with berries and hardened into cakes. One had to suck this rather than chew it, lest one's teeth splinter. With some in my mouth I shouldered my pack and started out.

Only the lines of brush protruding above the snow marked the outline of the old road, and this was a series of drifts, with wind scoured places in between. To wallow through the drifts was exhausting and I tried that for only a short time, then sought a way nearer the brush.

The struggle left me panting and blowing. And, in spite of my struggle to keep well aware of my direction, it was not long before the labor of merely walking, or rather skidding, slipping and falling, filled most of my world.

So it was that I nearly died. But the ice and snow which was my bane also was my enemy's. Ayllia, instead of impaling me neatly on her hunting knife as she had aimed to do, lost her footing, struck against me, carrying us both down into a smother of drift where I floundered free in time to meet her scrambling rush, prepared to kick the knife from her hand and send her sprawling a second time. The knife was gone, lost in the deep snow now furrowed by our scuffling. But she was at me with nails and fists in a whirlwind of fury, and I had to defend myself as best I could.

A hard cuff to the side of her head sent her down again. And this time I followed, kneeling over her, holding her down while she squirmed and spat and showed her teeth like a frantic animal.

I summoned my scraps of willpower, beamed them at her with all the decision I had in me, and at last she lay quiet under my hold. But in the stare she used to meet my eyes there was hot hate.

"He is dead!" She mouthed that as if it were both an accusation and an oath. "You killed him!"

Ifeng—had he meant that much to her then? I was a little surprised. Perhaps all my life I had depended too much on mind talk. I had not learned to judge people well by other signs as must those who do not have the ability. It had been my thought that Ayllia loved her place as second wife (perhaps almost first wife since Ausu's condition left her mainly a figurehead in Ifeng's tent) rather than the chief who had given it to her. But perhaps I had so wronged her and it was a true grief which had driven her to hunt down one who, by her reasoning, had as much blood debt as the raider who had actually loosed the ax to cut her husband down.

With some hatreds there is no reasoning and if Ayllia had gone past the point where I could reach her with logic, then I was given a burden I did not know how to solve. I could not kill nor disable the girl and leave her here; I was certainly not going to return to the tribe; and to go on with an unwilling prisoner was a very unhappy third choice.

"I did not kill Ifeng," I said with what reasoning force I could summon, seeking to impress also her mind.

"You—" she spat. "Utta was his shield; she foresaw rightly. He believed you do likewise. He depended upon you!"

"I never claimed to have Utta's powers," I told her. "Nor did I by choice choose to serve—"

"True!" she interrupted. "You wanted free of us! So you let the raiders come so you could run while they let their swords drink! You are a dark one—"

Her words bit into me as if they were the sharp edge of one of the blades she spoke of. I had wanted above all to escape the tribe; had I unconsciously therefore betrayed them to that purpose? Had I not remembered to consult the answer runes, take other precautions, because I wanted them rendered helpless? Dinzil had served the Shadow, and under his influence I had come very close to such deeds as would have damned me forever. Did the taint of that linger deep in me, rendering me now liable to such cold choices as Ayllia had accused me of?

I had been so keen on regaining my powers—for my own gain—as now I saw. And there is a balance in such things. Used for ill, good becomes ill, and that effect snowballs until even when one desires it greatly one cannot summon good, only something scarred and disfigured by the Shadow. Was I so maimed that from now on when I did aught with what I had in me it would injure others?

Yet one who has the Power is also constrained to make use of it. Such action comes as naturally as breathing. When I had been emptied of it I was a ghost thing, a shell walking through a life I could not feel or touch. To live I must be me, and to be me I must have what was my birthright. Yet if that also made me a monster who carried a fringe of the Shadow ever with me—

"I wanted my freedom, yes," I said now, and I was as much seeking an answer for myself as for Ayllia. "But I will swear on the Three Names that I meant no ill to you and yours. Utta kept me captive, even after her death, by her arts. Only lately was I able to break the bonds she used. Listen, if you were taken by raiders, kept a bondmaid in their camp, would you not use the means to freedom when it lay ready to your hands? I did not bring the enemy upon you, and I never had the means of clear foresight Utta controlled. She did not teach it to me. Ifeng came to me just before they struck; I used the answer runes and gave him warning—"

"Too late!" she cried.

"Too late," I agreed. "But I am not of your blood, nor sworn to your service. I had the need for freedom—"

Whether I could have made her understand I do not know, but at that moment there came a brazen sound, carrying. She tensed in my grasp; her head swung to look back down the drifted road where the marks of our scuffle broke the smooth dunes of snow.

"What is it?"

94

"The sea hounds!" She signaled for silence and we listened. That keening was answered from our right, to the west. There were already two groups and we might well be caught between them. I got to my feet to look ahead. There was no sun, but, though the day was cloudy, it was clear enough. Ahead was the beginning of the cape ruins and there my mind visualized many hiding places. It would take an army in patient search to find us there. I held out a hand, caught at Ayllia's wrist and drew her up beside me.

"Come!"

She was quick enough to agree and we pushed on for a step or two until she realized that our way led to that pile of buildings Utta had warned against. Seeing that, she would have fled, I think, had not the horn sounded closer from the west. The east was now walled against us by so thick a hedge of thorny growth as would need a fire to eat a path for us.

"You—you would kill—" She tried to break my grip. But barbarian though she was, tough and bred to struggle and warfare, she could not free my hold. And, as I propelled her along, the horns sounded again, much nearer.

There is bred into all of us a fear of such flights, so that once we began that retreat fear grew, swallowing up lesser terrors. Thus now it was with Ayllia, for she struggled no more, but rather hastened for the dark pile promising us refuge.

As we went I told her what I believed possible, that such ruins could not be easily combed and we would have a hundred hiding places to choose from until our pursuers would give up and leave us alone. In addition I assured her that, though my powers were crippled when compared to Utta's, they were still strong enough to give us fair warning of all Shadow evil.

I half feared, though this I did not tell her, that this might be wholly a place of the Shadow and so barred to us. Yet Utta had gone here and had returned. And a Wise Woman would not have risked all she was by venturing into a cesspool of ancient evil.

The road we followed led us between two towering gates. Their posts were surmounted by figures of fearsome nightmare creatures. As we set foot between those pillars on which they crouched there was a loud roaring. Ayllia cried out and would have fled, but I stood firm against her, shaking her sharply until a portion of her fear subsided and she listened to me—for such devices I knew of old. One of Es City's gates was so embellished. It was the ingenuity of their makers, since it was caused by the wind blowing through certain cunningly set holes.

I do not know whether she believed me. But the fact that I stood unshaken and that the creatures, in spite of the roaring, gave no sign of clambering down to attack us, seemed to reassure her so I could pull her on again.

Once within the gates some of the need for haste left me and I went more slowly, though I did not pause, and my grasp on Ayllia did not slacken. Unlike the village, these were not ruins, though, as in Es City, one had the feeling of long aging, as if many centuries weighed upon the massive stones, driving them yet farther into the earth. They did not crumble, only took on a patina of eternal, unchanging existence.

The outer walls were very thick, and seemed to have rooms or spaces within, for the passage through showed grilled openings on either side. Perhaps at some time guardians not human had lived there, for each had the appearance of a cage.

Then we were in a paved way which sloped up to the mighty pile of high towers and many rings of walls which was the heart of the whole city or fortress. Perhaps it had been a city, for between the outer gates and the inner core of castle many buildings were crowded. Now they turned dead window eyes, gaping mouths of doors, to us. Here and there, standing among the paving blocks, was a wizened, withered stalk of weed. Pockets of snow added to the dreariness of long desertion.

The stones were all uniformly gray, lighter than those of Es City. But above each door was a spot of mute color my eyes delighted in—the blue sheen of those stones which, throughout Escore, stood for protection against all which abode in the darkness we feared most. Whatever this stronghold had been, it had sheltered once those with whom I could have walked in safety.

Now I was conscious of something else: this street, sloping gently upward to a second pair of gates marking the keep, was somehow familiar to me, as if I now walked a way I had known of old and half forgotten. But it was not until we reached the second gate and I saw what was carved in the blue stone above it that I knew. There was the wand and the sword laid together. And this was the way I had walked in my dream when I had watched the opening of the gate.

Nor could I turn aside now and not complete my journey, for we were both drawn forward, following the same tracing of ways I remembered from the dream. I heard Ayllia give a small frightened cry, but when I looked at her her eyes were set and she moved as one under compulsion. That pull was on me, too, but not to the same extent, perhaps. I recognized it for the attraction of Power to Power. Whatever that adept had wrought here in the long ago had left a core of energy which would not be gainsaid.

As we went our pace grew faster, until we were half running. We entered doors, threaded corridors, crossed lesser rooms and halls, in greater and greater haste. Nor had Ayllia made another sound since her first cry.

We came at last into a high walled chamber, which must have been taller than a single story of that massive inner bailey. And, as we entered, it was into life, not dreary death. The weight of countless years felt elsewhere was lighter. There was a sense of awareness and energy, so strong it would seem the very air about us crackled with it.

Along the walls near us there were still some furnishings. Tapestries hung, their pictured surfaces now dim, but woven with such skill that here and there a face of man or monster peered forth with the brightness of a mirrored reflection, as if they were really mirrors and creatures invisible to us, marching up and down eternally viewing themselves on the surface of the cloth.

There were carved chests with symbols set in their lids. And those I knew for the keep-sake of record rolls. Perhaps it was from one like these that Utta had plundered her two. To go to the nearest, lift the lid and look upon such treasures was a vast temptation. But instead I linked hands with Ayllia and drew her with me in a slow circuit around the wall of that vast room, not venturing out upon the middle portion which was so clear and empty. But there was light enough to show the designs set in colored stones and metal strips which covered most of its surface.

Deeply inlaid, not just drawn for a single ceremony, were the pentagrams, the magic circles, all the greater and lesser seals, the highest of the pentacles. These lay a little out from our path around the walls. But beyond these symbols which were keys to so much knowledge were vaguer lines, not so well defined—as if when one advanced toward the center of the hall one advanced in knowledge, and concrete symbols were no longer needed as guides. Of those I did not know so many, and those I recognized had small differences from the ones I had seen before.

This might almost have been a school for the working of Power, such as the Place of Silence. But so much greater was this, and such suggestions did I read in those vague lines near the center, that I thought those who labored here might well look upon the Wise Women of Es as children taking their first uncertain steps.

No wonder a sensation of life lingered here. The stones of the walls behind these mirrored tapestries, those under our feet, must have been soaked in centuries upon centuries of radiation from Power; so that, inanimate though they were, they now reflected what had beat on them so long.

We were a good distance from the door we had entered

when I noted the chairs set out on the patterned floor. They were more thrones than chairs, for each rose above the surface of the pavement on three steps, and each was fashioned of the blue stone, having deep-set runes which glowed faintly, as if in their depths fire smoldered, unwilling to die.

They had wide arms and high, towering backs in which were set the glowing symbols. Laid across the seat of the middle one was an adept's wand, as if left there only for a few moments while its owner went on an errand elsewhere.

The symbol in the back of that chair was one I had seen on the seals, the broken bridge, the door of this citadel—the wand and the sword. And I was sure it stood for the man—or more than man—under whom this pile had held domination over the countryside. I did not doubt that this had been the principal seat of some ruler.

As I glanced at the chair I again remembered the details of my dream. This was where he had sat to watch the glowing presence of the gate he had opened. What had happened then? Had he, as legend told us was true of so many of the adepts, gone through his gate to seek what lay on the other side?

Now I looked past the chair, seeking for some trace of the gate itself, so vividly had the dream returned to my mind. Where that arch had presented itself there was bare pavement; no symbols, not even the vaguest, were discernible on the floor. Had the master of this hall indeed reached a point where he needed none at all for the molding of energy? I had thought the Wise Women, then Dinzil, represented heights of such manipulation. But I guessed that had I met the sometime master of that third and middle chair I would have been as Ayllia, as Bahayi, one simple and lost. And in me that was a new feeling, for though I had been emptied of much which had once been mine, I could remember how it had been at my command. However, here I was conscious of something else, the belief that all I had ever learned would be only the first page of the simplest of runes for the master of gates.

Realizing that, I suddenly felt very small and tired, and awed, though the hall was empty and what I reverenced was long gone. I glanced to Ayllia, who at least was human and so of my kind. She stood where I had left her when my hand dropped from her arm. Her face had a strange emptiness, and I knew a flash of concern. Had bringing her here, into a place where such a vast residue of Power was still to be sensed, blasted her as I with my safeguards need not fear? Had I again, in my stubborn self-centeredness worked evil?

I put my hands gently to her shoulders, turned her a little to look into her eyes, used my seeking to touch her mind. What I sensed was not the blasting I had feared, but a kind of sleep. And I thought this was her defense, perhaps it would continue to work as long as we lingered here. However it was well to go now lest that seeping of old Power was cumulative and would enslave us.

But to go was like wading through a current striving to sweep us in the opposite direction. To my alarm I discovered that there *was* an unseen current rising and that it swept around that third chair as if its goal lay somewhere near where I had seen the gate.

Ayllia yielded to it readily before I was fully aware that we might be in real peril. I had to grasp her tightly, pull her back, though her body strained away from me, her eyes stared unseeingly at that central emptiness. The arm I did not grasp swung out, the fingers of her hand groping blindly as if to seek some hold which would aid her to pull out of my determined grip.

I set up my mental safeguards. I was not strong enough to put a wall about both our minds, but if I could hold, surely I could keep Ayllia with me, work us both out of the hall. Beyond the door I thought we would be safe.

Only now it was all I could do to hold against that drag. And Ayllia pulled harder and harder until we were both behind the middle seat and I could have put my hand to its high back. There was the wand on the seat—could I snatch it up as we reached that point? And if so, what could I gain? Such rods of Power were weapons, keys governing shafts to be used in spells. But they also were the property of one seeker alone. What could I gain by trying to use it? Still, it remained so sharply in the fore of my mind that I knew it had some great importance, was not to be lightly overlooked in my present need.

We were level with the seat now. I must make my move to seize the wand or be pulled out of reach, for Ayllia was beginning to struggle against my hold and soon I must keep both hands on her.

I hesitated for a second and then took the chance. With a sharp jerk I dragged Ayllia closer to the chair, took the first step in a single stride, and groped for the end of the rod with my left hand.

IX

MY fingers closed about the wand, and then nearly did I drop it, for it was as if I had grasped a length of frosted metal, so cold it burnt the skin laid against it. Yet I did not release it—I could not—for at that moment it clung to me more than I grasped at it.

At the same instant Ayllia broke from my control. She threw herself forward, out of my reach before I could catch her again. As her feet touched the pavement she staggered and went down, falling on her hands and knees. Her weight upon those stones must have released some hidden spring, for a flash burst upward. As it had been in my dream, there stood the gate marked in fiery lines.

"No Ayllia!" If she heard my shout it meant nothing to her ensorcelled mind. She scuttled forward, still on hands and knees like some tormented beast, and passed between the gateposts of that weird portal.

Though through it I could see the hall beyond, Ayllia vanished utterly once she went through the arch. Still clutching the wand, I leaped after her, determined that no more lives would be lost because of my lack of concern or courage.

There was a feeling of being rent apart, not altogether pain but rather a hideous disorientation because I passed through some space which a human body was never meant to penetrate. Then I was rolling over a firm surface, and I found myself moaning with the punishment I had taken in that brief instant of time or out of time.

I sat up dizzily. Though I was now silent there was still moaning and I looked around me groggily. Against a tall object looming high in the gloom lay a crumpled bundle which cried out. I crawled to Ayllia's side, raised her head upon my arm. She lay with her eyes closed, but her body twitched and quivered. Now her head began to turn restlessly from side to side as I have seen in one who is deep in some burning fever. And all the while she uttered small sharp cries.

Pulling her closer to me, I looked back and up for the gate. To see—nothing!

I had oftimes heard of my father's coming into Estcarp through such a portal, and on this side he had found two pillars set to mark the entrance on Tor Moors. When he and my mother had gone up against the stronghold of the Kolder, that gate, too, had been marked in both worlds. But it would seem that this entrace or exit differed, for I could see nothing but a stretch of open land.

It was day here, but clouds hung low and the light was dusky. Whereas snow and ice had clothed Escore on the other side of that vanished doorway, here the atmosphere was sultry and I coughed, my eyes tearing, for the air seemed filled with noxious puffs of invisible smoke.

There was no vegetation. The ground was as uniformly gray as the sky, a sand which looked as if it had never given root room to any healthy growing thing. In some places there were drifts of powdery stuff which looked like ash. This might be a land cleared in some great burning. I glanced at the pillar Ayllia had fallen against.

It was tall, taller than any man. But it was no seared tree trunk nor finger of stone, but rather metal, a girder or support, now pitted and scaly as if something in the acrid air was reducing it little by little to flakes of its former self. Had it once been set to mark the gate on this side? But it stood too far from where we had come through.

I settled Ayllia on the ground, her head pillowed on my pack. Then I got shakily to my feet and I saw something gleaming on the ground and staggered toward it. The wand lay there, so white against this drab sand that it was like a beam of light.

Stiffly I stooped to pick it up. The icy cold of it was gone—now it was like any other smooth rod. I tucked it carefully into the folds of my belt sash. Then I made a slow turn, viewing what lay about us, hoping for a clue to the gate.

The sand was heaped in ashy dunes, each so like the next that it would be very easy, I believed, to be lost among them. There was no marker except the pitted pillar. But when I faced that squarely and looked beyond, I saw another one some distance away, in a straight line with the first.

Ayllia stirred, pulling herself up. I went to her hurriedly. Once more her eyes were blank; she was lost in some inner wilderness where I could not reach her. She clawed her way to her feet, holding to the broken pillar for support. Then she faced about, in the same direction as that second column. Her head was up and back a little, turning slowly from side to side, almost like a hound questing for some familiar scent. Then she began to stagger on, in the direction of that next pillar.

I caught at her shoulder. She gave no sign she knew me, but she struggled, with a surprising return of strength, against my hold. Suddenly, when I least expected it, she swung

103

around and struck out with a shrewdly aimed blow which sent me sprawling.

By the time I got to my feet again she was well ahead, her first staggering giving way to as firm a run as one could keep over this powdery footing. I scrambled after her, though I was loath to leave that spot without further exploration. I dared not believe that the gate was totally lost and we had no hope of return.

The second broken pillar stood near to a third and Ayllia was on her way to that. But it did not seem to me that she was being guided by them at all, but rather that she once more was led by something within her mind, an unseen compulsion.

We passed six of those columns, all as eroded and eaten as the first, before we came out of the place of sand dunes and into another type of country. Here there was a withered growth of grass-like vegetation, in sickly patches, more yellow than green. The line of pillars continued in a straight march across this landscape, but now they were taller and seemed less eaten—until we came to two which were congealed and melted into blobs of stumps. Around these were growths of the first vigorous vegetation I had seen, unpleasant looking stuff with a purple tinge, fine filaments of dusky red fluttering from the leaf tips, as if questing for life to devour. I had no desire to examine it closely.

Beyond the melted columns lay a road. Unlike the pillars, this showed no signs of wear: it might have been laid down within the year. Its surface was sleek and slick looking and of a dead black. Ayllia came to the edge of that and stood swaying a little, though she did not look down at what might be a treacherous footing, but still stared ahead.

At last I caught up with her. And, from behind, I grasped her shoulder, held her. But she did not try to attack me this time. I did not like the look of that road, nor did I want to step on it. And I was hesitating as to what to do next when I heard the sound. It was a rushing as if something approached at great speed. I set my weight against Ayllia, bearing her with me down against the gritty ground, hoping our dull colored garments would be one with the gray-brown soil.

It came along the road at such a speed as to leave me unsure of the nature of what had passed. Certainly not an animal of any kind. I had an impression of a cylinder, perhaps of metal, which did not even rest on the surface over which it skimmed, but perhaps the length of my arm above. It followed the roadway at a great speed, leaving a rush of air to cover us with dust as it vanished in the distance.

I wondered if we had been sighted. If we had, those controlling the thing had not bothered to stop. Perhaps they could not in this place. The speed with which they had swished by would not answer to a sudden halt.

But what manner of thing was it which would race so, not touching the ground, yet manifestly traveling by the roadway? The Kolder had lived with machines to do their work. Had we broken into the Kolder world, even as my mother and father had once done? If so we were in great peril, for the Kolder gave their captives to a living death such as no one could imagine without skirting madness.

I had in my pack very little food. And I carried no water, for I had intended to travel where snow and river could have satisfied my thirst at will. Here the acrid atmosphere and the dry blowing of the wind had awakened a thirst to parch my mouth, as if I had tried to swallow handfuls of the ashes about me.

We must have water, and food, to keep life in our bodies. From the look of the land so far we could not expect to find either—which meant we must risk the worst and travel along this road, perhaps in the same direction as the rushing thing.

I put my hand to Ayllia, but she had already turned in that direction, her eyes still staring blankly. Now she began to march along the edge of the road, while for want of a better guide I followed.

We saw it from far off. I had looked upon the towers of Es City, upon the citadel of the unknown eastern cape, and both had I thought major works of man's hand. But this was such as I could not look upon and believe that man alone had wrought. The towers, if true towers they were, arose up and up to tangle with the gray clouds of the sky. And they were all towers, with little bulk of building below to support them. From tower to tower there was a lacing of strung ways, as if their makers put roads high in the sky. And all this was of the same dun color as the ground. They might have been growths out of the ashy soil by some fantastic cultivation. Yet they had the sheen of metal.

The fluid looking road we followed fed directly into the foot of the nearest tower. Now we could see other such roads spreading out from the city, running from other towers. I have watched the webs of the zizt spiders with their thickly woven center portions, their many radiating threads of anchorage. And the thought came to me that if one were able to soar elsewhere overhead and look down on this complex, it would seem from that angle to be a zizt web—which was not a promising thought, for the zizt spiders are such hunters as it is well to avoid.

I ran my tongue over lips which were parched and cracked, and saw that Ayllia was in no better state. She had begun to moan again, even as she had when she first came through the gate. Somewhere there was water and it looked like we would have to enter that web of metal to find it.

There was another warning rushing sound and once more I pulled my companion to the ground. A carrier swept by, not on the road we had followed, but some distance away. And, as I levered myself up when it was safely past, I saw something else, a dark spot in the sky, growing larger at every beat of my thundering heart.

It could not be a bird. But what of my father's stories of the past? In his world men had built machines, even as did the Kolder, and in such they rode the sky, setting the winds to their commands. Had we—could this be my father's world? Yet such a city—he had never spoken of that, nor of a land reduced to cinders and sand.

The sky thing grew and grew. Then it halted its flight

to hover over a space between two of the towers. I saw a platform there, more steady than the lacy ways which provided passage between height and height. With caution the sky thing settled on that platform.

It was too far away for me to see if men came out of it to enter any of the four towers at the corners of the landing space. But it was so strange as to make me a little afraid.

Kolder lore, their machines and the men they made into machines to do their will, had so long been evil tales that we of Estcarp were tuned to an instant loathing for all their works. And so this place had the stench of vileness which was not like the evil of Escore which I could understand, since that came from the wrongful use of talents I was aware of—but this was of a monstrously twisted way of life wholly alien to all I stood for.

Yet we must have food and water or die. And there is always this: one does not willingly choose death when there is even a small chance of grasping life. Thus we stood and looked upon that fantastic city, or rather I looked, and Ayllia stared as if she saw nothing.

At ground level the only entrances to the nearer towers seemed to be those tunnels fed by the roads. In fact, there were no breaks in the walls until the first of the airy ways and those were higher than the highest spires I had known in Es City. No windows at all.

Therefore if we would enter we must do it by road. And I shrank from putting foot to that slick surface. Yet how long would my strength, or Ayllia's, hold without supplies? To delay was to weaken ourselves at a time when we must harbor all the energy we could summon for survival.

It was growing darker and I thought that it was not a coming storm but night which brought that dusk. Perhaps the dark would be our friend. I could see no lights aloft. But, even as I watched, there was a sudden outburst of sparkling radiance to outline each of the inter-tower ways, glistening like dew on a spider web.

There was a duller glow outlining the cave holes into

which the roads fed. And light in there could be more un-friend than aid. But I thought we had no choice, and what small advantage might lie with us grew the less with every passing moment.

So I took Ayllia's arm. She no longer led the way, but she did not hang back nor dispute with me when I pushed ahead, still beside the road, the glow of the entrance before us.

As we drew closer I saw, with some small relief, that the opening was wider than the span of the road so that there was a narrow walkway beside it and we need not get down on its surface. But was that wide enough to save us should one of those carriers make entrance when we were attempting the same? The wind of their passing had twice proved force-ful; in the confined space of the tunnel it might be fatal.

I halted at the mouth of that opening and listened. There was certainly no warning of such a coming, and we could not hesitate here for long. Best get inside and seek out a side way off the course of the road.

The surface under our feet as we passed into the base of the tower was, I believe, some sort of metal overlaid with a slightly elastic spongy stuff so that it gave with every step. We were in a tunnel as I had expected, and I hurried Ayllia along that narrow walk, hoping for a break in the wall beside us, some door opening from the tube.

We found such an opening, marked by a very dim light burning above it, and below that light a symbol foreign to me. The passage beyond was as narrow as a slit, leading off at a right angle. Once into it I breathed a little freer, relaxing my need to listen for destruction rushing from behind.

So relaxed, I sensed that other feeling in this place. The air was not as sultry as it had been outside, but it was still unpleasant to breathe, and now it carried odors which I could not identify, but which made me sneeze and cough.

At lengthy intervals along the wall were other patches of light; but so dim were they that the spaces between them were pockets of dark. We were midway in the second of those when I realized we had found this side burrow just in time.

For there was a mighty roaring from behind and the walls
and floor quivered. One of the carriers must have entered the
tunnel. There were blasts of air so fume-filled that we
strangled in our coughing fight for breathable air. Tears
streamed from our eyes until I was blinded, I only staggered
along instinctively, still pulling at my companion, trying to
escape that pollution.

When we reached the haven of the next light I leaned
against the wall, trying to wipe my eyes, regain my breath.
And so I saw that the footing under our boots was drifted
with a feathery deposit, as soft as the ashes of the outer
world, but black. Along the way we had come we had left
a well-marked trail. But ahead there were only untroubled
drifts. By such signs no one had passed this way for some
time—perhaps for years. And that thought was heartening,
but it did not bring us any closer to what we must have to
sustain us.

The narrow passage ended in a round space which seemed
like the bottom of a well. I could put my head far back on
my shoulders and look up and up into eye straining distance, as if this well space extended from here to the far-off
crown of the tower. There were openings along it at intervals,
as if it bisected various floors. Some of these were dim of
light, others shown brilliantly. There was no ladder, though,
no sign of any steps which would lead to even the lowest of
these openings. We had no choice, I decided, but to retreat
to the dangerous tunnel and try along it for a second possible
escape route.

Ayllia stepped forward suddenly, jerking me with her. I
threw out my hand to retain my balance, my palm slapping
hard against the wall.

There was an answer to that unplanned action. We were
no longer standing on our two feet at the bottom; instead we
were rising, our bodies soaring as if we had sprouted wings.
I think I cried out. I know my hand went to the wand at my
belt. Then I clawed at the smooth side of the space through
which we rose, striving to win some hold to stop our going.

My nails scraped and broke, but they did not even slow that ascent.

We floated past the first opening, which must mark the level immediately above the one we had entered. This was one of the dimmer lighted and I saw there was space on either side, as if this hole bisected a passage somewhat wider than the entrance into this trap.

I began to move my feet, kick out a little, and so I discovered that I could so push myself toward the side of the well. I must now make an effort at the next level to pull out, taking Ayllia with me. And to that I bent all my energies. We finally won free of the well, somehow pulling into another passage on the opposite side from where we had entered.

This was much better lighted and there was sound—or was it vibration, which seemed to come, not from any one direction, but from the floor on which we lay, or out of the walls about us. There was still a spongy coating on the floor, but no longer any drifts of sooty ash. We could have come into a portion which was in use. And that must make us more wary in our going.

I was conscious that Ayllia was sitting up, staring from me to the walls about us, then back to me again. That fixed look which had masked her for so long was gone and she shivered, her hands going to cover her eyes.

"The Paths of Balemat," she whispered hoarsely.

"Not so!" I put out my hand, not to lead her this time, but rather to give her what comfort might lie in human touch. "We live; we are not dead." For she had spoken then of their primitive belief in an evil spirit who waited beyond the final curtain for those whose rites were not properly carried out.

"I remember—" She still did not take away the fingers she used to blind herself. "But this is surely Balemat's land and we walk in his house. No place else could be so."

I could almost agree with her. But I had one argument which I thought would persuade her she had not joined the dead.

"Do you not hunger, thirst? Would the dead do so?"

She dropped her hands. Her expression was one of sullen hopelessness.

"Who can say? Who has ever returned to say this is this, that is that, behind the curtain? If not the House of Balemat, then where are we, witch woman?"

"In another world sure enough, but not that of the dead. We found an adept's gate and were drawn through it into one of the other worlds—"

She shook her head. "I know nothing of your magic, witch woman, save that it has ill served me and mine. And would seem to continue to do so. But it is true that I hunger and thirst. And if there is food or drink to be discovered I would like to find it."

"As would I. But we must go with care. I do not know who or what lives here. I only know it is a place of much strangeness and so must be scouted as we would a raiders' camp."

I opened my pack and brought out the remains of the food I had carried and we managed to choke some mouthfuls of it until our thirst proved too strong for us to swallow more. That little meal did give us a lift of energy.

As we went on we discovered that this hall was broken by the outlines of what must be doors. But all were without latches or ways of opening them. And though I was finally emboldened to push at one or two, they did not yield to pressure. So we finally came to the end of that way, which was a balcony open on the night. From it swung one of the skyways connecting the tower with the next farther in toward the heart of the city. And, looking at that narrow footway, which seemed to be the most fragile of paths, I knew I could not cross it. Ayllia covered her eyes and pushed back into the corridor.

"I can not!" she cried.

"Nor can I." But what else could we do? Trust again to the well and its upward pull to waft us to yet another corridor aloft where we might fare no better?

I asked her then what she remembered of our coming this far. And she replied with most of it, but said that it was all to her as a dream of which she was a spectator, not a part—save that earlier she had been moving by a drawing which ceased when we came to the road.

We started back toward the well, having no hope but to trust to it again. But before we reached that end of the hall there was a small snap of sound which sent us both into what very poor cover this way offered, flattening ourselves against the wall, standing very still.

One of those doors which had been so tightly shut opened and a figure stepped out. Stepped? No, it did not step; it rolled, or rather hovered above the floor even as the carrier had on the road. And that figure—

I have seen many mutants and monsters. Escore is plentifully inhabited by creatures who are the end results of long ago experimentation by the adepts. There are the Krogen, who are water men, born to live within that liquid at ease, and there are the Flannan, who have wings, the Gray Ones, who are an evil mixture of beast and man, and many others. But this—this was somehow worse than anything I had seen or heard described.

It was as if one had begun to make a machine which was also a man, metal and flesh grafted together. The lower half was an oval of metal, having no legs, though folded up against that ovoid shape were jointed appendages which ended in claws, now closed together as one might close fingers into a fist.

There were similiar limbs on the narrower upper section of the body, but above that was a human, or seemingly human, head, though there was no hair, only a metal capping ending in a point. And behind that ball-with-a-head came another mixture of man-machine, though this one walked on two legs, and had human arms. But the chest and the body were all metal, and the head again ended in a metal point.

Neither of the things looked in our direction, but one

floated, one walked, toward the well; there they simply stepped or rolled out into the empty space and were borne upward, past the roof of this level and out of our sight.

X

"NO!" Ayllia's denial of what she saw did not rise above a whisper. But she stood with some of the old blankness back in her eyes.

Meanwhile, I wondered how the magic force of that well might be reversed, taking us down the shaft and not up. After seeing what must inhabit the reaches of this tower city I had no desire to explore it further. And my hopes for finding supplies were already gone. Those things which were such an unholy mixture of flesh and metal could certainly not eat nor drink, nor furnish us with provisions even if we managed to find a storeroom in this maze.

I tried now to remember what had begun our float upward. My hand had fallen on the wall and now, as I tried to recall that memory more distinctly, I thought I had seen a plate of differently colored metal set there. My hand had scraped down it—but we had risen *up*! Could it be a uniform signal?

If so, could I find a plate somewhere which would reverse our course and send us safely down? We could only try. To remain where we were, I believed now, was only waiting to be discovered, and my whole being shrank from the thought of any close contact with those half and half things. It was just by the vast favor of fortune they had not looked in our direction.

"Come on—" I reached for Ayllia's arm in the old way.

She tried to elude me. "No!"

"Stay here," I told her grimly, "and they will find you."

"Go there"—she pointed to the shaft—"and they surely will!"

113

"Not so." Though I could not be sure of that. Hurriedly I explained what I thought had brought us up the shaft and the chance we might reverse the process.

"And if we cannot?"

"Then we shall have to try our fortune across the bridge." But that to me was almost as great an ordeal as facing one of the half-monsters of this place. And the only bridge we had access to led deeper into the city, not out of it.

I think that Ayllia liked that no better than I did, for she started on toward the shaft without further urging. But we went slowly, listening at each door marking, testing it with our hands before scuttling to the next, fearing each might open and we would have to face some inhabitant. When we reached the last opening, through which the two had come, we found the crack more pronounced. Under my fingers the barrier moved a little.

That hum which had been a part of the walls was louder and I saw, through a very narrow slit which was all I dared to open, sections of metal wrought into incomprehensible objects. But I did not linger for more than one hurried glimpse.

We reached the side of the shaft and I looked right and left. It was hard to detect the control plate, but it was there and I saw two depressions in it, one set above the other. I had passed my hand down before, now I would try up. So I did. But thereafter I lingered for a long breath or two, not quite wanting to put my guess to the test.

If we stepped out and were carried further aloft, following the grotesque metal pair, it might well be that we would be taken past any concealment straight into the hands of those who dwelt here. Then I remembered the pack. I could use that for a test. Though to part with the few supplies we had . . .

I loosed its straps and tossed it out. It reached the center of the shaft with the force of my throw and began to sink. I was right!

"In!" I ordered and stepped out, though that took some force of will, conditioned as I was to the fear of falling.

Ayllia gave a small, choked cry, but she followed me. Our descent was faster than our rise had been, though not to the point of actual falling. I worked my body until I reached the wall of the shaft where the openings were, ready to swing in, for I remembered that other dim level we had passed in our ascent. Now that I had a possible second exit I was emboldened to explore further where the lack of strong light suggested a deserted, or near deserted, level. And I said as much to Ayllia.

I think she would have refused, but she was in no mind to be left alone. We reached the level and I caught at its opening, while Ayllia, who had grasped my cloak, swung in beside me. We were perched in that opening as a Vrang might roost on a stone crag, the pack having gone past us to the bottom of the shaft—though I did not worry about that now.

We were not, I speedily discovered, in another corridor as we had been above, but rather on a narrow walk which ran out a short distance over a vast space. So dim was the light we could see little except that immediately around us, and of that I could make little sense. There were a number of large objects on the floor, each standing a little apart from its neighbor. Finally I decided that these were the carriers we had seen in swift passage on the road, though they were now at rest.

They were cylinders, perhaps twice the height of a tall man, and each was pointed into cone shape. I could see the marks of openings along their sides. But, as with the doors in the upper corridor, these were tightly shut, save for one in the nearest.

And that had not been easily opened. There were stains and sears and the metal was torn and rent, sticking out in points. It plainly had been forced and heat had been used in that forcing. Now, looking further, I could just perceive a similar tear was in the next cylinder. Though why the inhabitants of the city needed to break open their own containers, if that was what these were, was a puzzle.

Were they storehouses? Or were they used to transport

supplies to the city as the wains from the manors of Estcarp crawled at harvest time to Es? If so there might be food in them. I told Ayllia that.

"Water?" she asked hoarsely, "water?"

Though I could not believe any water supply was so housed, I was tempted to explore in that faint hope. We had to have water and soon, or we would not have enough strength to leave the city.

There were no steps nor ladders to descend from the balcony on which we stood, but the drop to the floor below was not too great and I made it. This time Ayllia did not follow. She swore she would remain where she was but not explore. And since I was already down there was no reason to return without at least a closer inspection of the nearest transport.

I longed for a torch—the half light was even less around the carrier. But now I saw something else. From that jagged cut in the side trailed a line, good proof that whoever had forced the opening had explored within.

It was not a braided nor woven cord I discovered, but fashioned of a mesh of small metal links, very strong for its size. And it had loops spaced along it in which I could just set the toes of my boots as an aid to climbing. So small were those loops I thought they had been made to support a foot less long than my own, unless they were only intended for handholds.

I looked back. Ayllia was pressed against the rail which walled the walkway. I raised my hand and she waved back before I climbed. When I reached the seared edge I crouched to peer in And was so startled I nearly lost my balance. For when I set hand on the wall inside there was an answering shaft of light in the interior of the cylinder.

There was a mass of tumbled boxes and chests, the covers of which had been torn away or beaten in, plainly for the purpose of plunder. But the contents were a disappointment, at least to me, for they consisted mainly of metal bars or blocks. And there was a foul smell coming from a sticky pool where a large drum had fallen on its side.

So strong were those fumes, even though the pool was almost dried to a greasy scum, that I feared to stay longer in the close interior. My head began to swim and perhaps I had breathed in some poison.

I backed away, wondering if it was worth my while to try one of the other plundered transports further on in the cavern. But I was beginning to cough and wanted nothing more than to be free, not only of this transport and the place where it was parked, but of the towers into the bargain.

Just as I reached the opening, set my hand to the rope again, I froze. From deeper in the cavern came a flash of light so vivid as to blind me temporarily. Yet I could not remain where I was; the fumes seared my throat and lungs. Blindly I went through the break, swung out and down to the floor. Then I was racked by such a spell of coughing that I could do no more than lean against the side of the transport, my hands pressed to my chest, my eyes blinking.

There was another flash of light, but this time I had not been directly facing it so was spared the assault on my eyes. This time it became a steady glow, and I guessed that perhaps those who had come to plunder were still at work, burning their way into another carrier. The determination of their search suggested that what they sought was of prime importance.

Were there others just as human as ourselves who also sought food and drink? After all, the gate in the citadel could have entrapped more then just we two throughout the years. And my mind fastened on that with a pitiful hope, so that I was determined to put it to the test here and now by spying on whoever was using that fire.

But to reach the place of the light I must go well away from the entrance, leaving Ayllia. To return to explain might be a waste of valuable time . . . .

I think now my mind was affected by those fumes I had breathed, but at the time all my decisions seemed logical and right. I did not return to Ayllia but instead rounded the nose of the transport I had entered, and began to work my way toward that distant glow.

At least enough sense remained to me to make that advance cautiously. I kept to cover with all the skill I had learned in Escore. The dim gloom of the place was an aid and the rows of transports provided many pools of shadow in which to halt before making a dash to the next.

My cough disappeared as I got into this air which, lifeless though it was, yet was free of that sickly odor. It had also increased my thirst to the point where I was frantic for water. And it seemed to me then that I need only reach those ahead to find it.

At last I huddled at the tip of another transport to watch the workers. Two of them clung to a webbing draped on either side of the door they were attacking. They hung there, watching the efforts of two more at floor level, aiming up at the metal beams of light which struck, to spray out, eating slowly into its substance.

I made the mistake of again looking at the light and so was blinded momentarily. I shrank back and waited for my sight to clear. A glimpse of those working to force the entrance had been enough to make me think they were not the same breed of half-things as I had seen above. They all appeared to have normal bodies, legs and arms.

Now I peered between my fingers, using them to shield against the glare. Was it fire they used as a tool, I wondered, or a force of light with the strength of fire? Fire I could and had summoned to answer my will, for it is a thing of nature and so must come at the call of a Wise Woman. But this was a different thing, for the beam issued from a pipe these workers held in their hands, and the pipe was connected by a limber hose to a box sitting on the floor between them.

The fire suddenly died, and now those on the webs swung closer. They smashed bars against the glowing opening, prying and working at the metal now softened a little.

But I no longer watched them. One of those who had held the pipe laid down the strange weapon and went to a pile of packs. He picked up a small container which he held to his mouth—drinking!

Water!

At that moment all the wealth of knowledge could have been mine for the taking and I would have passed it by for what the stranger held. What I was going to get!

He put down the container and went back to the pipe. As he raised that, ready to shoot the beam again, I moved, running along the side of the transport which sheltered me from their eyes. They were so intent upon what they did, though working openly as if they need have no fear of any inimical onlooker, that I did not believe I was in any danger then.

My world, my future, narrowed to that container. I made my way toward it, sparing only a short, searching glance now and then at the workers, to be sure none came my way. But they were engaged once more in burning, their attention all for the stubborn metal. My hand closed upon the container and I raised it to my lips.

It was not pure water, unless water in this world had a sour taste. But it was so refreshing to my cracked lips, parched mouth, and dry throat, that I had to fight myself not to swallow more than a few sips.

There was a cry from the working party and I turned in fear, sure they had sighted me. I discovered instead that the door had given away and those on the webs were kicking it loose.

I fumbled throught the packs they had stacked here. There were some packets which might contain food and two of those I took. But I could carry no more for I had chanced upon three more of the water containers, by their weight nearly full.

Slinging two carrying straps over my shoulders, clasping the third tightly to me with the packets, I faded back into the shadows, intent now on reaching Ayllia. We were in a good position by the door to watch these workers when they withdrew. If they were of our own kind, earlier victims of the gate, we could then claim meeting. Having drunk, my caution returned and I was not minded to surrender to any who prowled this world until I was sure it was not the enemy.

When I gained the entrance to the cavern there was no Ayllia. I dare not risk calling: my voice might carry back to the working party. And, burdened as I now was with the food and water I carried, I was not sure I could regain the upper level of the balcony.

At last I was forced to return to the ladder, reclimb into the fumes to unhook it, and drop in a jarring fall to the floor. Ayllia still did not show and I worked as fast as I could lest those beyond miss their water ration and trail me. There was a hook at the end of the ladder and I whirled a length around my head, let it fly, so it caught on the railing of the balcony. With this anchored I was able to climb, draw after me the containers I had made fast to the lower end.

Equipped with supplies, I sped down the short space to the well, but saw no sign of Ayllia. I hung over to peer down to the bottom of the shaft. She was not there either. But I was almost certain she had gone this way.

As my boots rapped against the floor of the shaft I looked around for the pack which had fallen ahead of us. There were many marks on the pavement, the gritty dust of these lower levels stirred and scuffed—more than could result from just our coming and going. The working party, had they come this way? I had not noticed too much on our entrance, but now I studied each foot of the way with care as I retraced the passage to where it gave upon the road entering the base of the tower.

I was now away from that sound or vibration which made floors and walls sing faintly on the upper levels, so I heard a sound ahead. Not the warning roar of the arrival of a transport, but a cry which I thought must be human. And I was greatly tempted to call out to Ayllia, save that suspicion warned me she might be in some danger which it was better not to walk into blindly.

As I started down the dusty passage leading to the entrance

I thought I saw movement ahead. I slowed, listened. If something or someone was coming toward me perhaps I would have to retreat, but if it went the other way I could follow.

Then in a small pool of glimmer I saw Ayllia. She was being dragged along by two figures shorter than she, creatures I could not see clearly. As I watched one of them dealt her a vicious blow across the shoulders which sent her staggering on. And they straightaway closed in on her again. She kept her feet but she went as one who was either only semiconscious or completely cowed, offering no resistance.

They were very close to the road tunnel and a moment or two later they were gone into it. I started to run, the heavy water bottles inflicting bruises as they banged my ribs, battering me as that blow had done for Ayllia.

At the tunnel I hesitated once more. Not only did I listen for the roar which would precede one of the transports, but I was undecided as to which way Ayllia and her captors had gone. Deeper into the towerways, or out into the country?

Though I listened and peered, I could find no clue. But at last I decided that it would be out. I hardly thought that those who inhabited the city would, by choice, take the dangerous road here. It was more likely to be the way of some invader.

Yet I was plagued as I began backtracking with the fear that my logical reasoning was at fault, that instead of following Ayllia I was heading in the opposite direction.

It was not until I was safely off that narrow footway and out in the night that I had confirmation as to the wisdom of my reasoning. That came when my foot struck against an object in the dark and sent it spinning into a shaft of moonlight—for I had not emerged into the blackness of complete dark but into a silvered world where a moon hung full and very bright.

What I had kicked into view was a packet I knew well, seeing as how I had made it up with my own hands, some of Utta's healing herbs tied into a small sack. That had not fallen from my pack when we had entered this place because, until I had opened it to share the food with Ayllia, the carrier had been well tied. Therefore, someone had opened the pack hereabouts and dropped this.

I went to one knee and felt around. If anything else had been dropped, I did not find it. I could only believe that those who had taken Ayllia also had the pack, had opened it for inspection and lost this.

The workers in the cavern, the shadow figures I had seen with Ayllia—I decided they were alike. They certainly had human bodies, even if they were over-small. I had an impression, when I took time to call to mind and assess all I had seen, of very thin legs and arms. And I thought of those of Escore—the Thas—bloated bodies, spider limbs, creatures who veered so far from the human they were now utterly loathsome to us who dwelt in the outer world above their tunnels and burrows.

Had Thas found their way through the gate? But their use of fire as a tool—that was no Thas doing.

So those I had trailed had come this way, but now where? In the bright moonlight, and I could not be too far behind them, could I track them? The packet had lain well beyond the edge of the road turning to my left as if those I sought had struck out between that highway and the next tower.

The ground had a hard surface, but across it were drifts of the ashy sand. Neither was good for my purpose but I quested on, searching for any hint of trail. And I found it, far plainer than I had hoped. This was another roadway, though cruder than those feeding into the towers. It was apparent that heavy weights had passed here to wear ruts in the soil. And where that upper crust had been broken, I found prints of feet. Some of the sharpest were from boots—Ayllia's, or so I believed. The others were smaller and narrower. The toes, instead of being rounded, speared out in points, unlike any I had seen. But they all pointed ahead and I followed.

That trail ended in a space where a new marking began and more and wider ruts cut very deep. I could only think of some vehicle which had carried a weighty cargo. There was no attempt to hide it and I marched along beside it.

The ruts approached the next road but did not cross it, rather paralleled it back into the country through which we had come on our way to the towers. This part of the land was more rolling and rougher than that we had traversed. The road was cut through hills, whereas the ruts veered and wove a way around such obstructions. It was impossible to see far ahead; I listened, hoping to hear something to tell me those I trailed were near, needing a warning if I were not to march blindly into captivity.

The hills rose higher all the time and crags of rock protruded from them—or what I thought to be rock, until taking shelter behind one when I thought I heard a noise, my hand rested on its surface, and detected a pattern of seam. And a closer look told me that these were not of nature's forming, but the work of man or some intelligent creature. These hills were not of earth but the remains of buildings half hidden by the shifting of the ash-sand dunes.

I had little time to think of that, for my belief that I had heard a noise proved to be true. There was a hissing, and then a soft crunching. Into the moonlight below my perch crawled a new form of transport. Beside the swift cylinders speeding along the highways this was a clumsy, ill-constructed thing, as if born from another type of brain and imagination.

It had no wheels as the carts of my own world, but huge bands which ran from the front to the back, turning so, their treads spinning on rods projecting from the box body. If it carried driver or passengers they were in that box which was ventilated only by a series of narrow vertical slits spaced evenly around it.

The pace it held was slow, ponderous, steady, and it gave such an appearance of a fortress able to move across the land that I wondered if that was how it had been conceived. But the route it followed was the rutted way to the towers; perhaps it had been sent to fetch those who plundered the cavern.

I kept to my hiding place in the corner of the half buried wall and watched it crawl on out of sight.

XI

CAN one say that there is a "smell" to Power? I only know that one can sniff the evil of the Shadow; whether that be done by the nostrils of the spirit, or ones of flesh I have never learned. But it is true that in Escore I could sense the places of the Dark to be avoided. In this world, however, there was an acrid stench always with one and foreseeing, even to the small extent I had regained it, was blunted. It was as if in passing through the gate I had shed the right to call upon what had once been a shield on my arm.

Now I had no more than my own five physical senses to depend upon, and it was like losing half of one's sight. Still I tried to see if I could not use even a little of my skills. Since Ayllia was also of my world there was a faint chance that there might exist a mind bond between us, and, using that, I could either gain from her some idea of where she went and the dangers which lay between us, or even, in a good meeting of mind, see through her eyes.

It was a very forlorn hope, but now I settled farther back into the ruined wall and concentrated upon Ayllia, building my mind picture of her, willing an answer.

Only—

What!

I sat up tense, gasping. Not the Vupsall mind. No! But I had touched, merely touched, on the edge of a mental broadcast so powerful that that small contact expelled me, buffeted me from its path, for it was aimed in another direction.

Not Ayllia, of that I was certain. Yet, was I also sure that what I had touched was of my world, trained in the Power? The gate—had my thought that others had come through it been right? But . . .

Part of me wanted fiercely to seek again that reassuring contact with the familiar. Another warned caution. I knew Escore history, and over and over had it been said that those who had used the gates were often of the Shadow, or the birth roots from which the Shadow had grown. To open communication with some dark power would doubly doom me.

I could not believe that those half-men of the city, nor those who had crawled past in the movable fortress, were of Escore. We have never depended upon machines. That is what we abhorred in the Kolder, who were in a way half-men, part of the machines they tended. And the Wise Women had believed us right in our choice, for in the last great battle at Gorm it had been mind power which had burnt out and vanquished those welded to metal.

But somewhere and not too far away was at least one from my world. And I longed to go seeking, but dared not until I knew more.

The rutted road of the crawler was very clear in the moonlight. And the sound of its crunching had died away. That was the road Ayllia had gone and the one I must follow. I drank sparingly from one of the water containers and slipped out to walk the ruts.

More and more of the hillocks and mounds around that roadway showed signs of being the remains of buildings. I could well believe that this had once been a city, unlike the tower one, but of some size and importance.

Then the ruts began to run between taller walls and suddenly into a vast open space like a huge crater or basin pocked deep into the earth. Here there were no remains of buildings, rather stretches of glassy material which the crawling tracks dodged around as if the treads of the fortress could not pass over their slick surfaces.

The ruts led to the center of the basin where there was a gaping blackness as if it were a mouth of such a shaft as we had found in the city, but as large as the base of one of the sky-reaching towers.

There was no cover to be found here. If I approached the well in the moonlight I would be as visible as if I sounded a warn horn at the verge of a manor. Yet it was into that hole Ayllia had surely gone. And it was laid on me, as heavily as if it were a geas, that I had a responsibility for her and must free her if I could.

I could not tell what spy searches might be laid about. But just perhaps—

Once more I hunkered down in the shadow of the last vestige of ruined wall. This time I covered my eyes with the palm of my left hand. With the right I touched the wand still thrust through my belt. I had no other thing of Power with me, and if it could add to my limited efforts I needed it badly.

I set the picture of Ayllia in my mind and sent out a search thought.

What I met was blankness. But it was a blankness I recognized and again I was startled into breaking my concentration. Ayllia was mind-locked against any such search. So alerted, I tried, very cautiously, as one might touch with only the tip of a finger, to find the source of the mind-lock. But what I fingered so very lightly was not what I expected to find, rather something entirely alien to all I knew.

A machine with Power? That was an anomaly I could not accept. Power was utterly opposed to machines and always had been. A Wise Woman could handle steel in the form of a weapon if some urgent need arose, as my mother had done upon occasion, though one relied mainly on the Power. But even so much a modification as a dart gun—that meant careful preparation in thinking patterns. We could not ally with a machine!

Yet touch here told me Ayllia was held in a pattern of mind-lock familiar to me, but that it was created by a machine! Could there have been some welding here of Escore knowledge with that native to this world to produce a monstrous hybrid?

To enter that hole ahead knowing no more than I did of what faced me there was utter folly. But neither could I turn my back on Ayllia. So was I one torn in two directions, unable to make up my mind. And such a state was so alien to my nature that I was perhaps easy prey to what followed, my mind so occupied with my dilemma that I was not ready, my safeguards down.

What struck was that seeking I had met before edge on. For a moment I received an impression of shock to the sender as great as that I had earlier experienced. And after that slight recoil, came a pouring out of a need so great that it actually pulled me on, out of the hollow where I had taken refuge, into the open. It was a current such as I had felt to a lesser degree in the hall of the gate.

My resistance awoke and I tried to fight with all I could summon, so I was a swimmer floundering in water rushing me madly toward sharp rocks of perilous rapids. And that which drew me on seemed triumphant, showing a kind of impatience which would not allow me any return of my own will.

Thus I came to the hole, which was a great mouth to gulp me down. And I saw a platform a little below me. But that did not fill the whole expanse, only a small wedge of it. Perhaps it was awaiting the return of the crawler that it might be lowered into the depths. Below I could see nothing else and it seemed to me this well reached so far toward the core of the earth that it was the length of one of the towers in reverse.

Beyond the waiting platform was the beginning of a stair circling down, hugging the wall of the shaft. I tried to fight the compulsion which drew me on, but there was no chance to free myself and I began the journey into the depths.

I discovered quickly that I must not look into the dusk

below, but must keep my eyes on the nearer wall to fight the giddiness which struck at me.

Time had no meaning; my world narrowed to the wall, the abyss on the other side into which I must not look. And it seemed to me that this lasted for hours, days. The wall was smooth in parts, with the slick look of those glassy patches in the basin; then again it would be rock, but rock dressed to a uniform surface.

The moonlight which had been silver bright in the outer world no longer reached me, and now I went more slowly, feeling my way from step to step. But never was I released from that drawing.

At last, when I felt for the next step, I met solid level surface. I leaned, shaking, against the wall, daring now to turn my head and look up to where the outer world was a segment of light, then around me in the dark. I was afraid to venture away from the wall I could touch and which so afforded me a sense of security, if there could be any security in such a place as this. But the pull on me never faltered.

So I began to feel my way along, hand to wall, testing each step before I took it. I was, I thought, perhaps a quarter of the way around that space from the point where I reached the bottom, before my hand on the wall met empty space. And it was into that opening the current drew me. But again I sought frantically for a wall and kept my fingers running along it, tapping one boot toe ahead, lest I end up in a pit trap.

After that first burst of recognition the mind beam which had entrapped me took on a mechanical sending. I longed to probe for what personality might lie behind it, but I was afraid to so open myself to invasion. It was known that an adept could take over a lesser witch or warlock, and such bondage was worse than any slavery of the body. It was what I had feared and fled in Escore, and to succumb to it here would mean I was wholly lost for all time.

There was a sound ahead, a faint hissing. Then there appeared a line of light which widened as I blinked against the glare. I had an open door and I walked through in spite of a last resistance to the pull. But, as I stepped into the light, the compulsion vanished and I was free.

Only I had no time to take advantage of my release, for as I swung around to retreat, the halves of the door were already nearly shut—too narrow a space was left for me to wriggle through. I stood, wishing for some weapon . . . .

As in the cavern of the stored transports, I stood on a balcony or narrow upper runway; before me was a scene of activity I could not take in all at once. There was a board or screen on which lights flashed, flickered, died, or flashed again in no discernible pattern. From that came a tinkling which was not of human speech.

The screen appeared to divide the whole of the space below into two parts, though there was an aisle with a low wall running from some point immediately below where I now stood, to a narrow arch in the screen.

On either side of that wall were cell-like divisions, all having partitions about shoulder-high and each like a room. Some of these were occupied, and seeing those occupants I recoiled until my back struck against the door now tightly closed behind me. I had thought those figures in the cavern, and with Ayllia had had some odd outlines which half denied humanity. Now I saw them in full light and knew that, though they might be travesties of men, they were such as made them worse than the monsters of Escore. My last hope that I might find here some others caught by the gate vanished.

They were small, and their skin was a pallid gray which in itself was repulsive. Where the half-men of the towers had had heads capped with metal, these had a thin thatching of yellow-white hair, but it had fallen from the scalps in places, to leave bare red splotches which looked sore and scabby. They wore clothing which fitted so tightly to their bodies and limbs that it was almost a second skin. This was uniformly gray, but of a darker shade than the flesh beneath it, so that their hands showed up as pallid sets of claws, for they were thin to the point of near skeletons.

I saw, when I forced myself forward a step or two again to look at them, that their faces had a great uniformity, as if they were all copies of a single model—save that here or there they were further disfigured by puckered scars or rough and pitted skin.

They moved sluggishly when they moved at all. Most of them lay on narrow shelf bunks within their individual cubicles. Others simply sat staring ahead of them at the low walls as if awaiting some summons which dim wits could not understand but would respond to. One or two ate from bowls, using their fingers to cram greenish stuff into their mouths. I averted my eyes hurriedly from them as they slobbered and sucked.

Men they might be in general outline, but they had become less than the animals of my own world.

The pattern of lights across the great board suddenly made a symbol and there was a clap of sound. Those lying on their bunks roused, stood straight by the doors of their cells. The eaters dropped their bowls to do likewise.

But only a few of them issued from their small private sections, gathering in the aisle. The line then faced in the opposite direction and marched, to file out of sight beneath the place where I stood.

The rest remained standing where they were. Nor did they show any sign of impatience as time passed and they were neither dismissed to their interrupted meal and rest, or alerted for some errand or labor.

The symbol on the board dissolved once more into running lights and I began to wonder about my own immediate future. It was plain that I was not going to break out through the door now closed so firmly behind me.

There was no sign of Ayllia in any of the cells below, though there remained the section behind the lighted screen—I did not know what was there, or beyond the exit through which the marchers had gone. Would any of those now at attention sight me if I were to go down to their level? I could not determine how unaware they were. And I was afraid to try to reach Ayllia by mind touch.

But I was not to be given time to put even my wildest half-plan into action. If it had seemed that the mind touch which had drawn me here had stopped at the door, there were other precautions in force at the command of he who ruled this underground enclave, as I speedily discovered. For, without warning, I was caught by a rigidity which would not yield to any of my attempts to break it. I could only blink my eyelids. For the rest I was frozen as if one of the legends of childhood had come true and I was turned to stone.

So imprisoned by a force new to me, I had to watch four of those standing at attention below turn and march, again under the shelf where I was. But now an opening appeared near me and through it raised a platform with the four guards. They crowded about me and one of them aimed a weapon not unlike a dart gun at my feet and legs. As he thumbed it the bonds which held that part of my body had vanished and I was free to move as they steered me to their platform, and on it we were lowered to face the aisle of the screen arch.

Seen from floor level and not from above, that screen with all its rippling lights awoke awe. It was alien, totally so to me, but there was that about it which I could recognize as well as a force influence wielded by a Wise Woman. Only this was not aimed at me, and it was not part of the current which had drawn me hither.

Shepherded by the guards, I went through the arch of the screen. Here were no cells, no divisions, just a four step dais. Around the bottom level of the dais were small screens: only two of those facing me sparkled with light. Below each screen jutted a ledge sloping toward the floor at an angle, and those were covered with buttons and small projecting levers. More and more was I unpleasantly reminded of the tales of Kolder strongholds.

Each of these ledges had a fixed seat before it. Gray-clad

men sat at the two which flashed lights, their eyes fixed upon the screens, their hands resting on the edges of the ledges as if ready at any moment to press one of the buttons, should the need arise.

On the dais itself, however, stood that which drew and held all my attention—in part the answer to the mystery which had entangled me. There was a tall, pillar-shaped box of clear crystal. And completely embedded in its heart stood a man of Escore. Not only one of the Old Race, I realized as I looked closer, but this was the man I had seen in my dream, he who had opened the gate and then sat to watch it.

Entombed, yes, but not dead! No, not mercifully dead. From the crown of that crystal coffin there fountained a series of silver wires which were never still, but quivered and spun, sparkling in the air as if they were indeed not metal but rising and falling streams of water.

The eyes of the prisoner now opened and he looked straight at me. There was a fierce brightness in his gaze, a demand which was cruel in its intensity, its force bent upon me. He tried in those few instants to beat down what was me, to take me over to do his will. And I knew that to him I represented a key to freedom, that he had brought me here for that purpose alone.

Perhaps if I yielded at once to his demand he might have achieved his purpose. But my response was almost automatic recoil. None of my breed yielded to force until we were overcome. Had he pled instead of tried to take—but the need in him was too great, and he could not plead when all life outside his crystal walls had become one with the enemy in his mind.

The silver strands tossed wildly, rippling as he fought to possess me as his slave thing. And I heard a startled cry. From before one of those ledges arose a man. He leaned forward and stared at the captive in the crystal. Then he swung around to look at me, astonishment speedily changing to excitement, and then satisfaction.

132

He was as different from the gray men as I was. But he was not of the Old Race. Nor had he any of the Power; I knew that when I looked upon him. But there was life and intelligence in his face and with that a detachment which said, though he looked human, he was not so within.

Standing a head taller than his servants, he was lean of body, though not reduced to such skeleton proportions as they. Nor did his face and hands have the gray pallor, though the rest of his body was covered by the same tight-fitting clothes as they wore, distinguished from theirs by an intricate blazon on the breast worked out in colors of yellow, red, and green.

His hair was almost as brightly yellow as that blazon, thick and long enough, though he wore it tucked behind his ears, to touch his shoulders. That was the hair of a Sulcarman. But when I studied his face I knew that here was no sea-rover trapped by the gate. For his features were very sharply angled about a large and forward thrusting nose, giving him almost the appearance of wearing one of the bird masks behind which the Falconers rose into battle.

"A—woman!"

He touched a button on his board and then he came around to face me, standing with his hands on his hips, eyeing me up and down with an insolence which made my anger rise.

"A woman," he repeated and this time he did not speak in surprise but thoughtfully. And he glanced from me to the prisoner in the crystal and then back again.

"You are not," he continued, "like the other—"

He gestured to the other side of the dais. I could not turn my head so I saw no more than the edge of a cloak. But I knew that to be Ayllia's. She did not move and I thought perhaps she was caught in just the sort of web as now held me.

"So"—now he addressed the prisoner—"you thought to use her? But you did not try with the other. What makes this one different?"

The man in the crystal did not even turn his eyes to his

133

questioner. But I felt that deep wave of hate spread from the box which held him, hate that froze instead of burned, a hate such as I had at times sensed in my brothers, but never in such a great tide.

His captor walked around me, though I could not turn my head to see him. I had learned this much, however, that he could not instantly recognize Power as his prisoner had done. Therefore he was devoid of any trace of that talent. And that thought gave me a spark of confidence, though looking upon the prisoner, I could not hope too much. . . . For as he had known me as witch, so did I know him as more than warlock, as one of the adepts such as no longer existed in Escore and had never been known on Estcarp, where the Wise Women carefully controlled all learning lest just such a reckless seeker after forbidden learning rise.

"A woman," the stranger repeated for the third time. "Yet you aimed a sending at her. It would seem she is far more than she looks, bedraggled and grimy as she is. And if there is any chance that she is even a little akin to you, my unfriend, then this is indeed a night when fortune has chosen to give me her full smile!"

"Now"—he nodded at my guard and they crowded in upon me, though there seemed to be some barrier so they could not really lay hand on me—"we shall put you in safekeeping, girl, until we have more time for the solving of your riddle."

They continued to crowd me along the steps until I was on the opposite side of the room from the entrance, behind the prisoner in the crystal, so he could no longer see me, though I knew he was as aware of me as I was of him. The guards then stepped away and from the floor arose four bars of crystal like the pillar, but only as thick as my wrist. They slid up above my head and then they began to glow. As they did so the force which had held me rigid vanished, but when I put out my hand I found that there was an invisible wall between one bar and the next and I was boxed.

There was room within my square of unseen walls for me

to sit down and I did, looking about me now with the need to learn all I could of this place—though I could not begin to guess the reason for it, what great project it was necessary to.

I could see Ayllia now. She sprawled as one unconscious or asleep on the second step of the dais, her head turned from me. But I could see the rise and fall of her breast and knew she still lived.

I needed sleep too. As I sat there all the strain and fatigue of my hours in this world closed about me as a smothering curtain and I had to have ease and relaxation of mind and body. Thus I concentrated on setting certain safeguards to alert me against any new attempt on the part of he who stood in the pillar to take command. With that done I rested my head on my knees.

But between my palms, hidden from sight, I held that wand I had brought out of Escore. Did it belong to the man in the pillar? If so, it might have been what he had noted instantly at my coming and wanted to get, though how he might reach it through his walls I could not see. That he was of value to my new captor was certain. And it might be that I would also end so. This thought I willed away, for sleep I must have if I would be quick of wit when such was needed.

XII

WHILE I slept, I dreamed. But this was no second assault upon my will, no harsh order to obey. Rather a hand slipped into mine to lead me to a place of safety where one could speak mind to mind without chance of being overheard; it was the prisoner of the pillar whom I faced in that place which was not of our waking world. Somehow he seemed younger, more vulnerable, not filled with white hate and the need to burst bonds and rend the world about him to satisfy the revenge his spirit craved, all of which I had read in him before.

That he was an adept I already knew, one above the Wise Women of Estcarp as I was above Ayllia in the scale of Power control. Now I learned his name, or rather the name by which he went, since that old law that the naming of true names was forbidden lest it offer some enemy a straight course into mastery held. He was Hilarion, and once he had dwelt in the citadel of the gate.

He had created the gate because his seeking mind ever pushed on and on for new learning. And, having opened it, it followed that he was constrained to explore what lay beyond. So he came, arrogant and proud in his power—too arrogant, because of the past years of his supremacy in his own sphere, to take precautions.

Thus he had been caught in a web which was not spun from such learning, learning that would not have held him for an instant. But this danger was born of a machine, or a different path of Power, and one he did not understand. Only it was a strength which could incorporate him into it, even as I had seen the half-men in the city of towers, part flesh, part machine.

Between the towers and this underground hole was a long war. It would seem that the present inhabitants of the towers made no overt attacks against the underground; but the gray men, under the orders of he who dominated this chamber, raided in the cities, bringing back the supplies which were needed to sustain this installation. And this life of raid and struggle had lasted for untold years—so many that Hilarion could not list them, for it was old before he had been entrapped, and he had dwelt here long. This I well knew, for the days of the adepts in Escore were past perhaps a thousand years ago.

The machines here had been set in place a millennium ago for the waging of a great war and had continued to function although the world on the surface had been blasted so that nothing remained there save the towers. The machines had been faltering when Hilarion had come, but at his capture they took on new life from his Power, so that now he in a measure controlled them, though in turn he was controlled by Zandur, who was master here, who had always been master. At hearing that I showed disbelief that a man could exist so long.

"But he is not truly a man!" countered Hilarion. "Perhaps he was, long ago. But he has learned to make other bodies in a growth vat and transfer to them when the one he wears grows old or ails. And the machines weave such a protection around him that he cannot be reached by any impulse I have been able to summon. Now he will soon know that you are of a like nature to me and he will imprison you to add to the power of his machines—"

"No!"

"So said I once: 'No' and 'No' and 'No!' Yet my 'Nos' could not stand against his 'Yes.' There is this, that together we may—I need only be free of this crystal which negates anything I send against him, and then we shall see which is stronger, a man or machine! For now I know these machines as I did not before, all their stresses and weaknesses; I know they can be attacked. Loose me, witch. Give me your Power for my backing, and we shall both win free. Deny me your aid and you shall be entrapped as I have been for all these weary reaches of time."

"He has me entrapped now," I pointed out warily. Hilarion's arguments were well ordered, but I had not forgotten his first try at making me, not an ally in his struggle, but a weapon in his hand.

He read that now and said; "Such imprisonment is said to build impatience in a man. But if that same man sees before him a key to his cell, perhaps in easy reach, will he not put out his hand to seize upon it? You brought here what is mine, and which, in my hands, will be worth more than any steel, any fire-spitting rod such as these people turn upon each other in their deadly dealing."

"The wand."

"The wand, which is mine and which I had never hoped to see again. It will not serve you to any purpose. But me—to me it will give the power this world withholds!"

"And how do you get it? I do not think your pillar will be easily broken—"

"It looks solid but it is a field of force, force which can be seen. Put the wand to it—"

"Then so I can also loose me!"

"Not so! You know the nature of such a wand. It will obey the one who wrought it, in the hands of another it is a feeble thing. It is not your key, but mine!"

And he spoke the truth. Yet was I now a prisoner and so his wand was as far from me as if it too were encased in crystal.

"But—" What more he might have said was lost. For suddenly he was gone, out of my dream, as a candle might be blown out in a puff, and I was alone. Whether I slept then, or whether my waking thereafter was as quick as it seemed, I do not know. But when I opened my eyes all seemed just as before. I sat guarded by the pillars of light, even as Hilarion was in his casing, and I could not look upon his face, only his back.

However, there was this much of a change: those silver trails which sprouted from the top of the pillar were weaving rhythmically, and I saw the flicker and flash of lights on more than one board which, when I had fallen asleep, had been dark and untended. There were gray men at them now. And around the dais paced Zandur, pausing now and again behind one of those lighted sections, as if he read the lights as runes. There was a tenseness about him, though the gray men worked automatically, as if they were concerned by nothing but their immediate labors.

There was a loud crack of sound, and Zandur spun about to face the large screen which walled this division from the cells of the gray men. A rippling of light ran across its surface, glowing in portions that had been dead and dull moments earlier.

Zandur studied that display and then ran to an empty seat before one of the small boards. His fingers sped across the buttons there. Instantly, in response, I felt such a blow as if someone had laid a lash across my bared body. We were not in the dream now. What demand or disciplining torment was given Hilarion, I also felt, though, I thought, in lesser extent.

So this was how Zandur used controls to make his captive do as he desired. And yet Hilarion had not told me of that. I marveled at the spirit of a man who had been kept so long captive by such pressures.

There are measures one may take in one's mind to elude the pains and needs of the body, a discipline my kind learns early, for if one would use Power one must learn rigid self-control. Hilarion had these to call upon for his protection, unless the machine, being wholly alien, could negate them. And I thought that perhaps that was at least partly so.

Not only for pity, though that was awakened in me, must I do what I could to aid Hilarion, since there was an excellent chance of my being set with him, to be played upon by the same demands and stresses. I had the wand; now I turned it over in my hands. Hilarion had warned that it would not serve me, only him. But I had little chance of getting it to him now. And I was sure that when Zandur released me, he would be well prepared to counter any bid for freedom I might make.

There remained Ayllia. I glanced at where she still lay. How much of mind sending could Zandur detect? I had respect for the machines here, the more so because I did not understand them in the least.

Were there among them some to pick up mind sending, alert our captor to any efforts in that direction? And mind send itself was the part of my own talent which I had not

139

regained to any extent. I was a cripple forced to rely on my maimed talent for support.

There was this, that unless Ayllia was also locked in some invisible cover, then she was teachable. That she was unconscious might perhaps be in my favor. The Wise Women's hallucinations and dreams were principal ways of moving others to their purposes. Now—if I could work on Ayllia, and *if* my mind send was not detected . . .

As far as I could see Zandur was completely absorbed in what was happening on the screens. The Vupsall girl still lay where I had seen her last, but now she had turned upon her side, her head pillowed on her crooked arm, much as one in a natural sleep. If that were so it was even better for my purpose.

I began to blank out, bit by bit, the room about me. This was the traditional method of thought control, and I went at it as cautiously as I had walked in the dark of the outer passage leading here, now testing the strength of my forces, as I had then tested for pitfalls ahead.

This was an exercise known to me for years, but never before had I to hold to it with such uncertainty. Good results depended upon the receptiveness of the person to be influenced. And in Estcarp there had been no such distractions as surrounded me here. I did not want to touch the band Hilarion operated upon, lest such interference be instantly apparent in some way to Zandur.

I closed my eyes, not in truth, but as I had been taught, upon all but Ayllia's body. There was no need for the mental picture; she was there before me. I began to reach, questing for the right line to her brain. Seemingly they kept no watch on her, but that, too, might be deceptive.

The strain was very great; I was forcing my mutilated power. "Ayllia!" I beamed my call at her as if I shouted that aloud.

"Ayllia! Ayllia!"

I have seen many times a patient fisherman casting out a line, letting it drift, bringing it back, to cast again, and yet with no result. And so it was with me. I fiercely fought the rising despair, the feeling that it was no longer in me to succeed in this thing which had once been such a small exercise.

"Ayllia!" No use—I could not touch her. Either I was lacking in force, or else something blanked my questing.

But if that was so how had Hilarion been able to make me dream true? Or had I? Was that all a hallucination spun by Zandur?

Some of the adepts had not walked in the Shadow, but more of them had. Could I believe that he was one of the Dark Ones? I wavered, lost, drew in upon myself, and knew bitterness from my failure.

For a space did I so retreat, and then once more I began to think, with more clarity. My fellow captive was a part of whatever Zandur did with these machines. To be such a part it was necessary for mental contact, since his body was imprisoned. And it was plain to my eyes that the gray men who pressed buttons below the dais did that by rote and not because they thought. Therefore there was an energy here, enough akin to our Power to be able to link to it. Suppose I could so link in part, build thus a backing for my crippled mind sending.

Such a course was tempting, but there was danger in it, too. For such a touch might well draw in the whole of me, as a magnet draws steel. And it was plain that what chanced here now was demanding from Hilarion a high amount of force. Did Zandur have a need for sleep, or was his synthetic body without fatigue known to the human kind? Did there ever come a time when the energy here was at a low ebb? And if so, how far were we from such a period now? Too long for me, that Zandur might be reminded he had a second captive and turn to my humbling?

I set myself to watch what was going on—and discovered that in the time I had been concentrating on Ayllia there had come a change: the extra boards which had been alight

141

and tended by the gray men were once more dark, the seats before them empty.

Zandur—I caught sight of him on the other side of the dais, where he must be facing Hilarion. He looked up at the adept and there was a satisfied smile on his face. He spoke then and his words, though low-pitched, reached me.

"Well done, my unfriend. Even if not by your will, yet you have added to our accomplishment. I do not believe those in the towers will try that again: they have no liking for losses." He turned his head slowly from side to side as if he surveyed all within that huge chamber with pride. "We wrought better than we first guessed when we set these here. Machines they were then, extensions only of our own hands, eyes, brains. Now they are more. But still"—his face was suddenly convulsed; he grimaced as if some inner pain gnawed at him—"but still they are ruled, they do not rule! And that is how it must be as long as one tower stands! They wrought worse than they thought, those builders of towers, giving themselves to the machines. We knew better! Man"—he beat one fist into the palm of his other hand—"man exists, man abides!"

Man, I wondered. Did he speak thus of himself, who Hilarion had said was certainly not human as we judged human, or the gray men who were but things operating under orders with no will or minds of their own? He spoke as one waging a battle in a rightful cause, as we spoke in Escore against the Shadow, as they spoke in Estcarp when they mentioned Karsten and Alizon.

In such bitter struggles there is a pitfall which few seldom avoid. The time comes when to the fighters the end justifies the means. So it had been when the Wise Women had churned the mountains and put an end to Karsten's invasion; but they had been willing to pay a price in turn, giving up their lives to that end. It was a very narrow path on which they had set their feet and they had not overstepped— they had summoned the Power to that blow, but they had not trafficked with the Shadow.

Here it might have gone otherwise. Perhaps in the beginning Zandur had been one such as my father, my brothers, and then he had taken Dinzil's road, seduced by the thought of the victory so badly needed, or by the smell of power, which, as he handled it, became more and more sweet and needful. He could also still deceive himself that what he did was for a high purpose, thus making him the more to be feared.

"Man abides," he repeated. "Here—man abides!" And he threw up his head, looked to Hilarion as if he taunted his captive with that, dared him to deny his saying.

The silver wires which had stood so erect and had rippled with force and energy now hung limp, with no life at all, about the pillar providing a thin veil for the prisoner within. And if Hilarion had any way to answer he did not.

For the first time a new thought crossed my mind. How was it that I so understood Zandur's speech? It was certainly not the tongue of the Old Race, even modified and changed as it was in Escore. Nor did it resemble that of the Sulcarmen. Why should it? This was another world—unless Zandur, too, was one who had passed through a gate.

Then it came to me that this was some magic of the machines. They must pick up the words he said, then translate them for us. The machines—what could they not do? I had been momentarily shaken from my plan by what happened here, but now I turned to it. The energy of the machines was linked to Hilarion. My need of it—

But time—I needed time! Zandur moved away from the dais, coming toward me. Luckily I had not altered my position. If I could deceive him into believing me still sleeping . . . even so small a deception should be to my advantage.

I closed my eyes. With most of the thrumming lights stilled I could hear the sound of footfalls drawing closer. Was he standing now to stare at me? Though I did not look to see, I thought that he was, and I waited tensely for some word to tell me that this was the end of what small freedom I still possessed.

But he did not speak, and, a moment later, I heard foot-falls again, this time receding. I counted fifty under my breath, and then another fifty to make sure. When I opened my eyes it was to find him gone. A single gray man sat at one bank of buttons, the screen before him alive. But, left to right, all others had been shut down. And, save for Ayllia, the prisoner in the pillar and myself, there was no one else in the chamber I could see.

Hilarion—no! To mind touch him with purpose would be to bring the very recognition I must be most careful to avoid. However, I did not quite know how to go about my search, except to conduct it as the mind quests which had once linked me with Kyllan and Kemoc when we were at a dis-tance from one another.

There are bands of communication which perhaps one can best visualize as bright ribbons laid horizontally edge to edge. To touch these is indeed a kind of search. My brother Kyllan had always been able to find those of animals and use them; but I had never sought any save the bands best known to those of my own craft.

Now I must range higher or lower and to do so took time, which perhaps I could ill spare. For the sake of a beginning point I chose the old one so well known to me, my brothers'.

I do not think I cried out. If I did the gray man at the one live bank of buttons did not turn his head to show that the cry alerted him. I had touched for an instant so clear and loud a call that I was shocked into relinquishing touch, even as I had when Hilarion's mind had earlier met mine.

Kyllan? Kemoc? Once before Kemoc had followed me into the terrors of an unknown world, far more alien to those of our heritage than this one. Had he been drawn after me again?

"Kemoc," I called.

"You—who are you?" The demand was so sharp that it rang in my head as loudly as if the words had been shouted in my ears, deafening my mind for an instant the way my ears could be dulled.

"Kaththea," I answered with the truth before I thought. "Kemoc—is that you?" and a part of me wanted *yes*, a part of me feared it. For, I thought, to have the burden for his safety laid on me once more was more than I could bear.

I was not answered now in words, rather did I seem to look, as through a window, into a room with rock walls, gloomy and dark. There was a stone bowl set on a pedestal. In that bowl blazed a handful of coals, giving limited light to that portion of the chamber immediately about it. Standing in that light was a woman. She wore the riding dress of the Old Race, breeches and jerkin of dark, dull green, and her hair was braided and netted tight to her head. At first I could not see her face: it was turned from me as she looked down into the fire. Then she turned around as if she could look through that window at me.

I saw her eyes widen, but her surprise could be no greater than mine.

"Jaelithe!"

My mother! But how—where? Years lay between our last meeting, when she had ridden forth to seek my father, vanished apparently from the sea. She had searched for him by a trail of magic in which all three of us had played a part, the first time we had been drawn into a formal use of our gift.

Time had not touched; she was the same then as now, though I was a woman and not the girl child. But I saw that she was not confused by the change, but knew me.

"Kaththea!" She took a step toward me, away from the brazier, lifted her hands as if across that strange space between us we might touch fingers. Then her face took on an urgent expression and she asked quickly: "Where are you?"

"I do not know. I came through a gate—"

She made a gesture with her raised hand as if to wave away unimportant things. "Yes. But now describe where you are!"

I did so, making as short a tale as I could. When I was done she gave a sigh which might be half of relief. "So much it

145

is to the good; we are in the same world at least. But now—
you searched with thought for us?"

"No, I did not know you were here." And I went on to
tell her what I must do.

"An adept who wrought a gate kept prisoner!" She looked
thoughtful. "It would seem, my daughter, that you have
stumbled by chance on that which may save us all. And your
plan of using the girl, that is well reasoned. But that you
need help from outside is also true. And we shall see what can
be done. Simon," she called with her mind, "come quickly!"
Then she turned her full attention to me again. "Let me see
this girl through your eyes—the room as well . . . ."

And I did for her what I would not do for Hilarion; I sur-
rendered my will so that her mind linked fast to mine and
I knew she viewed all I saw. I turned my head slowly from
side to side for her benefit.

"Are these Kolder?" I asked.

"No. But there is a likeness. I think that this world was
once close to the Kolder and something of their Power
spread to the other. But that is of no consequence now. I
know where lies the entrance to the burrow in which you
are. We shall come to you with what speed we can. Until
then, unless you are in great need, do not link. But if this
Zandur would work on you, as he has upon Hilarion, link
at once."

"Ayllia?"

"You have read rightly that she may be your key to freedom. But again we cannot use her as yet, not if we are to
have time. Above all, the adept is necessary. He knows the
gate; it was of his creation and will answer him. If we are
ever to return to Estcarp we must have that gate!"

Suddenly she smiled. "Time seems to have run more swiftly
for you, my daughter, than it has for us. Also, I appear to have
borne one who is as I wished for, a child of my spirit as well
as my body. Take you care, Kaththea, not to throw away
now, by some chance, that which will work to save us all.

Now I will break link, but you shall be in mind and if you have need, call at once!"

The window into that place of stone was gone. And I was left to wonder—how had my mother and father come here? For she had spoken to him as if he were some distance from her but no world away. Had he stumbled on another gate into this world, she following him thereafter? If so, it would seem that portal had been closed to their return.

That led me back to Hilarion. The gate he created must answer to him, my mother had said. Then we must free him in order to win back. But time—was time our friend or enemy? I fumbled in my cloak and drew out the packet of food I had taken from the gray men's supplies. It was a square of some dark brown substance which crumbled as I pinched it. I smelled the scrap I held in my fingers: a strange odor, not pleasant, not unpleasant. But it was the only sustenance I had to hand and I was hungry. I crunched it between my teeth. It was very dry and gritty, as if made of the ashy dust which covered the surface of this world. But I drank from one of the containers and swallowed it somehow. There was now only the need to wait, and waiting can be very hard.

XIII

BUT I could think and speculate. Time, my mother had said, ran less swiftly in this land than it had for us. It was true that in the mind picture she seemed no older than she had when she had ridden forth on that quest for my father. But then we three had been children not yet started upon our life paths. Now I felt immeasurably older than I had at that hour.

It would seem that she and my father, having once reached

this world, were imprisoned for lack of a gate. So her eager-ness concerning Hilarion. But if they dared to come to this pit, could they not also be sucked into the same net? It was in me to call a warning by mind link—until I remembered that she had spoken of knowing this place in which I was captive. If she did, then surely she also knew of the perils it had to offer.

I finished the food and drank sparingly. About me the pillars still blazed, the silvery strands continued to veil the adept's prison. Perhaps he slept.

But suddenly I caught slight movement on the dais where Ayllia lay. They had apparently put no bonds on her, no visible ones. Now she was rousing from whatever state of consciousness had held her for so long. She sat up slowly, turning her head, her eyes open. As I watched her closely I thought she did not seem wholly aware of her surroundings, but was still gripped in a daze, as she had been during our journey to the tower city.

She did not get to her feet, but rather began to crawl along the step on which she had lain. I watched the gray man on duty. He sat inert before his board, as if he could see nothing but the lights on the screen.

Ayllia reached the corner of the step, rounded that, began to crawl at a sluggish pace down the far side. In a moment or two she would be out of my sight. And perhaps out of reach when I needed her. I sent a thought command to halt. But if it touched her mind there was no answer. Now she was out of my sight on the far side of the dais.

Then I noted that one of the silver tendrils about the pillar stirred, enough to touch the one next to it to the right, and that to the next, and the next, before those, too, were hidden from my observation. That movement carried with it a suggestion of surreptitiousness, as if it must be hidden from any watcher. I could not remember whether there had been any movement of the tendrils before Ayllia's apparent waking, or if it had begun only when she moved. Was Hilarion put-ting into practice what I had earlier attempted, contacting the barbarian girl's mind and setting her under his orders to try a rescue attempt?

Two sides of the dais were hidden from me. The third I faced, where Ayllia had lain, and the fourth I could also see. But any advance along that would be in plain sight of the gray man. And he could hardly fail to notice if she passed directly before him.

I waited tensely to see her come into view. But she did not. The arch in the big screen was in my view; if she tried to leave through that I could see her. Then—then I must contact Jaelithe in spite of the danger lest my one possible aid be taken from me.

But Ayllia did not creep to that door. Instead there was another bright ripple of lights along the screen, followed by that sound which had earlier alerted the gray men to march. I saw the tendrils on the pillar stir and rise slowly, so slowly that watching them one had a feeling of a great weight of fatigue burdening each and every one of them.

Through the arch in the screen now marched a squad of the gray men, while from some point behind me came Zandur.

I did not have time to play asleep, it was too sudden. And I was frightened when I saw that the gray men marched straight for me, making a square about the lighted rods of my small prison.

Zandur approached more slowly, but he came to a stop directly before me, and stood as he had earlier before Hilarion, his hands on his hips, staring at me intently. Instinctively I had risen to my feet as the guards closed in. Now I met his gaze as steadily as I could.

It was not a duel of wills as it might have been with one of my own kind, as it had been with the adept, for we had no common meeting of Powers. But I was determined that he would not find me easy taking for his purposes. Yet I also waited before beaming a call to my mother, since I would not do that unless I had no other course.

Zandur appeared to come to a decision. He snapped the fingers of his right hand and one of the gray men crossed to

149

the other side of the dais, to return, pushing before him wha looked like a chest set upon one end. Down one side was a narrow panel of opaque substance, not unlike the screens, and this was put to face me.

Behind it Zandur stood and his fingers played across it surface, first hesitatingly, and then with an air of impatience as if he had expected an easy answer and had not received it. He said nothing, nor did the gray men even show interest in their master's action. Rather they simply stood around me as a guard fence.

Three times Zandur touched his panel. Then, the fourth time he did so, that opaque length came to life. Not with the rippling patterns of the screens but with a weak blue glow.

That color! It was—it was that of the rocks which spelled safety in Escore! To look upon it now was almost reassuring. I had a strange feeling that could I but lay my hand to the screen over which it crawled, I would be far more re- freshed than from the food I had just eaten.

But Zandur jerked his fingertips away from the block with a sharp exclamation. He might have been burnt where he expected no fire.

He hastened to press a new place. As the blue spread it also became darker. And I thought he must be focusing upon me some test of Power. For long moments he held fast until the color reached the top of the panel. There it remained steady, neither darkening nor lightening again. Zandur gave a nod of satisfaction and took away his finger. Straightaway the color disappeared.

"The same, and yet not the same." For the first time he spoke. He could have been addressing me, or only speaking his thoughts aloud, but in either case I saw no need to answer.

"You,"—he gave another wave of hand which sent one of his followers moving off the box—"what manner of thing are you?"

Manner of thing! It seemed that he now equated me with his machines. To him I was a thing, not a person. And I felt some of the rage which ignited Hilarion. Did Zandur only

ecognize force as coming from machines, and therefore see
us, because of what we held in us, as machines?

"I am Kaththea of the House of Tregarth," I made answer
with those words I could best summon to underline the fact
that perhaps I was even more human than himself.

He laughed. There was that in his scornful mirth which
ed my anger. But a warning alerted me within: *Do not let
him play upon your emotions, for in that way lies danger.
You must guard each step you take.* So I fell back upon the
discipline of the Wise Women and ordered myself to look
upon him objectively as they would have done. Perhaps it was
their old feeling that the male was the lesser creature which
now came to my aid. I had not accepted such a belief—I
could not when I knew my brothers and my father, all of
whom had a portion of my talents—but when such an idea
is held constantly before one, it is easy enough to accept it
as a pattern of life.

This was a man—at least one who had been a man. He
was not born to the Power, but must depend upon lifeless
machines to serve him as our minds and spirits served us.
Therefore, for all his trappings, he was not really one to
stand full equal to a witch out of Estcarp.

Yet there was Hilarion, an adept, who had fallen into Zandur's web. Yes, my mind rationalized swiftly, but Hilarion
had come here unprepared, had been entrapped before he
was truly aware of the danger. I—I could have safeguards.

"Kaththea of the House of Tregarth," he repeated as one
would mock a child by reiterating a simple statement. "I
now nothing of this Tregarth, be it country or clan. But
t would seem that you have that which I can use, once we
ix you even as we have this other—" He waved to Hilarion.

"And it is best for you, Kaththea of the House of Tregarth,
that you do as we would have you, since the penalty for
doing otherwise is not such as you would wish to face a
second time—though it is true you are a stubborn lot if you
re akin to this other."

I did not answer him; best not be drawn into any argument.

151

Many times is speech weakness, silence strength. I was sure
that Zandur could not read my mind without his machines
which I distrusted deeply. Thus I could plan and not be uncovered in that planning.

It would seem that his gray men did not need spoken orders,
perhaps he controlled them as I had tried with Ayllia. They
split into two parties and marched into the obscurity of the
chamber somewhere behind me. I did not turn to see them
go, not wishing to lose sight of their master.

He seated himself before one of the small boards, releasing
the chair to turn and face me. There was about him an air
of ease which to me spelled danger . . . . If he deemed me
so well in his control perhaps I had against me more than I
could imagine.

Ayllia? She had not come into sight at the far corner of
the dais, nor had she headed for the arch. Therefore she
must now be before Hilarion. And Zandur and a single gray
man, still in his own seat, were alone—for the moment.

I did not close my eyes in strict concentration, but at that
moment I aimed my call, seeing that I might have no better
moment for attack.

"Jaelithe—Simon!"

Instantly came their answer, full, strong—as if protecting
arms were about my shoulders, a shield moved to stand between me and sword point. There is an old tale that if one
with Power wishes to sever two who have caused tears and
heartache to one another for all eternity he or she shakes a
cloak between them. I could almost believe in that moment
that the cloak was before me, that I could see, feel it. Still
that sense of protection, though it continued to abide with
me, did not cloud my present purpose.

"What need you?" came my mother's quick question.

"To deal with Zandur—now!"

"Draw." She gave both consent and order in that word.

I drew because of my crippled need, and there flowed into
me such strength as I had not known since the days I walked
with Dinzil. All I had regained through Utta's teaching and

my own seeking was as a single pale candle's shine compared to the full sun of midday. And that power I pulled and shaped into a beam of command, seeking again my answer to Zandur.

"Ayllia!"

This time there was no failure: my command, my enveloping force swept into the barbarian girl. I filled her with my purpose, not daring in my extremity to remember I was doing this to a living person, for she was my only weapon for all our safety.

There were a few moments of strange disorientation when I looked through my own eyes at the lounging Zandur and the dais, but I also had another glimpse of the fore of the pillar as Ayllia must be seeing it.

Then I concentrated on that second seeing. I had never before ruled another so, save under carefully controlled experimentation in the Place of Silence when I was a novice. This was so dire a thing that one's spirit sickened as might one's body if put in a place where no human had a right to be. But I fought that sickness and kept my place in Ayllia.

At first her body answered me clumsily. It was as if I were one of the traveling puppet masters who used to come on harvest feast days to the manor markets—yet an inept one, as I handled the strings controlling the arms and legs awkwardly, making them slew in the wrong directions.

Still, I dared not be clumsy if I could help it. So I did not try to totter to my feet, but turned and crept as Ayllia herself had earlier crept, heading in the direction from which she had come. If I could so reach the same step where she had been I would be able to make my move at the right time.

Now I was no longer conscious of Jaelithe and Simon, only of the strong, ever-flowing current they gave to me. And I hurried faster, each passing breath of time giving me more control over Ayllia's body, though I did not try as yet to do more than take it back to the spot not far from Zandur.

I came to the far side of the dais, and along that to the

corner from which I could see Zandur in his chair still facing the four blazing rods which held—*me*.

Seldom is it given one to look upon one's self save in a mirror. And now when I tried it I had a sensation of dizziness, of whirling into some space which was neither here nor there, that I speedily averted my eyes and kept them fixed on Zandur.

Fear marched forward with every measure I gained. Why the master of this prison had not already turned to sight me I could not understand. It seemed to me that the generation of such energy as had brought me to this desperate move would touch him. It was almost as if an invisible line spun across the open air tying the me in the cage of light rods to the me who crawled in Ayllia's body.

At last I came to the place where Ayllia had lain when first I saw her. There I paused for some long breaths. If Zandur turned now and sighted me, I might still be safe. But if I proceeded, as now I must, to a point behind him, I had a long, or what seemed a very long space of open to cover—during which journey I would be instantly suspect if sighted.

He stood up and, involuntarily, I cringed. But he did not turn his head. He was instead looking into the depths of the chamber to a point beyond the cage of rods. There was a stir there as his gray men returned. Now he came to stand before the cage. Could he tell that I was not in my rightful body? I must depend upon the fact that he had none of the real gift, and things instantly visible to an adept would not be so to him.

Now I must dare my last move along the step, rising to my feet at last and running to a point directly behind him, willing all the way that he would not turn to see me. Now much would depend upon expert timing. I made my last impressions on Ayllia's sleeping mind. This must she do when the time came; I set that command as deeply and strongly as all the renewed strength I could call upon gave.

Then I returned to myself. Between my hands, ready, was the wand. The gray men had reached an area where I could see them without turning my head. They bore, some singly, some together, a number of objects. And these Zandur went to sort, sending some to one side of the dais, assembling the burdens of others closer to my cage.

Instinct told me that I would only have a few moments at the best, no more than a heartbeat or two at the least. And for that I must be ready. I waited. I could see Ayllia standing on the dais. Her eyes were open, fixed on mine, and a touch assured me that she was filled with the need to obey the last command I had left in her.

Zandur came to stand before me again.

"Now, my Kaththea of the House of Tregarth," he said mockingly, "and well do I call you mine, since you shall do my will from this hour forth. But be not downhearted at such a fate. Will you not now be one to live forever, knowing life as you have not been privileged to taste it before? No, you will have much to thank me for, once you have learned to accept my wisdom, Kaththea of the House of Tregarth."

He must have given one of those voiceless orders to his followers for they began to open boxes and casks and set out on the corner of the dais a gleaming circle, making it fast to that base.

It pleased, or amused Zandur to explain what they did for two reasons: to let me know there was no escape from what he planned for me, and to have an audience. Perhaps he had long gone lonely for one still sentient enough to match him in brain power, for it was plain to see that the gray men were no companions, rather servants and extra hands and legs for his use.

What they were doing was preparing a second pillar, this to encase me as Hilarion was held. And so encased I would add what Power I held, even as the adept did, to protection and renewing of Zandur's precious machines. He seemed almost to believe, as he talked, that once it was all explained to me I would indeed understand the justice and need for this action, and go docilely into the cage which would be far more permanent than the one which held me now, going so because I agreed that this was necessary.

The very ancient war between the towers and this place had existed so long as a way of life that he could not think of any other pattern. And aught which would make more secure his position was to be seized upon and incorporated in his defense. Thus I was another sword for his hand.

His followers worked with precision and no wasted motions, as if they were so much a part of the machines here that they needed little direction to the task. They had embedded the ring in the floor of the dais, and now they set certain small machines about it.

When they had done and stepped away, I made ready. They must release the force of my rod cage to free me from one trap before putting me in another. I would have seconds then to act. I tensed, ready, the wand now in my right hand. Yet I strove to give Zandur the impression of one cowed and easy to control.

Perhaps he thought speed best, to use surprise as a counter to any attempt at escape on my part. The glow from the rods flicked out without warning. Only I had been watching, was ready.

I did not try to leap away as he probably expected. Instead I hurled the wand and joyfully saw Ayllia catch it. Then, without hesitation, she turned and leaped up the last step to the top of the dais, dashing for Hilarion's pillar with the wand held point out, as she might hold a sword against a human enemy.

Perhaps Zandur was not aware at once of what I had done. Or he could have been so sure of his own defenses and safeguards that such cooperation between me and one he believed utterly useless came as a shock he did not at first absorb. I think that absolute control for so many centuries had given him such confidence in his own power to rule his world that he could not foresee nor understand what had happened.

The point of the wand struck the pillar. In that moment all the installations in the chamber went wild, as if some vast storm, such as the Wise Women working in concert could summon, burst upon our unsheltered heads.

Flashes of raw light which blinded and hurt the eyes, noise as might have been thunder multiplied a thousand times, swept down and held us. Smoke rose in acrid clouds to make a stinking fog.

I moved now, running for the arch in the wall screen. I heard Zandur shouting, saw gray men blundering here and there as light whips of raw energy struck at them. There were things I saw only briefly, marveled at afterward, when I remembered them. There were worms of fire crawling on the floor, or dropping from air to writhe with a semblance of living creatures. I leaped over one and reached the front of the dais.

"Ayllia!" With mind call I pulled her and she came stumbling down to me. I need not so summon that other; he was already running for the arch, free as he had not been for untold centuries. In his hand was the wand, which he used as a pointer, aiming with it to send those serpents of fire hither and thither behind us. Whether they attacked Zandur and his men I could not see, for the stifling smoke was a yellow fog to set one coughing, with streaming eyes, but they did build behind us a formidable rear guard.

Hilarion looked at me and I read in his eyes something of what he felt in his moment of triumph. With his free hand he gestured us on toward the opening through the big screen; there was an alert wariness about him which told me that we were far from rid of what Zandur might summon.

On the other side of the screen we met the first of these ranks of the gray men, in their hands fire tubes such as I had seen used by those who cut their way into the transports. I drew upon the tripled power within me and built an hallucination. It was hastily contructed, unfinished, but for the moment it served. Ayllia, by my side, took on the appearance of Zandur. Seeing him with us, the gray men did not loose their fire, but fell back to give us an open passage, down which we fled.

We came to a plate in the floor beneath the balcony and huddled on this at Hilarion's gesture. Once we were upon it, it rose under us, taking us to the higher level. None too soon, for the gray men had taken heart, or learned the deception, and were firing at where we had been only seconds earlier. As those fiery trails whipped back and forth under the rising plate, I saw smoke float out from behind the screen and heard the clamor of that storm Hilarion's freeing had induced.

"Well done, sorceress," For the first time he spoke. "But we are not free yet. Do not think that Zandur is one as easily handled as this girl you have so aptly used."

"I do not underrate any enemy," I told him. "But help comes—"

"So!" It appeared that with that I had startled him. "Then you did not come through the gate—you two—alone?"

"I am not alone." I made him an answer, but more than that I did not say. Hilarion was a key now as Ayllia had been the key earlier, and I did not trust him. Only with my mother and father to stand with me would I dare to set any demands on him . . . for the old question stirred and dwelt ever at the back of my mind: some of the adepts, many, had turned to the Shadow. Was Hilarion even faintly so tainted, though he might not have been wholly of the dark? I had believed in and trusted Dinzil, who had in turn seemed one with the Valley people, been accepted as friend by them. And yet he had proved in the end to be one with the enemy. So it would seem there were those on the other side of our war who could take on the semblance of light while they were truly of those choosing to walk in the great dark.

A common danger can make temporary allies of unfriends and this might be true here. Suppose Hilarion did return us through the gate he had created, enter with us into Escore, and then prove to be such a one as those there had to fear? No, we must be ever on our guard until we knew—and how could we learn?

XIV

WE faced now what seemed a solid wall, and I remembered how that had parted when I had been drawn here and closed behind me. How could we force our way out when this must be controlled by Zandur's machines, and we had not even the fire shooting weapons of his followers? It would not take them long to reach where we stood, and then we might be crisped to ashes with no escape.

But Hilarion had no doubts. He approached the wall, though I noticed how he moved stiffly, as if long imprisonment in the pillar had frozen his body. But even if his muscles obeyed him slowly, he had every confidence in his Power. As Ayllia had done he used the wand in a swordsman's move, laying its tip against that portion of the wall where we could see a fine line of division.

And I felt, though I did not add to it, the surge of will which emanated from him at that moment. From the tip of the wand leaped a blue spark which fastened to that line, sped down and up, running along it. There was a trembling through the floor on which we stood. Then the portal gave, very grudgingly, affording us only a narrow slit of passage. I pushed Ayllia through and followed myself, to have Hilarion bring up the rear.

We were in the dark passage through which I had groped with such care nights—days—earlier. In the narrow strip of light from the door I saw Hilarion aim the wand once more at the portal. Again blue light moved, and, as falteringly as it had opened, the door began to close. When a slit only the width of a finger remained, I saw a flash of blue, this time not aimed at the opening but along the floor, rising to run in the same fashion overhead.

"I do not believe they can force that too soon." There was satisfaction in his voice, but something else, such a spacing of words and slurring of them as I have heard in the voices of men who have been pushed very close to the edge of endurance in both body and spirit.

"Kaththea?" he called. I could not see him in the dark.

"I am here." I answered swiftly for it seemed to me that this was a call for either reassurance or aid. It astonished me greatly—unless the battle he had waged for his freedom, and incidently ours, had truly exhausted him.

"We. . . must . . . reach . . . the . . . surface—" The hesitation, the slurring were stronger. And I could now hear heaving breath, a rasping as a man might make after he had just climbed a steep rise at his best speed. I put out my hand, touched firm, warm flesh, and felt my fingers taken into a grasp which was not strong, but which held. Straightaway I sensed a draining from me into him.

"No!" I would have broken that hold but, weak as it seemed to be, there was no loosing of my fingers.

"Yes, and yes!" There was more energy in his denial. "My little sorceress, we are not yet out of this pit, and perhaps our first skirmish was the least of those to be faced. I must have what you can give me, as I do not think you could carry me if you would. Nor do you know the pitfalls herein as I do; remember I have been an unwilling part of them. I have been too many ages pent within that prison to be as able on my feet, or as fast as a master swordsman. You will give me what I need, if you truly wish to be free of Zandur."

"But the machines—the fires—" I drew upon what had happened in the chamber to add to my stubborn resistance.

"No worse hit than they have been many times before. There are fast methods of repair, and Zandur will have already put those into action. Remember, this place was made to wage war, such a war as I do not believe you have dreamed of, my lady sorceress. For it is not a war those of our blood have ever seen. This place has many defenses and most of them shall now be turned on us, as speedily as Zandur

can make the repairs to activate them. So give me of your
strength and let us hurry."

Then I, recalling that long descent which I had made,
wondered if we could reclimb it. Ayllia came willingly enough,
but as at first, she must be led. I did not try to control her
mind again.

"Let him have what he now needs," my mother's thought
rang in my head. "Feed, and we shall feed you! He speaks
the truth: time now marches, heavily armed, against us all!"

So I let my hand remain in his grasp as we went on down
that dark way, and felt the energy flow out, to be soaked up
by him as a sponge soaks up water. But into me came what
Jaelithe and Simon released to my aid, so that I was not
drained as I might well have been. Again I wondered whether,
had that not been so, Hilarion would have indeed plundered
me, and then what he would have done with Ayllia and
myself. My distrust of him grew the stronger.

We reached the foot of the long climb, but the adept did
not turn to the stair. Instead, in the half-light (for there was
no moon above, rather a clouded sky, very far away, gray
and forbidding), he again raised the wand, pointed it at
that part of the well which seemed to be cut by a half cap.

As slowly as the doorway had obeyed him, so did that
segment begin to descend, and I recognized it as the platform which ferried the vehicles up and down. But it moved
very slowly, and, though he said nothing, I knew that Hilarion
was disquieted. He turned his head now and then as if listening. I could hear a humming, feel a vibration such as I had
heard and felt in the tower. But of the clamor we had left
behind there was no whisper, nor could I hear anything moving after us. I was afire to be away, and would even have attempted the curve of the stair had not a dependence
upon the superior knowledge of Hilarion and the guess that
he chose now the best and easiest way, kept me where I
was.

The platform finally reached the bottom and we three
scrambled onto it. Then it began to rise again, this time

more swiftly than it had descended, and I felt a small relief. Once we were in the open we might be able to use the broken nature of the land as a cover for our escape—if we could cross the basin fast enough.

But we were not to reach the surface. We were still well below the point of possible leap or climb when the platform stopped. For a very short space I believed that halt only temporary. Then I saw Hilarion pointing his wand to the center of the surface beneath our feet. Only this time the spark of blue from its tip was gone before it touched. He tried again and the effort he made was visible. Yet the quickly dead flash did us no service. At last he turned to me.

"There is a choice left us," he said, his face expressionless. "And it is one I shall make. I advise you to do the same."

"That being?"

"Leap." He pointed into the well. "Better that than be taken alive."

"You can do nothing?"

"I told you, there are strong defenses here. We are now trapped, to await Zandur's pleasure as surely as if he had put his force fields about us. Leap now—before he does do just that!"

Having said this Hilarion moved to carry into action exactly what he had suggested. But I caught at him and such was the drain which exhausted him that, though he was the larger and normally stronger, he swayed in my hold and nearly fell, as if my touch had been enough to destroy his balance.

"No!" I shouted.

"I tell you yes! I will not be his thing again!"

But my call had already gone forth and I was answered.

"The help I promised—it comes," I told him, dragging him back to the center of the platform. "There are those who bring us aid."

Though at that moment I could not have told what manner of aid came with my parents; I only had confidence that they would have it to give.

"This is folly." His head dropped forward on his breast;

he lurched against me as if at that moment the last drop of his strength had run from him. I was borne to the floor under the limp weight of his body. So I sat there, Ayllia dropping down beside me, Hilarion resting against my arm and shoulder. And I stared up at the rim of the well, tantalizingly out of reach, waiting for the coming of the two who sought us.

What outer defenses Zandur might have I did not know, and I began to fear that perhaps they were too many for any quick rescue. It could well be that Hilarion would be proved right and his solution, grim though it was, was the better one. As my mother said, time was our enemy.

And time, as it has a way of doing in moments of great stress, walked or crept on leaden feet as I watched that rim and waited. I listened, too, for sounds from below. And I watched the wall in quick sideward glances to mark whether we might be descending on some order from Zandur. To lose what distance we had gained might mean we had lost all.

Then I marked movement above. I waited in fear to learn who or what leaned over there to view us. The light was less dim than it had been. Perhaps we had come here at dawn and the day now advanced. So I at last saw what dangled toward us from above, striking the wall with a sharp metallic clink that I longed to order to silence lest it alert some lurker below.

When it came a little lower I saw it was a chain ladder such as had been in use in the transport cavern. And, as it touched full upon the platform, my mother's mind send reached me.

"Up, and speedily!"

"Ayllia—" First I turned my mind control on her. She rose and went to the ladder without question, began to climb.

"Well enough!" my mother applauded. "Now, hold to the adept."

That I was already doing, but now I felt that inflow and outflow. This time it was not my own strength being so

163

drained, but that which came from the two aloft. Hilarion struggled out of my hold, got slowly to his feet.

"The ladder—" I guided him to it. But once his hands closed on it he took on new life and, as Ayllia, he climbed, steadily, if more slowly than my impatience wanted to see him go.

As soon as he was well above my head I put my own feet and hands to use. I could only trust that the chain would support the weight of the three of us at once, for Ayllia, though continuing to move, was still well below the rim.

"Hold well!" My mother's command came for the third time and I held. Now the ladder moved under me, not me over it, as if that tough but slender strand to which we all clung was being hoisted.

There sounded a grating noise from below. I looked down, startled, at the shadow which was the platform. Surely we were not ascending that swiftly? No, the platform was sinking, down into the depths where Zandur's forces doubt-lessly waited. We had left it just in time.

Up and up we went. I soon found it better not to look up, and surely not down, but to cling as tightly as I could to that swinging support and hope it would hold for time that was a measurement to lessen my fear. Thus it was that we came at last, one by one, into a gray and clouded day.

And for the first time in so long I looked upon those two from whose union I had come. My mother was as she had appeared in my mind picture, but Simon of Tregarth was so long lost in the past I had half forgotten him. He was there beside her, his head bare of helm, but about his shoulders the mail of Estcarp. He, too, had not aged beyond early middle life, yet there was a thin veil over his features which could be read as much weariness and endurance under great and punishing odds. He had the black hair of the Old Race, but his features were not the regular ones of inbreed-ing you saw in those men, being blunter, a little heavier. And his eyes were strange—to me—startling when he opened them wide to look intently upon one. As he did at me now.

It was a constrained meeting between the three of us. Though these were my mother and father, as a child I had never been close to either. Caught up as they had been in the duties of border guardians, they had spent little time with us. Then, too, our triple birth had prostrated our mother for a long time, and, Kemoc had once said, that had earned us our father's dislike. Therefore, while our mother lay fingering the final curtain, not sure whether or not she would lift it to go beyond, he had not been able to look upon us at all.

Anghart of the Falconers had been our mother by care, not Jaelithe Tregarth. So that now I felt strange and removed from these, not racing to open my heart and my arms to embrace them.

But it would seem that it was not in their minds to make such gestures either, or so I then thought. My father raised one hand in a kind of salute, which straightaway altered into a gesture beckoning us all on to where stood one of those crawling machines which I had seen moving toward the towers.

"In!" he urged us, stopping only to coil together the ladder and carry it over his shoulder as he shepherded us before him. There was a door gaping in the side of the box and we scrambled in.

The interior was indeed cramped quarters. My father slammed the door and pushed past us to take his seat at the front behind such a bank of levers as I had seen under the screens below. There was a second place to his right, and in that my mother settled. But she turned halfway around to face the three of us where we sat upon the floor.

"We must get away fast," she said. "Kaththea, and you, Hilarion, link with me. It will be necessary to maintain the best illusion we can lest we pull pursuit after us before we dare to turn and fight."

In the half-light of that small chamber I saw Hilarion nod. Then he gripped his wand by one end, allowed the other to touch the back of Jaelithe's seat. His left hand he put across Ayllia to me and I grasped it.

As we had linked, Simon, Jaelithe and I, so now did the four of us combine when my mother put the fingers of one hand on my father's arm. And our minds came together with one purpose, though for Hilarion and myself it was merely a lending of thought force to be molded and used by those other two as they saw best. I do not know what they wrought outside our crawling box, but at least no attack came. I guessed that perhaps they had chosen to produce a simulation of our machine headed in another direction.

There was a screen set before the two seats at the front, and on this appeared a picture of the basin over which we traveled, so that while the window slits were too narrow to see through, the outer world was thus made plain to us.

I had been so intent upon what lay before me when I had tracked Ayllia hither that I had not noted much of the country. But I could see on the screen the crunched tracks of the transports that had gone out from the well and returned to it. We soon veered from that course, heading at an angle over ground which was not so marked. Would we not then leave tracks doubly easy to follow? one part of my brain questioned as I bent my energy to supplying what was needed for the weaving of the hallucination.

My father had a reputation for being a wily and resourceful fighter, a leader of forlorn hopes which usually ended in success, as he had gone up against the Kolder to bring an end to them. One must have confidence now that he knew what he was doing, even though it seemed errant folly to the onlooker.

Ayllia had lapsed into the same sleep or loss of consciousness which had held her in the underground, lying inert between Hilarion and myself. The adept sat with his back against the wall of the cabin. His eyes were closed and there were signs of strain on his face, even as they were painted upon my father's. But his hold upon the wand, his grip on my hand, were firm and steady.

166

That we could depend upon his aid as long as we were in this haunted land I was certain, for failure would mean an even worse fate for him if we were taken. But what if he did activate the gate again and we won back into Escore? Could it be that his return would then bring upon my brothers and the people of the Valley such danger as they could not stand against?

I had no globe of crystal for foreseeing, nor had I Utta's board to summon the *possible* future—for no one can see the future exactly so and say this and this shall be. There are many factors which can change, so one can see a possible future and perhaps alter it thereafter by some action of one's own.

But I determined that I must speak in private with my mother, not trusting mind speech, which Hilarion could easily tap. And I would beg her aid and that of my father to make sure we did not bring new danger through the gate—always supposing that Hilarion *could* find and unlock it once more for us. I did not believe that I could find the place where we first burst into this world (unless by some concentration it could be traced by a mind search—such troublings of the fabric of time and space ought to leave a "scent" which the talented could perceive).

It was not an easy ride in that box, for once we crept from the basin there was a jolting, a slipping, a sickening up and down swing of the floor under us. Meanwhile, we were deafened by a throb which marked the life of the thing, and the acrid air of this world was rendered even worse to our nostrils by fumes which gathered in our close quarters. But all these discomforts we had to ignore, concentrating only on supplying the energy necessary to provide our flight with what cover we manage to maintain.

The screen now showed again those remnants of ancient buildings which ringed the basin. They were even more noticeable on this portion of the rim than they had been where I came in. Truly this must have been a city of such size that Kars or Es would have been swallowed up in one small district.

We followed a weaving path, keeping to what lower and clearer ground was visible. Our pace could not be any faster than a man's swift walk. I thought we might make a better escape if we trusted to our own feet and not to this stinking box which swayed and rumbled over the blasted ground.

Then, suddenly, we ground to a stop. And a moment later I saw what must have alerted my father, movement on the top of a crumbled wall. Not a man, no, but a black tube which now centered its open core upon us. My father stood on his seat, his boots planted firmly, his head and shoulders disappearing into an opening directly above. What he did there I could not guess, until fire crackled across the screen, struck full upon that tube. Under that lash of flame the tube was no longer black; it began to glow, first dull red, then brighter and brighter.

After that our weapon began a wide sweep over the ground from side to side as far as we could see on the screen. And it was several long minutes before my father settled back at the controls.

"Automatic weapon," he said. "No hallucination can confuse that. It was set, I think, to fire at any moving thing which did not answer some code."

In the world in which he was born my father had known such weapons, and it would seem that in this nightmare country he was fitted to conduct such an alien type of war.

"There are more?" asked my mother.

I heard my father laugh grimly. "Were there any around here we would know it by now. But that there are more between us and open land I do not doubt in the least."

On we crawled and now I watched the screen for the least hint of movement which would mark the alerting of another metal sentry. Two more we found and destroyed in a like manner, or rather my father so destroyed them. Then we left behind the traces of that forgotten city and crawled into the open country he sought, where that ashy ground was broken only here and there by the withered vegetation which seemed either dead or filled with loathsome life.

Our journey appeared to continue forever. And the cloudy sky began to darken. Also, I was hungry and thirsty, and the supplies which I had drawn upon in the caverns had been left behind in our dash for freedom.

At length we stopped and my mother shared out some sips of water and a dried meat with a bad smell. One could chew and swallow it, and hope it would mean strength and nourishment. My father leaned back in his seat, his hands resting on the edge of the control board, a gray tiredness in his face. Still he watched the screen as if there were never to be any relief from vigilance.

My mother spoke to Hilarion. "We seek your gate," she said straightly. "Can it be found?"

He had raised a water container to his lips; now he made a lengthy business of swallowing, as if he needed that extra time for thought or to make some decision. When he spoke he did not answer her but voiced a question of his own: "You are a Wise Woman?"

"Once, before I chose to take another path." She had turned as far as she could in her seat that she might see him the better.

"But you did not so lose what you had had." This time it was no question but a statement of fact.

"I gained more!" My mother's voice held pride and a kind of triumph.

"Being who you are," Hilarion continued deliberately, "you understand the nature of the gates."

"Yes—and I also know that you created the one we seek. Indeed, we have long been hunting you, having some small hint you were where you were. But they kept you lapped in something hostile to our seeking so we could not speak with you—until Kaththea reached you and so opened a channel of mind seeking between us. Having created the gate you can control it."

"Can I? That I shall not know until I try. Once I would

169

have said yes, but I have been warped by that which is alien to my own learning. Perhaps it has twisted me so askew that I cannot again summon the true Power to answer me."

"That rests on one side of the scales," agreed Jaelithe. "But we do not know what lies upon the other until we set to the weighing. You were truly adept or you would not have made the gate. That you have been a prisoner to other purposes is your bane; it need not be your end. Can you take us to your gate?"

His eyes dropped from hers to the wand, and he turned it about with the fingers of both hands, looking upon it as if he now held some new and totally strange thing he did not recognize.

"Even that," he said in a low voice, "I cannot be sure of now. But I know this much, that I cannot have a guide to follow if I remain in this machine: the taint of the other is too strong and able to warp what I would try."

"Yet if we leave it"—my father for the first time took part in that exchange—"we go out as men naked to a storm. This has defenses enough to provide us with a moving fortress."

"You asked me," Hilarion returned in sharp impatience, "and I have told you the truth. If you want your gate we must be away from this box and all it stands for!"

"Can you go forth a little," I began, "and do what must be done to find the direction, then return?"

Both my father and mother looked at Hilarion. He continued to slip the wand back and forth for a long moment of silence but at length he answered.

"There can be but a trial to see . . . ." There was such hesitation in his voice, such weariness there, that I thought that any seeking of that nature would be a task he must force himself to. Yet a moment later he asked, this time speaking directly to my father, "If you name this country safe as you can see it, there is no better time for my efforts. We cannot wait and hope and let Zandur loose his might on our tail. Also, those of the tower have their own brand of terror when dealing with aught walking the surface here. And since you travel in this thing which is of Zandur's people, their air scouts will be ready to use lightning against us if they sight it."

So it was that we came forth from the crawler into the darkening night and stood looking about us at the desolation which was the countryside here.

XV

THE bare bones of this land, which was all that was left, were stark under a night sky. And the moon, so bright and full when I had come into the basin, was now on the wane. Yet it gave enough light for us to see what was immediately about us. My father waved an order to stay where we were for the time being while he flitted—I can find no words to really describe his swift movements—blended with the landscape, spiraling away from the halted vehicle. And I realized that he now put into use the training of a border scout. He had disappeared when my mother spoke.

"There is no danger close by. Which way?" This she asked of Hilarion.

He lifted his head; I thought I almost saw his nostrils expand as might a hound's testing scent. Then he raised the wand, setting its tip to his forehead midpoint between his eyes, which were closed, as if he must see the better inwardly instead of outwardly.

The wand swung, pointing to the right from where we stood. When he opened his eyes again there was a spark of new life in them.

"That way!" So certain was his pronouncement that we did not doubt he had managed to find us a guide through this ash-strewn wilderness.

171

When my father returned, which he did shortly (I think in answer to some mind search call from my mother, not within my range), he studied the direction Hilarion's wand had indicated and then, within the crawler, made adjustments to the board of controls.

But we did not set out at once, taking rather a rest period, with one of us, turn about, on guard. I slept dreamlessly. When I awoke the moon had vanished, but so clouded was the sky that the light was that of dusk. Once more we ate and drank sparingly from our scanty stores. And my father said that he was sure that we had not been seen in any way, especially as the mechanical sentries of the crawler machine also registered naught.

We crept on, now following the path Hilarion had set us. But within the hour my father turned the nose of the machine abruptly and, at a rocking pace we had not used since we left the basin, sent it under a ledge, or at least most of it into that protection. There came a loud buzzing from the controls until he swept his hand down, hastily thumbing buttons and levers. The throb of life stilled, we sat in silence unable even to see much, for the screen now displayed only the bare rock of the crevice into which we were jammed.

My father's back was rigid and he did not turn to offer any explanation, only stared at the controls. I feared some danger he thought beyond his ability to counter. And I found myself listening, though for what I had no idea.

It was Hilarion who moved as if to ease his long body, cramped in the inadequate space beyond the still sleeping Ayllia.

"The tower people." He did not ask that as a question but made it a statement of fact.

"One of their flyers," agreed my father.

"This machine," Hilarion continued, "it answers you easily, yet she"—he pointed with his chin to my mother, not loosing his grip on the wand—"is of the Old Race and those love not machines. . . ."

"I am not of Estcarp," my father answered. "Gates upon

172

gates seem to tie worlds together. I entered through such a one into Estcarp. And in my own time and place I was a fighting man who used such machines—though not exactly like this one. We found this on the shore of the sea when first we came here through a gate which would not open to us again. And since then it has been our fortress.

"Only if you keep away from the towers," Hilarion commented. "For how long have you roamed so, hunting a gate to take you back?"

Simon shrugged. "The days we had numbered, but it would seem that time here does not march at the same pace as it does in Estcarp."

"How so?" Hilarion was surprised. How much more stunned would he be when he discovered just how many years had passed in Escore if or when we returned?

"I left a daughter who was a child," my father said, and he turned to smile directly at me, shyly, ill at ease, but somehow as a plea, "and now I face a grown woman who has gone her own way to some purpose."

Hilarion looked to me, more surprise in that glance, before he stared again at Simon and my mother.

Jaelithe nodded as if she were answering some unvoiced question.

"Kaththea is our daughter. Though we have long been apart. And"—now she spoke to me—"it would seem much has happened."

I must pick and choose my words well, I thought. To tell them of what had chanced in Estcarp and perhaps somewhat in Escore, that I could do. But while I distrusted Hilarion, and there was no chance to talk apart with my parents, I must speak with care.

Now I told them of what had chanced with the three of us after Jaelithe had gone seeking my father—of my own taking by the Wise Women and the years spent in the Place of Silence. Then of that last blow which the witches of Estcarp aimed at Karsten, and of how Kyllan and Kemoc had come to free me and of our escape into Escore. Thereafter I did not change the truth, I only told part of it—that we had come into a land which was also under the cloud of an ancient war, and that we had united there with those akin to us in spirit, though I mentioned no names or places.

My own misfortunes I dealt with as best I could, saying mainly that I had been ensorceled by one deceiving us and had headed back to Estcarp for treatment. Thereafter I spoke of the Vupsall and of the raiders, and lastly of how Ayllia and I had come to the citadel on the cape and of our passing through the gate.

I dared not use mind touch, even to let my mother know there was more which should be known between us. But something in her eyes as they met mine told me that she had guessed it was so and when opportunity arose we would speak of it.

Mostly I feared that Hilarion might be one to turn on me with questions of how Escore had fared since his leaving there. But strangely enough he did not. Then I began to see in that abstraction a suspicious silence, and I liked even less the thought of his return, though without him we could not go either.

When I had done my father sighed. "It would seem that indeed our carefully numbered days here are not to be trusted. So Karsten is now behind a barrier and the Wise Women brought themselves to naught in so building it. Who then rules?"

"Koris, by our last hearing, though he suffered an ill wound in the latter days of the war—so that he no longer carries Volt's ax."

"Volt's ax," my father repeated as one who remembers many things. "Volt's abiding place and the ax . . . . Those were brave days. Their like will not come again for us, I believe. But if Karsten lies low, what of Alizon?"

"It is said by those who have come to join Kyllan," I told him, "that Alizon, having seen what chanced with Karsten, walks small these days."

"Which will last only for years enough to match my fingers."

He held out his right hand. "And then they shall think big and begin to rattle swords out of sheaths again. Koris may rule, and well will he do so, but he can also do with old friends at his back or right hand. And if he holds not Volt's ax, he shall need them even more."

As well as if I could read his mind I knew my father's thought. Though he was not of the Old Race born, yet by will he had become one of them. And between him and Koris of Gorm there was a strong tie forged by blood and sweat during the struggle with the Kolder. He willed with all his might now to ride once more into Es City and be there at his friend's need.

"Yes," agreed my mother. "But before we ride west to Es, we must be in the same world."

So she summoned us back to the matter at hand. My father shook his head, not in denial, but as if to thrust away thoughts which were now a hindrance. Then he looked at the control board, seeming to read plainly there what was a puzzle in my sight.

He asked of Hilarion, "Have you any knowledge of how far we are from your gate?"

"This will tell." Hilarion spun the wand between his fingers. "We have yet some distance before us. And what of your flyer?"

"It is going." Once more my father's attention was for the board. "We can travel as soon as the alarm ceases."

It was indeed not long before the crawler backed out of the pocket in which my father had set it. Then it trundled on its way and all we saw was the unchanging bleakness of this world.

This was a place of dunes and hillocks and we were forced to pick a roundabout way among them; our view of what might lie ahead was thus foreshortened. But my father had other warnings built into this machine and upon those we depended.

It seemed long, that night during which we bumped along until our bodies were as one huge bruise, though in the seats my mother and father fared a little better. Then we pulled to another rest stop and Hilarion thereafter took my mother's seat, as the wand now showed that we were not too far from our goal. Jaelithe came to sit beside Ayllia. We had been able to dribble water into the girl's mouth, but she had not eaten since she and I had divided our supply in the corridor of the tower city, and I wondered how much longer she could exist. My mother reassured me that, remaining in this unconscious state as she had for so long, her body had less demands.

We lost the crawler up a ridge, teetered there for a minute, and began a downward slip. I heard my father give a shouted exclamation and saw his hands move quickly on the controls. The screen showed us what lay ahead—one of those black ribbon roads. And we were sliding straight for it as my father fought to halt our precipitous descent.

He managed to turn the blunt nose of the vehicle sharply left so we skidded to a stop pointing in that direction parallel to the road. I heard what I was sure was his sigh of relief as we came to rest without touching the pavement.

"What now?" But he might be asking that of someone or something beyond our own company.

"That way!" Hilarion squirmed impatiently in his seat, pointing the wand directly across the highway.

My father laughed harshly. "That takes some considering. We cannot cross in this—not and want it to be of service thereafter."

"Why?" Hilarion's impatience was stronger, as if, so close to the goal, he would not be gainsaid in making a straight line to reach it.

"Because that is no ordinary roadway," my father returned. "It is rather a force broadcast meant to keep the tower transports in motion. This tank was never designed to touch it. I do not know what will happen if we crawl out upon it, but I do not think that it would survive such a journey."

"Then what do we do? Seek a bridge?" demanded Hilarion.

"We have no promise any exists," my father answered

bleakly. "And to hunt a bypass or overpass may take us many leagues out of our way." He turned away from the screen to look directly to the adept. "Have you any knowledge of how close you now are to the gate site?"

"Perhaps a league, or less. . . ."

"There is a chance—" my father began hesitatingly, as if while he spoke he was measuring in his mind one ill against another and trying to assess which was the least. "We might perhaps use this tank as a bridge. But if it fails, and leaves us caught midway . . ." Now he shook his head a little.

"I think, Simon," my mother broke in, "that we have little choice. If we seek a way around there may be none, and we shall only be putting such a length of journey between us and the gate as will defeat us. If this half plan of yours has any merit at all, then we must prove it here and now."

He did not answer her at once, but sat looking to the screen as one studying a weighty problem. Then he said, "I can promise you no better odds than if you throw the tip-cones with Lothur."

My mother laughed. "Ah, but I have seen you do that very thing, Simon, and thereafter, having made your wager, take up two handfuls of round pieces from the board! Life is full of challenges and one may not sidestep even the worst of them, as we well know."

"Very well. I do not know the nature of this force but I think that it flows as a current. We must set the controls and hope for the best."

But there were more preparations for us to make. Under my father's orders, we climbed out of the crawler, taking Ayllia with us; and then we loaded into that small section where we had crouched as passengers, and into the seats in front, all the loose rocks we could gouge from the ground about us, setting such a weight in the interior as would give the vehicle some anchorage against any flow of force. My father brought forth the chain rope which had aided us out of the well. With that we made handholds on the flat roof of the crawler, taking with us what was left of our supplies and water. Once we were all atop, save for my father, he entered the cabin, crawling through the small space he had left for that purpose. Under us the machine came to life, edged back and around to once more face the road directly. It was partly upslope, tilted toward the black surface on which my father read such danger.

As it began to crawl and slide down again, my father swung out and up to join us. He had been right in his fore-boding. As the heavy vehicle rammed out onto that surface it was struck with an impact like the anger of a mighty river current, half turned from its course.

Would it be entirely turned, bearing us, as helpless prisoners on and on to the towers this road served? Or would the power my father had activated win across for us? I lay grasping the rope until its links bit painfully into my flesh, while under me the machine trembled and fought. It traveled at an angle to the right, but it still had not been sucked into the complete turn which would mean disaster. I could not be sure that we were still making any progress toward the other side.

We had already been swept on, well away from the point where we had entered. And what would happen if one of the transports for the towers came down upon us? So vivid was the picture of that in my mind that I fought to blank it out, and so perhaps missed the turning point of our battle.

I was suddenly aware of the fact that my father was no longer stretched flat beside me, but was on his knees freeing the packs of supplies. With a quick toss he hurled them both to his left so that, raising my head, I saw them strike the ground beyond the road, on the side we wished to reach. Then his hand gripped my shoulder tightly.

"Loose your hold!" he ordered. "When I give the word—jump!"

I could see no hope of success. But this was a time when one must place faith in another, and I struggled with my fear long enough to indeed loose my frantic hold and rise to my knees, then, with my father's hand drawing me up, to my feet. I glanced around to see my mother and Hilarion also standing, Ayllia between them, stirring as if awaking.

"Jump!"

I forced my unwilling body to that effort, not daring to think of what my landing beyond might mean. But luckily I struck on the edge of a dune of ash-sand and, while I sank well into it, I was uninjured, able to struggle out, spitting the stuff from between my lips, smearing it out of my eyes and nostrils.

By the time I was free of it and able to see, I marked other dust-covered figures arising from similiar mounds. And, as I stumbled toward them, I discovered we were no worse off than bruises, choked throats and grit-tormented eyes.

But the tank had now been turned wholly about, caught tight in the mid-current, and was fast disappearing from our sight, whirling on to the distant goal of the towers.

We slipped and slid back through the dunes to find and dig out the supply packs. Then Hilarion took out the wand which he had stowed in his tunic for safekeeping. Once more he held it to his forehead.

"There!" He pointed into the very heart of the dune country.

Ayllia was walking, though it was needful to hold her by the hand, and I knew my mother had taken over her mind to some extent. This was a burden on Jaelithe, so that I straight-away joined with her in that needful action.

Footing in the shifting ash-sand was very bad. Sometimes we waded in the powdery stuff almost knee-deep. And the dunes all looked so much alike that without Hilarion's wand we might have been lost as soon as we left the side of the road, to wander heedlessly.

But all at once I saw something tall and firm loom up and I recognized it as one of the metal pillars which I had seen when we entered through the gate. With that in sight part of my fears were lost. Only, would Hilarion really *know* when we reached the proper spot? There had been no marking on this side that I had been able to perceive.

However, our guide appeared to have no doubts at all. He led us in a twisting hard-to-travel path, but always he came back to the way the wand pointed. At last we stood at the base of another of those pitted pillars. I could not be sure, for there was a terrible sameness to this country, but I thought that we had indeed reached the place we had first entered.

"Here." Hilarion was certain. He faced what seemed to me merely air full of dust (for a breeze had arisen to blow up whirls of acrid powder).

"No marker," commented my father. But my mother, shielding her eyes with her hands half cupped about them, stared as intently ahead as the adept.

"There is something there," she conceded, "A troubling—"

Hilarion might not have heard her. He was using the wand in quick strokes, as an artist might paint a scene with a brush, moving it up and down and around, to outline a portal.

And in its track the dust in the wind (or was it dust? I could not be sure.) left faint lines in the air following the path of the wand tip. This outlined an oblong which was center crossed by two lines each of which ran from the two upper corners to the two lower ones. In the four spaces thus quartered off the wand tip was now setting symbols. Two of these I knew—or at least I knew ones like them, as if those I learned had somewhat changed shape in time.

The others were new however, as was the last, drawn larger to cross all the rest. When Hilarion dropped his wand we could see what he had wrought, misty and faint, yet remaining steadfast in spite of the rising wind and swirling sand.

Now he began again, retracing each and every part of that airborne drawing. This time that wispy series of lines glowed with color, green first, darkening into vivid blue—so that once again I saw the "safe" color I had known in Escore. But that color did not hold and before he had quite completed the entire pattern the first of it was fading, as a dying fire leaves gray-coated coals behind.

I saw his face and there was a grimness about it, a set to his mouth as you may see on a man facing odds which will try him to the dregs of his strength. Once more he began the tracing, with the color responding to the passing of his wand. A second time it faded into ashiness.

Then my mother moved. To me she held out one hand, to my father the other. So linked physically we linked minds also. And that energy which was born of our linking she sent to Hilarion so that he glanced at her once, startled, I think, and then raised the wand for the third time and began again that intricate tracery of line and symbol.

I could feel the pull upon my power, yet I held steady and gave of it as my mother demanded. This time I saw that there was no fading, the green-blue held, glowing the brighter. When Hilarion once more lowered his wand it was a brilliant, pulsating thing hanging in the air a foot or so above the sand. Around it the wind no longer blew, though elsewhere it spread a murky, dust-filled veil.

For a moment Hilarion surveyed his creation critically, I thought, as if he must make sure it was what he wanted, having no flaw. Then he took two steps forward, saying as he went, though he did not look back at us: "We must go—now!"

We broke linkage and my mother and I snatched up our packs, while my father gathered up Ayllia. Hilarion put wand tip to the midpoint of those crossed lines on the door, as one would set a key in a lock. And it opened—I saw him disappear through. I followed, my mother on my heels, my father behind us. Again was that terrible wrenching of space and time, and then I rolled across the hard stone of pavement and sat up, blinking with pain from a knock of my head against some immovable object.

I was resting with my back against the chair which had dominated the hall of the citadel. And the glow of the gate was the only bright thing in that room where time had gathered as a dusk.

Someone near me stirred; I turned my head a little. Hilarion stood there, his wand in his hands. But he was not looking toward the gate through which we had just come, rather from one side of the long hall to the other. I do not know what he had expected to see there, perhaps some multitude of guards or servitors, or members of his household. But what or who he missed, that emptiness had come as a shock.

His hand went to his forehead and he swayed a little. Then he began to walk away from the chair, back into the hall along the wall, walking as someone who must speedily find that which he sought or else face true fear.

As he went so I felt a lightening of my inner unease, for it was plain he had no thought of us now—he was caught in his own concerns. And what better chance would we have for a parting of the ways?

So, in spite of the wave of dizziness which made me sway and clutch at the arm of the chair, I somehow got to my feet, looking around eagerly for the rest of our party. My father was already standing, Ayllia lying before him. He stepped over her body to join hands with my mother, pulled her up to stand with his arms about her, the two of them so knit together that they might indeed be one body and spirit.

Something in the way they stood there, so enclosed for this moment in a world of their own, gave me pause. A chill wind blew for a single instant out of time, to make me shiver. I wondered what it would be like to have such a oneness with another. Kyllan—perhaps this is what he knew with Dahaun, and this was what Kemoc had found with Orsya. Had I unconsciously reached for it when I went to Dinzil, to discover in the end that what *he* wanted was not me, Kaththea the maid, but rather Kaththea the witch, to lend her power to his reaching ambition? And I also learned, looking upon those two and the world they held about them, that I was not enough of a witch to put the Power above

182

all else. Yet that might well be all which lay before me in this life.

There was no time for such seeking and searching of thought and spirit. We needed to be aware of the here and now, and take precautions accordingly. I stood away from the supporting chair to waver over to my parents.

XVI

"PLEASE—" I felt shy, an intruder, as I spoke softly, for I feared that my words might resound through that hall, perhaps awaken Hilarion from his preoccupation and bring him back too soon.

My mother turned her head to look at me. Perhaps there was that in my expression which held a warning, for I saw a new alertness in her eyes.

"You are afraid. Of what, my daughter?"

"Of Hilarion." I gave her the truth. Now I had my father's full attention as well. Though he still had his arm about my mother's shoulders his other hand went to his belt as if seeking a weapon hilt.

"Listen." I spoke in whispers, not daring to use mind touch—such might be as a gong in a place so steeped in sorcery.

"I told you part of the tale, but not all. Escore is rent, has long been rent by warring sorcery. Most of those who wrought this have either been swallowed up in the darkness they summoned, or else have gone through gates such as this into other times and places. But it was they who started this trouble in times far past, and upon them rests the blame for it. We do not know all concerning Hilarion. It is true that I do not believe him to a master of darkness, for he could not control the blue fire were he such. But there were those here who followed neither good nor ill, but had such

183

curiosity that they worked ill merely in search of new learning. Now we battle for the life of Escore . . . and I had a hand in reviving this old war when I unknowingly worked magic to trouble an uneasy old balance. Also, I did other damage and that not too long since. I will not have a third burden to bear, that I brought back one of the adepts to meddle and perhaps wreck all that my brothers and our sworn comrades have fought to hold.

"Hilarion knows far too much to be loosed here and taken to the Valley. I must learn more of him before we swear any shield oath for his company."

"We have a wise daughter," commented my mother. "Now tell us, and quickly, all you did not say before."

And that I did, leaving out nothing of my own part in Dinzil's plans and of what came of that. When I had done my mother nodded.

"Well can I understand why you find this Hilarion suspect. But . . ." Her face had a listening look, and I knew that she was using then a tendril of mind search to find him.

"So—" Her gaze from looking inward was turned outward and we had her attention again. "I do not think we need fear his concern with us, not for awhile. Time must be far different between this world and that other. Even more so than we had guessed. He seeks that which is so long gone even the years themselves have lost their names and places on the roll of history! Because he must believe this is so, he is now lost in his own need for understanding. Ah, it is a hard thing to see one's world swept away and lost, even while one still treads familiar earth. I wonder whether— Do you really believe, my daughter, that Hilarion can be so great a menace to what you must cherish?"

And I, remembering Dinzil, crushed down any doubts and said yes. But it would seem that my mother was not yet fully convinced. For, at that moment, she opened a mind send between us that I might read, though maybe only in part, what she had learned from Hilarion. And the pain and desolation of that sharing was such that I flinched in

body as well as mind, to cry out that I did not want to know
any more.

"You see," she said as she freed me, "he has his own
thoughts to occupy him now and those are not such as we
can easily disturb. If we would go—"

"Then let us do it now!" For in me arose such a desire to
be out of this place which was Hilarion's, and away from
all thought of him (if I could so close my mind on part of
the past), that I wanted to turn and run as if rasti or the
Gray Ones hunted behind.

But though we did go it was at a more sober pace, for
we still had Ayllia with us. I began to think about her and
what we would do with her. If the Vupsalls were still at the
village perhaps we could awaken her sleeping mind and leave
her nearby, maybe working some spell which would cloud
the immediate past so she would not remember our journeying,
save as a quickly fading dream. But if the raid had indeed put
an end to the tribe I saw nothing else but that we must take
her with us to the Valley wherein Dahaun and her people
would give her refuge.

My father left one of the packs of food and water where
it had fallen on the floor. But the other he shouldered,
letting my mother and myself lead Ayllia. So we went out
into the open. Then I, too, learned the surprises time can
deal: I had entered here in the coldest grasp of winter, but
I came out now into the warmth and sun of spring—the
month of Chrysalis, still too early for the sowing of fields,
and yet a time when the new blood and first joys of spring
stir in one, bringing a kind of restlessness and inner excitement. Still, to my reckoning, I had only been away days,
not weeks!

The snow, which had lain in pockets in this long deserted
place, was long since gone. And several times our passing
startled sunning lizards and small creatures, who either froze
to watch us with round and wary eyes, or disappeared in an
instant.

I was a little daunted by the maze of streets and ways

before us, for I could not clearly remember how we had found our path through the citadel. And after twice following a false opening which brought us up to a wall, I voiced my doubts aloud.

"No way out?" asked my father. "You came in without hindrance, did you not?"

"Yes, but I was drawn by the Power." I tried not to remember each and every part of how Ayllia and I had come here. Looking back it seemed that our road had been very easy to find from the time we entered twixt those outer gates where the carved guardians gave tongue in the wind. This sprawl of passages and lanes I did not recall.

"Contrived?" I asked that aloud.

We had come to a halt before that last wall when an opening which seemed very promising had abruptly closed. About us were those houses with the blue stones above their doors, their windows empty and gaping, and something about them to chill the heart as winter winds chill the body.

"Hallucination?" my father wondered. "Deliberate by bespelling?"

My mother closed her eyes, and I knew she was cautiously using mind seek. Now I ventured to follow her, fearing always to touch a cord uniting us to Hilarion.

My mind perceived, when I loosed it, what the eyes did not. Simon Tregarth was right, that a film of sorcery lay over this place, erecting walls where there were none, leaving open spaces which were really filled. It was as if, upon closing our eyes, we could see another city set over the one which stood there before. The why of it I did not know, for this was no new spell set for our confounding by Hilarion; it was very old, so that it was oddly tattered and worn near to the first threads of its weaving.

"I see!" I heard my father's sharp comment and knew that he in turn had come to use the other sight. "So . . . we go this way—" A strong hand caught mine, even as with my other I held to Ayllia, and on the other side of the Vupsall girl my mother walked. Thus linked we began to defeat the spell of the city, going with our eyes closed to the light and the day, our minds tuned to that other sense which was our talent.

So we came to a street which sloped to the thick outer wall, and that I recognized as the one up which we had come on our flight before the raiders. Twice I opened my eyes, merely to test the continuance of the confusion spell, and both times I faced, not an open street, but a wall or part of a house. I hastened to drop my lids again and depend upon the other seeing.

One without such a gift could not have won through that sorcery as we discovered when we came at last to the gate. For within an arm's length of escape lay a body stark upon the ground, arms outflung as if to grasp for the freedom the eyes could not see. He had been a tall man and he wore body armor, over which thick braids of hair lay, while a horned helm was rolled a little beyond. We could not see his face, and for that I was glad.

"Sulcar!" My father leaned over the corpse but did not touch it.

"I do not think so, or else not of the breed we know," Jaelithe returned. "Rather one of your sea rovers, Kaththea."

As to that I could not swear for my glimpses of them on the night they had come to Vupsall had been most limited. But I thought her right.

"He has been dead some time." My father stood away. "Perhaps he trailed you here Kaththea. It would seem that for him this trap worked."

But for us it failed and we passed through the wall, between the brazen beasts who would howl in the tempests. There we found signs that this was indeed a place others found awesome: set up was a stone slab, dragged, I thought, from the ruined village. And on it lay a tangle of things, perhaps once placed out in order and then despoiled by birds and beasts: a fur robe now stiff with driven sand and befouled by bird droppings, and plates of metal which might once have held food. Among all this was something my

187

father reached for with a cry of excitement, a hard ax and a sword. He had never been more than an indifferent swordsman, though he had put much practice into the learning of that weapon's usage, swords not being used in his own world. To a warrior, however, any weapon, when his hands are empty, is a find to be treasured.

"Dead man's weapon," he said as he belted on that blade. "You know what they say—take up a dead man's weapons and you take on perhaps also his battle anger when you draw it."

I remembered then how Kemoc, when he came to seek me in Dinzil's Dark Tower, had found a sword in the deep hidden places of a long vanished race and had taken it, to serve us well. And I thought that since a man's hand reached instinctively for steel, one had better judge it for good instead of ill.

But my mother had taken something else from that offering table and stood with it in her two hands, gazing down into it with almost a shade of awe on her face.

"These raiders plied their looting in odd places," she said. "Of such as this I have heard, but I have not seen. Well did they treasure it enough to offer it to the demons they believed dwelt here!"

It was a cup fashioned, I think, of stone, in the form of two hands tight pressed together save for an open space at the top. But they were not altogether human hands: the fingers were very long and thin; the nails, which were inlaid with gleaming metal, very narrow and pointed. In color it was red-brown, very smooth and polished.

"What is it?" My curiosity was aroused.

"A mirror for looking, to be used as one does a crystal globe. But into this one pours water. I do not know how it came to this place, but it is such a thing as must not remain here for— Touch it, Kaththea."

She held it forth and I laid fingertip to it, only to cry out. I had touched, not cold stone as I expected, but warmth, near to the heat of a live firebrand. Yet my mother held it

188

firmly and seemed not to feel that heat. Also from that light touch I felt an instant inflow of Power, so I knew it for one of the mighty things which could be as a weapon for us, even as the sword came naturally to my father's hold.

My mother pulled loose a wisp of tattered silk which also fluttered on the offering table and wrapped it about the cup, then she opened her tunic a little and stowed the bundle safely within. My father belted on the sword openly and also thrust the ax into that belt for good measure.

The finding of that pile of plunder outside the gates suggested one thing, that the raiders and not the village people had been the victors in that snowbound struggle. I was sure that the raiders had left this here; never had I seen the Vupsall willing to leave their treasures behind, save in the grave of Utta. Yet I must make sure Ayllia's people were gone before we left this place.

When I explained, my parents agreed. It was mid-morning now and the sun was warm, pleasantly so. As in the city, there were no pockets of snow left, and some early insects buzzed lazily; we heard the calls of mating birds.

Until we were well down the cape, setting foot on the mainland, I walked tensely, expecting at any moment to be contacted by Hilarion, to feel his summons, or his demand as to where we went and why. But now that we were back in the budding brush and in a world normal in sight and sound, a little of that strain ceased. I was still aware, however, that we might not be free of that companion I wanted least to see.

It was plain, when we scouted the village, that it was deserted, and not by the regular wandering of the tribe. The torn skins of the tent-roofs of those tumbled stone walls flapped here and there.

As scavengers in search of what we might find to make our journey westward easier, we went down into the ruins. I found the hut from which I had fled—when? Weeks, months earlier? To me that period was days only. The sea raiders had been here. Utta's chests had been dumped open on the floor, her herb packets torn, their contents mixed as if someone had stirred it into a perversely concocted mess.

My mother stooped to pick up a leaf, dry and brittle, here, a pinch of powder there, sniffing and discarding with a shake of her head. I looked for those rune rolls which had guided me to the citadel. But those were gone, perhaps snatched up as keys to some treasure. We did find, rolled into a far corner, a jar of the journey food of dried berries and smoked meat pressed together into hard cakes. And at the moment this meant more to us than any treasure.

Ayllia stood where we had left her by the outer door, nor did she seem to see what lay about her, or understand that we had returned to the village. My father went to hunt through the other tent-huts, but he was quickly back, motioning us to join him.

"A place of death," he told us bleakly. "One better left to them."

I had had no friends among the tribe, but rather had been their prisoner. Neither would I have willingly been their enemy, yet in part would these deaths always rest on my shoulders; they had trusted in my gift and I and it had failed them. My mother read my thoughts, and now her arm was about me as she said, "Not so, for you did not willfully deceive them, but did what you could to leave them to their own destiny. You were not Utta, nor could you be held to a choice which she forced upon you. Therefore, take not up a burden which is not yours. It is an ill of life for some that they feel blame lying upon them when it comes from an act of fate alone."

... Words which were meant to comfort and absolve and yet which, at that moment, were words only, though they did sink into my mind and later I remembered them.

We had no snow sleds with mighty hounds to drag them, nor real guide except that we knew what we sought lay to the west. But how many days' travel now lay between us and the Valley, and what number of dangers could lie in wait there was a guess I did not care to make as a challenge to fate.

I thought I could remember the way upriver and across country to the place of the hot stream. But my father shook his head when I outlined that journey, saying that if the hot stream valley was so well known to the nomads it was better we avoid it and instead strike directly west. This was thought best even though we could not make fast time on foot, especially with Ayllia, who walked to our control but must be cared for as a mindless, if biddable, child.

So we turned our backs upon the sea, and upon that cape with the citadel black and heavy between sea and sky when I gave a last glance northward to it. Our supplies were very few, the ill-tasting meat we had brought out of the ashy world, and the jar we had found in the village. At least there was no lack of water, for there were springs and streams throughout this land, all alive now in the spring, having thrown off their winter's coating of ice.

My father, picking up two rounded stones from the ground, fashioned an odd weapon such as I had never seen before, tying them together with a thong, and then swinging the whole about his head and letting it fly in practice at a bush. There it struck and with the weight of the stones the cord wove around and around, to strip small buds from the twigs. He laughed and went to unwind it.

"I haven't lost that skill, it seems," he said. And a few minutes later he sent the stones winging again, not at a bush, but at an unwary grass dweller, one of the plump jumpers which are so stupid they are easily undone. Before we stopped for the night he had four such, to be roasted over a fire and eaten with the appetite which comes when one has been on sparse and distasteful rations for too long.

The warmer air of the day was gone. But after we had eaten we did not stay by the fire in spite of its comfort. My father fed it a final armload of the sticks he had gathered, and then led us to a place he had already marked for our

191

night camp, well away from that beacon which might draw attention to our passing.

He had chosen a small copse where the winter storms had thrown down several trees, the largest landing so as to take several others with it and providing a mat of entangled limbs and trunks. In that he hacked out a nest, into which we crowded, pulling then a screen of brush down to give both roof and wall to our hiding place.

I wished we had some of the herbs from Utta's store, but those had been so intermingled by the raiders that I could not have sorted out what was needed most. So the spell barrier they might have given us was lost.

But my mother took from her belt a piece of metal which glowed blue, very faintly, when she passed her hands caressingly up and down its length. This she planted in the earth to give us a wan light. I knew it would blaze if any of the Shadow's kin prowled too near. But against the common beasts or perhaps even the raider and nomads, we had no defense which was not of our own eyes and ears. Thus we divided the night into three parts; I had the first watch while the others slept, so closely knit together that we touched body to body. And I grew stiff because I feared to move lest I rouse those who so badly needed their rest.

My eyes and ears were on guard and I tried to make my mind one with them, sending out short searching thoughts now and then—but only at rare intervals, since in this land such might be seized upon and used to our undoing. There were many sounds in the night, whimperings, stirrings. And at some my blood raced faster and I tensed, yet always did it come to me at testing that these were from creatures normal to the night, or the winds . . . .

And all the time I strove to battle down and away the desire to think of Hilarion and wonder what he did at this hour in that deserted pile which had once been the heart of his rulership. Was he still lost in his memories of a past time which he could never see again? Or had he risen above that blow, and drew now on his talents—to do what? He would not chance the gate again, of that I was sure: his long bond-age to Zandur had decided that.

Zandur . . . I turned eagerly, defensively, from those dangerous thoughts of Hilarion, to wondering what had chanced with Zandur. Had our ripping forth from his place of Power put far more strain on his machines than Hilarion believed, perhaps crippling his stronghold? We had expected him to follow us; he had not. Suppose he was left so weakened that the next time the tower people struck they would put an end to his underground refuge, finishing the imme-morial war that had caused a world of ashes and death.

But Zandur memory, too, might be an opening wedge for a searching by Hilarion, so I must put it from me. There remained the farther past, the Green Valley, Kyllan, Kemoc—I had been months out of Escore. Was the war still a stale-mate there? Or were those I cared for locked in some death struggle? I had regained my mind search in part—enough to reach them?

Excitement grew in me, so much so that I forgot where I was and what duty lay upon me. I closed my eyes, my ears, bowed my head upon my hands. Kemoc! In my mind I built his face, thin, gaunt, but strong. There—yes, it was there! And having it to hold, I reached beyond and beyond with my questing call.

"Kemoc!" Into that summons I put all the force I could build. "Kemoc!"

And—and there was an answer! Incredulous at first, then growing stronger. He heard—he was there! My faith had been right: no death wall stood between us.

"Where? Where?" his question beat into my mind until my head rolled back and forth and I strove to hold it steady in my hands.

"East—east—" I would have made more of that, but my head was not moving now with the struggle to mind send; it was shaking with a shaking of my whole body. Hands on my shoulders were so moving me, breaking by that contact my mind touch so that I opened my eyes with a cry of anger.

"Stupid!" My mother's voice was a cold whisper. I could not see her as more than a black bulk, but her punishing hold was still on me. "What have you done, girl?"

"Kemoc! I spoke with Kemoc!" And my anger was as hot as hers.

"Shouting out for any who listens," she returned. "Such seeking can bring the Shadow upon us. Because we have not sniffed out its traces here does not mean this land is clean. Have you not already told us so?"

She was right. Yet, I thought, I was right also, for with Kemoc knowing that I lived aid might come to us. And if some gathering of evil stood between us and the Valley we would be warned by those wishing us well. As I marshaled my reasons, she loosed the hold on me.

"Perhaps and perhaps," she said aloud. "But enough is enough. When you would do this again, speak to me, and together we may do more."

In that, too, she spoke what was right. But I could not put from me the exultation which had come with Kemoc's reply. For in the past, ever since I had shared in Dinzil's defeat, I had been severed from that which made one of three. As I had painfully relearned my skills from Utta it had been working alone. But to be again as I was—

"Will you ever be?" Again it was my mother's whisper, not her thought, to strike as a blow. "You have walked another road from which there may now be no returning. I demanded for you three what I thought would serve you best in the world into which you were born: for Kyllan the sword, for Kemoc the scroll, for you, my daughter, the Gift. But you shared in a way I had not foreseen. And perhaps it was worst for you—"

"No!" My denial was instant.

"Tell me that again in the future," was her ambiguous reply. "Now, my daughter, trouble us with no more sendings. We need rest this night."

Although it went sore against my impatient desires, I made her that promise. "No more—tonight."

Again I settled to scanning only the outer world, that of the night about us, until that hour when Jaelithe roused to take the watch and I willed myself resolutely into slumber.

Shortly after dawn my father awakened us all and we ate of the jar cakes. It was more chill than it had been the day before. Now there was a rime of frost on the branches about us.

Though my father had been much afield along the borders, my mother riding with him as seeress for the rangers, yet they had not gone afoot. Neither had I ever before this time traveled for any space in that fashion, for the nomads had made use of their sleds, walking and riding in turn when they were on a long trek. So now we all found this a slow method of covering the ground, one which wearied us more than we would have guessed before we began it. We tried to keep an even pace, slowed as we were by Ayllia.

The Vupsall girl would walk at our direction, just as she ate what we held to her lips, drank from the cup we gave her. But she went as one walking in her sleep. And I wondered if she had retreated so far from reality that she might never be whole again. As she now was we could not have left her with her people, even had we found them. They would have given her only death. Such as she were too much of a drag upon a wandering people. Utta had lasted so long only because of her gift, and Ausu, the chief's wife, because she had had a devoted servant to be her hands and feet.

XVII

SIMON TREGARTH had the skill of one who had long laid ambushes, or avoided those of the enemy, in the wild lands of the Karsten mountains. He scouted ahead, sometimes ordering us to remain in hiding until he had explored and then hand-signaling us on. I could not understand what had so aroused his suspicion, unless it was something in the very lay of the land, but I trusted in that suspicion as our safeguard.

We did not use mind touch because this was a haunted land. Twice my mother ordered us into hasty detours around places where her arts told of the lurking of the Shadow. One of these was a hillock on which stood a single monolith of stone, dusky red under the sun. No grass or shrubs grew there; the earth was hard and had a blackened look as if it might once have been burnt over. And the pinnacle itself, if one looked at it for more than an instant, flickered in outline, appeared to change shape. I averted my curious eyes quickly, knowing it was not well to see what might reform from that misty substance.

Our second detour nearly plunged us into disaster. It was caused by a spread of wood wherein the trees were leafless, not as might normally be because of the early season, but because the foliage had been replaced by yellowish lumps or excrescences with pinkish centers, sickening to behold. They might have been open sores eating the unwholesome flesh of the vegetation. One had a queasy feeling that not only were those trees deformed and loathsome, but that something crawled and crept in their shade, unable to issue forth into the sunlight, but waiting, with an ever ravening hunger, for the moment it might grow strong enough to leap.

To pass this ulcerous mass we had to strike south, and the wood proved then to be much wider than we had first suspected, with fingers of leprous vines and brush. It was like a beast, belly-down on the earth it contaminated, crawling ever forward by digging those fringe growths into the soil to drag its bulk along. At one point those holds were on the river bank and we halted there in perplexity.

We would either have to batter our way through them, a task we shrank from, or take to the water, unless we could negotiate a very narrow strip of gravel below the overhang of the bank. And with Ayllia to care for that would be far from easy.

Then sounds carrying over the water set us all to lying low on the earth of the upper bank, a thin screen of growth between us and the water below. I choked as a breeze blew toward me, passing over the tainted growth nearby—the stench nearly drove all the wholesome air from my lungs. Yet we had no chance to withdraw, for out on the far bank of the river came those whose voices carried, not with distinguishable words, but rather as a rise and fall of sound.

For a moment or two I believed them survivors of the village raid, as they were certainly of the same breed as the Vupsalls. But as the newcomers splashed into the shallows to fill their water bags, I did not recognize any face among them. And I noted that while their dress was generally the same, they wore a kind of brightly woven blanket folded into a narrow strip across one shoulder, rather than the cloaks of Utta's clan.

They were in no hurry to move on; in fact the women and children settled down, preparing to make a fire and set up their three-legged cooking pots. Some of the men pulled off their boots and took to the water, crying out as they felt its chill, but persevering, to spread a net among them and sweep it for water dwellers.

For the first time I felt Ayllia stir on her own and I turned quickly. That blankness of now expression was fading; her eyes focused with intelligence on that busy scene, and I saw recognition in them. She raised her head, and I feared that, though these newcomers were not Vupsalls, yet she knew some among them, and would call out for their attention. I tried to grasp her hand, but she twisted away, striking out at me, her blow landing on the side of my head to momentarily daze me. Then she was on her hands and knees, not trying to reach that party overstream, but scuttling away from them, as if she saw not friends but deadly enemies— which could well be with the many feuds in existence.

Had she merely headed back, away from the river's edge, all might still have been well. But in her blind haste she went west, straight for that nightmare growth. And we all knew that she must be stopped before she reached it.

My father threw himself in her direction and an outstretched hand managed to close vise-tight about her ankle, jerking her flat on her face. At least she did not cry out—perhaps her fear of the tribesmen was such that it kept her silent. But she curled around to attack her captor with teeth, nails, all the natural armament she possessed.

But what was worse than that fierce struggle (in which Simon was plainly winning the upper hand) was that the evil vines toward which their battling carried them began to stir. Not as if any wind had brushed them into motion, but as if they had serpents' awareness of what moved close by and were preparing to attack.

In that moment both my mother and I united in a blanketing mind send meant to subdue Ayllia, whose frantic struggles might not only betray us to those across the stream, but could carry her and my father into the grip of those vines now poised in the air as if about to strike.

Ayllia went limp as our mind bolt struck her deeply into bondage. My father lay an instant or two panting, half across her. But it was the vines which frightened me.

They, too, were studded with those loathsome bulbous knots. And now, as the stems set up a wild writhing, the bulbs cracked open. My mother cried out and rose to run forward, with me following.

We caught at whatever portion of the two bodies was the nearest, jerking them away from proximity to the vines. And we were none too soon, for at least one of the knots burst across, loosing in the air a stream of menacing motes. Luckily they did not float toward where we scrambled frantically to get out of range, but drifted to the ground under the writhing stems.

It seemed we had escaped some grave danger only to fall into another. There were sudden shouts from the river bank and I looked hastily around. The fishermen had dropped their net, were splashing toward us, steel in hand.

"Link!" My mother's command rang in my head. "Link—hallucinate!"

I do not know what manner of picture she had selected to give us cover, but what came out of our joining of Power was indeed enough to stop the tribesmen short in midstream, set their women and children screaming and running. Before my eyes, and I was one who was giving Power to raise that guise, my two conscious companions became monsters. Such was their being that I knew these mental pictures had not taken shape by any will of ours. Nor did I doubt that I, myself, must equal them in horror. Of us all only Ayllia, lying as if dead under my father's hands, remained in human seeming.

There was a sudden faltering, lasting only for a breath, in my mother. Her astonishment must have been equal to my own. She stood erect on two misshapen clawed feet, great taloned paws swaying menacingly, her demon's mask of a face turned upon those in the stream. And from her throat came a roar which was enough to crush eardrums.

Seeing her, the tribesmen broke and ran after their women-folk. And we were left, trying to avoid viewing one another.

"Break." My father pulled himself to his feet, stooped to swing Ayllia up over a horn-plated shoulder. "We have served our purpose—so break."

Break the illusion? But we had instinctively tried that as soon as the tribesmen ran. However, though we no longer fed the hallucination, it remained in force. The monster who had been Jaelithe turned slowly to stare at the hideous wood.

"It would seem," she mouthed between thick purple lips, "that we have wrought our spell too close to that which could twist and turn it to unsightly purpose. We did not achieve invisibility but went far too far in the opposite direction. Also, I do not see the means of breaking this yet—"

And in me then arose a sharp sword of fear to cut and thrust, so that I shivered and quailed. For once before I had worn the stigmata of the Shadow, and so harsh had been that burden that it had driven me to things I hated to remember. Kemoc, by his own blood, shed in mercy, had won me back then to human kind. But at first I had known terror and self-disgust. Were we doomed again to carry such befoulment?

"Let there be a time for shedding later," my father agreed. "I think we are better off the farther we get from this growing cesspool of vileness."

We trailed him down to the river wherein he boldly splashed. I thought that for now we need not fear the return of the tribe. The water rose about us, and in a way that was reassuring, as it is one of the fundamentals of the Power as opposed to the Shadow, that running water can, in itself, be used as a barrier to evil. I almost expected my monster-seeming to vanish as that current washed strongly about my warted and scaled skin. But it did not and we came ashore unopposed in the half-set camp of the tribe.

Seeing some of their packs lying there I became practical and went hunting, finding and filling a sack with what dried foodstuffs were spilled out and around. But my mother passed me, her horned and horrible head down and bent as if she sniffed a trail. At last her taloned paws rent open a tightly lashed basket, turning out dried herbs, which her long and filthy nails sorted until she scooped up a scant handful of twigs and leaves, dried and brittle.

We lingered no longer at the river, but turned westward again. Now my father did not scout ahead, relying on his monster-seeming to be a defense, carrying Ayllia, while we flanked him on either side. A strange and forbidding company we must have made if any of the tribe lurked in hiding to watch our going. I doubted that for even the great hounds had caught the contagion of their masters' panic and had joined in the rout.

"When it is safe"—my mother's words were almost as distorted as the new mouth which formed them—"I think that I have that which will return us to ourselves again."

"Good enough," was Simon's answer. "But let us have more distance traveled behind us first.

On this side of the river the country opened out into a mead-owlands. Perhaps these had once been farms, though we came across no signs of walling or any hint of buildings. But my belief that man had once lived here in peace and plenty was affirmed when we came to lines of trees. These were not the twisted, evil things of that terrible wood, but were flushed with the petals of early flowering, and they formed an orchard which had been planted so.

Some were dead, split by storm, battered by the years. But enough still flowered as a promise that life did continue. And life did, for birds nested among them in such numbers as to surprise, unless they depended upon early fruit to sustain them.

Just as that other wood had been a plague spot of evil, so here was a kind of benediction, as if this had been a source of good. I could smell the scent of herbs, faint but unmistakable. Whoever had once planted or tended this orchard had also set out here those growing things which were for healing and good. There were no blue stones of security set up, only a peace and wholesomeness to be felt.

And there we took our rest. While Ayllia slept, my mother brought out the cup made as clasped hands. Holding it in her talons, she turned her head slowly from side to side, until as one who sees a guide point directly ahead, she went down one of the lines of trees until she came to a dip in the ground. I went after her, drawn by the same elusive scent.

A spring bubbled in a basin which my two arms might have encircled. About it stood the first tender growing green ringed by small yellow flowers—those which in my childhood we had called "stareyes" and which are very frail and last but a day, but are the first blooms of spring.

My mother knelt and filled the cup half full from the spring. Carrying it with care, she returned to our temporary camp under the trees.

"A fire?" she asked my father.

His horned and fanged head swung from side to side. "Is it necessary?"

"Yes."

"So be it."

I was already gathering from under the dead trees their long shed branches, choosing those I knew would give forth sweet-smelling smoke, dry enough to burn quickly and brightly.

My father laid a small fire with care, and once done he put spark from his lighter box to it. At my mother's nod I fed to the rising flames some of those herbs she had taken from the tribe's packets.

Jaelithe leaned above the fire, holding the cup in her two hands. Now she stared into its depths. I saw the water it held cloud, darken, then serve as a background to throw into bright relief a picture. It was my father who stood in the depths of that cup, not as the monster who tended the fire, but as the man. I realized what we must do and joined my will to hers. Even so it was a struggle. Slowly that picture in the cup changed. It grew misshapen, monstrous, as we watched and willed. Finally it was completely the thing which had led us across the river.

When that was so my mother blew into the cup so that the picture was broken and only water remained, as clear as it had been at her first dipping. But when we raised our heads and tried to straighten the cramp in our shoulders, my father was again the man.

Then my mother passed the cup, not to me, but to my father. Though she looked at me somewhat ruefully, if such an expression could be read on the twisted countenance which was now hers, and she gave me an explanation: "He who is closest—"

I was already nodding. She was right—to my father would the mind picture be the sharpest now.

So in turn I lent my will to his, while she rested. But I was growing more and more tired, must force myself to the struggle. In the cup my mother slowly changed from a woman of great and stately beauty to monster, until we were sure it was safely done, and my father blew the demon mirrored on the water into nothingness.

"Rest," my mother then bade me, "for what is left we two shall do together, even as we gave you life in the beginning."

I lay back upon the ground, saw my mother and father lean above the cup, and knew that therein they would paint me as they had seen me. But we had been so long separated, was the "me" they would build there the "me" I myself would see in any mirror? It was an odd thought, a little disturbing. I looked away from where they wrought their spell, up into the flowering branches of the tree under which I rested. In me arose such a great desire to remain where I was, to lose all the burdens I had carried, that I yearned to remain here always at rest.

There was tingling along my body, yet I did not care. My eyes closed then and I think I slept. When I awoke the sun was far warmer and lay in slanting beams which told me that a goodly portion of the day must now be behind us. I wondered that we had not gone on.

But as I raised my head and looked along my body I saw that I had indeed returned to my proper guise. My mother sat with her back to the trunk of a tree, and my father lay prone, his head in her lap. He slept, I thought, but she was awake, her hand stroking his hair gently, smoothing it back from his forehead. She did not look at him, rather into the distance, though there was a smile on her lips which softened her usual stern expression—it was even tender, as if she remembered happy things.

In me awoke again that faint desolation, that sense of emptiness which had come before when I had witnessed the expression of their feeling for one another—as if I were one who looked into a warm and comfortable room from outside, where the dark of a chill night closed about me. I almost wanted to break that contentment which I read in my mother's face, say to her, *what of me, of ME? Kyllan has found one who is so to him, and Kemoc, also. But me*—I thought I had such in Dinzil. Is it true, what I learned from him, that any man who looks upon me sees only a tool to further his ambition? Must I turn my mind resolutely from such hopes and follow the narrow, sterile road of the Wise Women?

I sat up and my mother looked to me. I had indeed broken her dream, but not by my full will. Now her smile widened, reached also to me, in warmth.

"It is a thing to weaken one, such spelling. And this is a good place in which to renew body and spirit."

Then my father stirred also and sat up, yawning. "Well enough. But it is not good to dream away the whole day. We need to make more distance for what remains of the sun and light."

It seemed that our rest period had been good for Ayllia too, or else my mother had released her from the full mind block that she might not be so great a drag on us. She roused enough to walk after we had eaten a portion of the supplies we had taken from the tribe.

So we left that oasis of good in the old orchard. As I passed beneath the last of the flowering trees I broke off a twig, holding the blossom close to my nose so I could smell its fragrance, tucking it then into my hair that I might bear with me some of the peace and ancient joy of that place. Oddly enough, the fragrance, instead of growing less as the flowers wilted, became stronger, so that I might at last have laved my whole body in some perfume distilled from their substance.

Our camp that night was on the top of a small hill from which we could keep watch in all directions. We did not light any fire, but when the dark closed about us we could see a distant point of light which was a fire, or so Simon believed. And since it lay to the south he thought it might mark the camp of the tribe, though it was well away from the river; perhaps they had not returned there, even to gather up what they had abandoned in their flight.

Again we slept in turn. But this time I had the middle hours of the night. And when I was aroused by my mother to take that watch, I found it chill enough to keep my cloak tight about me. Ayllia lay a little beyond, and it was shortly after my mother had gone to sleep that I heard the barbarian girl stir. She was turning her head from side to side, muttering. And that mutter became whispered speech as I leaned closer to listen. What I heard was as much a warning of danger as if she had rung some manor alarm.

"West—to the evil wood—across the river south—west again—to the orchard—then west to a hillock among three such, but standing higher than the other two. West—to what they name the Green Valley—"

Three times she repeated it before she was silent. And I was left with the belief that she herself was not trying to memorize our route, but rather reported it to another. Reported it! To whom, and for what reason?

Her people had been killed or scattered and taken captive by the sea raiders, and I did not believe that any among them could evoke the mind send anyway. Her actions today had been those born in fear when she had seen the other tribe. Did they by chance have some seeress like Utta who had traced us thus? It could be true, but that was not the first and best answer I imagined.

Hilarion! He would not have tried to contact me, or my parents, knowing that any such contact, be it the most tenuous, would have been an instant warning. Then he would have had to try complete take-over. But Ayllia, by our standards, was a weakling, to be easily played upon by anyone learned in sorcery. Therefore he could reach out and work upon her—and now he was using her to keep track of us.

All my fears of what he might be or could do flooded back. But at the same time there was a weakness in me also, for I remembered that touch my mother had made for me, how I had tasted the terrible loneliness which had rent him as he understood what had happened to the world he had known and dreamed of returning to while he stood in Zandur's pillar.

I had never believed him actively evil, only one of those who, following a trail which interested them, could be ruthlessly self-centered, acting recklessly out of curiosity and confidence in themselves. So had he been once, and if he remained so, then he was a threat to what was being built here anew in Escore. If he could track us to the Green Valley . . . !

We could mind block Ayllia completely again. But if we did so she would be only an inert bundle, needing to be carried and constantly tended. And there surely lay many dangers ahead which would make such a captive our bane and perhaps even our deaths. We could abandon her, but that, too, was unthinkable. And the final decision was not mine but to be shared by the three of us.

During the rest of my hours of watch I listened, not only to the noises of the night, but to any sound from Ayllia. She slept untroubled, however.

When I roused my father to take the final watch I warned him of what I had heard, that he might be alert in turn, even though there was certainly little more that she could report.

In the morning we took council together. My mother was very thoughtful as she considered my ideas.

"I do not believe in a tribal seeress doing this," she said. "Your Utta must have been unique among those people. Hilarion *is* the more reasonable answer. Upon us may now rest an error in judgment for leaving him behind."

"But—" I protested.

"Yes, but and but and but. There are many ifs and buts to be faced in every lifetime and we can choose only what seems best at the moment when the choice is to be made. We have the Power, which makes us more than some, but we must be ever on the alert not to think that it makes us more than human. I think we dare not mind block her. It would render her too great a burden on us. Also, I would set no rearguard cover spell. Such can be as easily read as plain footprints in muddy earth by one like Hilarion. Better to let him think we suspect nothing while we plan ahead for a defense needed at our journey's end."

My father nodded. "As ever, you put it clearly, my witch

wife. Our first need is to cross this country to where we shall find friends. To be thought less than we are, not more, is a kind of defense in itself."

They were logical, right. Yet as we started on in the first daylight, I had a feeling that I must now and then look behind me, almost as if some barely perceptible shadow crept behind, always fluttering into hiding just upon my turning so that I never saw it, only sensed it was there.

XVIII

WE found no more sweet and sunlit spots such as the orchard; neither did we again chance upon a pool of vileness as the wood. Rather we journeyed over what might have been a land where man had never set foot before. A wild country, yet not too difficult to travel. And for two days we headed steadily west over this. Each night we listened also as Ayllia reported in whispers her account of that day's traveling, as if she had walked with a knowing mind and open eyes scout-trained to see. Nor when I urged that she be blocked did my parents agree, for fear of rendering her helpless that we could not transport her.

On the third day distant blue lines against the sky to the north and west broke into individual mountain peaks. And I was heartened, for by so much were we closer to a land I knew, at least in part. And perhaps I could, within this day's journeying or tomorrow's, pick out some landmark which would guide us into a land the Valley riders patrolled.

We surmounted a ridge at midday, to look down and away into a meadowland, though the grass was now a drab, winter-killed mat through which only a few spikes of early green stuff broke. But man had been here, for there were very old stone fences, so overborne by time that they were mere lines of tumbled rocks. Yet those lines in one direction marked out a road, and the road ended in piers water-washed by a languidly flowing river, some planted in the water, jagged stumps above its surface, and one on an island midway between the two shores.

But it was what occupied that island which froze us, startled and staring, on the ridge crest, until my father's fiercely hissed warning sent us down flat, no longer to be noted against the sky. What we had chanced upon was a sharp skirmish between two bands of sworn enemies.

On this side of the stream reared, pawed, galloped up and down, black keplians—those monsters with the seeming of horses that served the Sarn Riders. The Sarns—I had thought them all dead in the defeat of Dinzil, but it would seem that enough had survived to make up this troop at least—were human appearing, their hooded cloaks flapping about them. Padding along the margin of the water were the Gray Ones, pointing their man-wolf muzzles into the air as they slavered and screeched their hatred. But, as ever, running water kept them both from full attack. Not so the others of that Shadow pack. From the air shrieked the rus, those birds of ill omen, flying with talon and beak ready to harry the party on the island. And I saw, too, the troubling of the water as rasti swam in waves of furred and vicious bodies, struggling out into the jumble of rocks which was the only defense the island party had.

And running water did not hold others of that foul regiment. Well above its surface floated a swirl of yellowish vapor which did not travel fast, yet made purposefully for the island. Only the sharp crackle of the energy whips of the Green Riders on the island kept all these at bay. Yet perhaps what the forces of the Shadow fought for was only to hold until support came, since we could see movement on the ground at the other side of the river, an ingathering of more of the Sarn Riders and the Gray Ones. Behind those something else moved with intent, but was so covered by a flickering of the air that I could not truly see it. I believed it, however, to be one of the strong evils.

Once Kemoc and I had been so beseiged in a place of stones, with a monster force ringing us in. Then Kyllan and the Green People had broken through to our rescue. But here it would seem that some of the Green People themselves were at bay.

Kemoc! His name was on my lips but I did not cry it aloud, remembering that such a betrayal of my recognition might be caught by one of the Shadow and used as another weapon against the very one I would protect. Now I saw a boiling of water about the island and wondered if the Krogan, alienated as they had been, had also now come fully under the Dark Ones' banner.

My father had been surveying the scene below with critical measurement. He spoke now.

"It would seem wise to provide some diversion. But these are not Kolder, nor men—"

My mother's fingers moved in gestures I understood. She was not really counting those of the enemy between us and the river; rather she was in a manner testing them. Now she answered him.

"They do not suspect us, and among these there is knowledge of a sort, but they are not of the Masters, rather creatures born of meddling in pools of the Power. I do not know whether we will turn them by spelling, but one must try. An army . . . ?" And of those last two words she made a question.

"To begin with, yes," he decided.

She brought out of the fore of her tunic some of the herbs which she had used to break the counter spell of the monster-seeming while my father and I clawed loose the earth of the ridge about us. Using spittle from our mouths, we made of it small balls, into which Jaelithe pressed some of the bits of dried leaf and broken stem. When she had done so, she set them out in a line before us.

"Name them!" she ordered.

And my father did so, staring long and hard at each one as he spoke. Some of the names he uttered were ones I had heard:

"Otkell, Brendan, Dermont, Osboric."

And a great name that last was! Mangus Osberic had held Sulcar Keep and taken its walls and Kolder attackers with him when there was no hope of relief.

"Finnis . . ." On and on he spoke those names, some of Old Race Borderers, some of Sulcarmen, one or two of Falconers. And I knew that he so chose men who had stood beside him once, though now they were dead and so could not be harmed by our magic.

When he had done, and there were still some balls remaining, my mother took up the tale. The names she called sounded with a particular crackle in the air. Thus I knew she raised, not warriors, but Wise Women who had gone behind the final curtain.

She was done and a single ball remained unnamed. I was—possessed? No, not in reality, for another will did not enter into me to direct my hand or take over my brain, yet I did that which I had no forethought to do. My finger went out to the last ball and the name I gave it was not that of the dead, but of the living, and a name I would never have voiced had not that compulsion out of nowhere brought it to my lips.

"Hilarion!"

My mother sent a single direct and measuring glance. But she said naught, rather put then her force to the summoning, and my father and I joined with her. Then from the small seeds of soil, herbs and spittle, gathering form and solidity as they did rose, came the appearances of those named.

In that moment, they were so very real that even putting forth a hand one might feel firm flesh. And one could indeed die under the weapons they carried, ready for battle.

But that last seed, that which I had so intently named, did not bear fruit. And I had a fleeting wonder if it had been only my fear of him, perhaps a desire to think him dead and safely removed from us, which had led me to that act.

There was no time left for idle speculation as down from the ridge marched the army we had summoned, the warriors to the fore, behind them a half a dozen gray-robed women, each with her hands breast-high, holding so her witch jewel, in its way as great or greater a menace to the enemy that the steel the others bore.

So great was the hallucination that, had I not seen the spell in progress, I would have accepted the sudden appearance of a battle-ready force as fact. Yet that one ball of mud remained. I would have pinched it into nothingness but I discovered that I could not, so I left it lying as we four got to our feet to follow the army our wills commanded down the slope to the river.

I do not know which of those in the lines of beseigers first looked up to see us coming, but suddenly there was an outward surge, mainly of the Gray Ones leaping at us. Among them our warriors wreaked slaughter, though at first I thought that perhaps the enemy could sense they were not normal and meet them as illusions.

Now the Sarn Riders wheeled and rode, and from them sprang lance points of fire. Yet none of those at whom they aimed shriveled in the flames or fell in death. And as our warriors had met the Gray Ones, so did the Wise Women of the second line send forth beams from their jewels. These touching upon the head of keplian or rider appeared to cause madness so that keplian ran screaming, stopping now and then to rear and paw wildly, throwing riders who had not already been crazed by the touch of jewel beams.

Our advantage was a matter of time, as I knew well, and I struggled along with my parents to hold fast the flow of energy which fed our illusions. For, if we faltered or tired, they would fail. And soon we marched less quickly, and I felt drops of sweat gather on my forehead, to roll as tears of strain down my cheeks. But still I gave all I had to this task.

The regiment of illusions reached the river bank. Then the drifting swirls of mist floated back from the island toward us. These were in fact so insubstantial they were naught which could be hewed nor did the jewel beams appear to harm them, though they would swing away from any aimed at their centers.

And, if these were not enough, that curious "thing" we had seen advancing on the other side of the river was drawing closer. But the Sarn Riders and the Gray Ones on that side of the water made no attempt to cross and join the fighting here, nor even to reach the island. It could be they only waited to cut off retreat, leaving the strange thing to do the battling.

Suddenly my mother flung out her hand, and, as suddenly, my father was at her side, his arm about her shoulders, supporting her. I caught only the sidewash of that chaotic confusion which struck at us obliquely, so that my mother must have taken far more of its force. And I knew without being told that it was a blow from that flickering unseeable. However, if it had thought to contemptuously sweep us into nothingness by such tactics, it was soon to learn that we had more, or were more, than it expected.

Our illusionary troops did not fall dead, nor fade away; they simply ceased to be, as we withdrew that energy which gave them life and being in order to defend ourselves. Still, they had cleared a path to the river bank and those on the island were quick to take advantage of what relief we could offer them. I saw renthan arise from where they had lain, men swing onto their backs, energy whips lashing, to sweep the rest of the rasti away. Then, with great leaps through the water, they came to us.

Kemoc was well in the van, and sharing his mount was Orsya, her hair and pearly skin still water-sleeked. Behind them were six of the Green People, four men, two women.

"Mount!" My brother wheeled his renthan close, his order clear. I saw my father half throw Ayllia to one of the Green Riders, and then aid my mother to mount behind another.

I took the hand of one of the women and rose to sit behind her, seeing my father behind another.

The keplians and Gray Ones who had been so scattered by our illusions were not united to stand yet, and we rode southeast, keeping along the river bank. We rode knowing that behind us that flickering menace was coming, and, of all the enemy we had fronted this day, that was the most to be feared.

I glanced back, to see that it was out over the stream now—though it made that journey quickly, as if it cared little to cross running water. Then it was on the same bank. And how swiftly it might travel could mean the difference between life and death for us. We dared not halt again to make a new army, even if we could summon strength anew to call it into life.

I had never really known just how much speed the renthans could summon, but that day I learned, and it was such learning as I would not care to face a second time unless the need was very great. I only clung to the one who sat before me and centered all my determination on holding that seat, while I closed my eyes to the wild sight of the world flashing by so fast that it would seem we bestrode a flying thing which never touched hoof to solid earth.

Then we were running not over land but in the river's wash, and still east, away from our goal. With the water-covered gravel under them the renthan slowed, though they kept a pace the fastest horse of Estcarp could not have bettered. I dared not look behind again, for ever and anon something reached out at us, a kind of nibbling rather than a blow designed to bring us down. To me that insidious touch was worse that a sword cut. There was a tenacious spirit to it which meant that once it had set upon a chase nothing would turn it from the trail.

The renthan could not be tireless, and what would happen if they must mend their pace or were forced to rest?

Our river travel ended as suddenly as it had begun, the renthan having crossed the stream at a long angle, to come out on the opposite shore, miles from the island. Now they faced about to run west again. But there were long shadows lying across our path and sunset could not be too long ahead—and night was the time of the Shadow. It could then summon to our undoing creatures who never dared face the light of day. We must, I was sure, find some stronghold we could defend during the dark hours. And I only hoped that those with whom we rode had enough knowledge of this land to do so.

When the renthan came to a halt I was amazed, and could only believe that their energy had at last failed, to leave us in as great, or almost as great, a place of danger as we had fled. For we were now in the midst of open, level land, with dried grass brushing knee-high on our mounts. There was no sign of any outpost of the Light—no blue stones, not even such a memory of good as had hung in the orchard. We were in the open, naked to whatever attack our enemies might launch.

But the Green People slid down from the backs of their allies, and perforce we did the same. Then I saw the meeting of Kemoc and our parents. Kemoc stood as tall and straight as Simon, though he was more slender. And he looked my father eye to eye until he put forth both arms and my father caught them in the grip of the Borderer's greeting, drawing him close till their cheeks met, first right and then left. But to my mother Kemoc went down on one knee and bowed his head until she touched it, and he looked up, to have her make one of the signs upon his forehead in blessing.

"A good greeting at an ill time," said my father. "This seems a place in which we have no defenses." That was a half question.

"The moon is at full," my brother answered. "In this night we need light, for that which follows can twist dark to its own purposes."

But we had more than the moon to serve us. The Green People moved with the swift sureness which said that they had done this many times before, marking out a star upon

214

the ground by laying the fire of their whips accurately, a star large enough to shelter our whole party. Upon its points they set fires which were first kindled from twists of grass and then had planted in the heart of each a cube of gum as big as a man's clenched fist. This took fire but did not blaze fiercely nor was it quickly consumed; from it instead pillared a tall shaft of blue radiance, making us safe against evil.

So sheltered we ate and drank, and then we talked and there was much to say. Thus I learned that Kemoc and Kyllan had been flung by the force of the avalanche well to one side, and with them Valmund, but he had been sore injured. They had later found Raknar's crushed and broken body, but me they could not locate. And they had been forced away by a second avalanche which buried deeper that part they had frantically dug into. In the end they had returned to the Valley, but, as I had done, they clung to the hope that because of our bond they would have known of my death.

Thereafter, in the winter, matters grew more difficult for the Valley. Cold brought boldness to the evil things and they kept such a patrol about the borders of that part of the land the Green People and their allies had cleared, that each day saw some struggle or clash—as if the Shadow force planned to wear them down by such a constant keeping of alarms ringing them in. To my brothers this was the old way of Borderer life and they fell back easily into its pattern.

It appeared that those besieging them weakened with the coming of spring, however, and patrols from the Valley ventured farther and farther afield. Kemoc had been on one such mission when my mind touch reached him. And instantly he had ridden to seek us. We were well outside the influence of the Valley here and we must ride swift and hard to gain its shelter.

So had life been with him. Then we must add our own story, both separately and together, and this took time to tell, though we kept to the bare bones of fact. He was startled to hear of Hilarion and straightaway looked at me. I knew what moved in his mind, that he wondered if again we must arm ourselves against another Dinzil, and one perhaps ten times more powerful. And I could not say yes or no, for I had fear only, not proof.

By his side sat Orsya, also watching me. I flinched from her eyes remembering only too well how, tainted by Dinzil's teaching, I had once wished her so much ill. Could I ever be sure that she, too, could look at me and not see the past rise as a wall between us?

But when we would sleep at last, she came to me and in her hand she had a small flask, no longer than the smallest of her fingers. She unstoppered it with great care and held it close so that a delicate fragrance reached my nostrils.

"Sleep well, sister, and be sure that such dreams as may come will have nothing of the Dark rooted in them." I knew she was giving me of her own magic. And now she put fingertip to the vial and moistened it. With that moisture she wet my forehead, eyelids and, at last, my lips.

I thanked her and she smiled and shook her head, restoppering the vial with the same care. Then she gestured to Ayllia, who sat staring at nothing with unseeing eyes.

"This one needs a safe world for a while," Orsya commented. "She is not of our breed and what she has seen rests too heavy a burden on her. Once in the Valley Dahaun can bring her better healing than we can offer." She lifted her head higher and turned her face to meet a breeze out of the night.

There was no effluvia of evil in it, though it was chill. But in it was the hint of renewing life. Breathing deeply of that air, and doubtless helped by Orsya's cordial, I felt as one from whose shoulders a weight of burden was loosened.

I saw that most of our party was already at rest, the renthans kneeling to chew their cuds and think their thoughts, which are not those of my kind, but as meaningful. Orsya still sat between me and Ayllia, and now her hand came and we clasped fingers.

She looked at me searchingly. "It is better with you, my sister."

As if she had meant that as a question, I answered her with perhaps more firmness than I was inwardly sure was the truth. "It is well. My Powers have well nigh returned."

"Your Powers," she repeated. "If you have regained or found what you treasure, cherish it well, Kaththea."

I did not understand what she truly meant by that but, bidding her then good sleep in turn, I rolled in my cloak and sought that state myself.

If there was virtue in Orsya's fragrant liquid, it did not seem to work for me. For straightaway when I closed my eyes I was back on that ridge where we wrought in mud to raise our small army. Once more my finger touched that last ball and I uttered the name I did not want to say.

But this time those other small balls remained earth only, and he whom I so summoned arose—not as I had seen him last in his deserted and time-worn citadel, but rather as I had viewed him in that other dream, when he had sat upon his chair and looked at the gate he had opened.

He turned to look at me with something in his eyes that made me wish to turn away and quickly, only I could not.

"You have named me in the field of death." He did not speak those words but I read them mind to mind. "Do you then hold me in such fear—or dislike?"

I brought all the boldness I had into my answer, giving him the full truth. "I fear you, yes, for what you may do, being who and what you are. Your day is past in Escore; seek not to raise your banner here again."

As if my very thought conjured up what I feared the most, I saw then a banner form in the sky behind him. It was as yellow as the sunlight across gold sand, and on it were the wand and sword crossed.

"Raise not my banner," he repeated thoughtfully. "For you think my day done, do you, Kaththea, sorceress and witch maid? I lay no geas on you, for between us there must never be ruler or ruled. But this I foresee, that you shall wish for this banner, call for it in your need."

I marshaled my thoughts to drown out his, lest he influence

me. "I wish only that you keep your own place, Hilarion, and come not into ours. No ill will do I call upon you, for I think you are not one who has ever marched with the Shadow. Only let us go!"

Now he shook his head slowly. "I have no army, naught but myself. And you owe me a boon, since you death-named me. The balance will be equaled when the time comes."

Then I remembered no more, and the rest of the night I did sleep. I awoke with a vague foreboding that this day, new come to use, would be full of trial and danger. For the first hour or two after our leaving the star camp, though, it would seem I was wrong.

We rode steadily westward. Then renthan did not race as they had the day before, but they covered ground at an awesome pace, seeming not to feel the burden of their riders. Before long, however, we knew that if Sarn Riders and Gray Ones did not sniff behind us, that flickering thing did. And we also knew that it was more than matching our speed, though it labored to overtake us.

I saw the two Green Riders who formed our rear guard look now and then behind. When I did likewise I believed there was the flickering to be sighted far off. It also cast some influence ahead, slowing our thought, clouding our minds, and affecting even our bodies so that each gesture became a thing of effort. And under that drain the renthan, too, began to give way.

The sunshine which had seemed so bright was now a pale thing; there might have been a thin cloud between it and us. Cold gathered about our shivering bodies as if the Ice Dragon breathed, months after he had been driven to his den.

Our run became a trot, then a walk in which the renthan fought with great effort to achieve some of their former speed. Finally their leader, whom Kemoc rode, gave a loud bellow and they came to a halt as his thought reached us.

"We can do no more until this spell is lifted."

"Spell!" My mother's reply came quickly. "This is beyond

my skill. It is born of another kind of knowledge than I have dealt with."

Hearing this, the cold of my body was matched by the chill of inner fear. For she was one I believed stood ready to challenge and fight aught which walked this tormented land.

"Water magic I do have," Orsya said. "But it is no match for what hunts us now. Kemoc?"

He shook his head. "I have named great names and have been answered. But I know not what name can deal with this—"

And at that moment there came into my mind that I alone knew what—who—might face our pursuer. I had named him to death on that ridge, not understanding why. If I called him now it was to death—for the breath of that lay on us, and whoever faced it in battle must be mightier than any I had thought on. Even the Wise Women of Estcarp must work in concert for their great bespelling.

I could call. He would answer—and death would be the end. So did my fear tell me. To summon one to his death—what manner of woman could do that, knowing before that she did so?

Yet it was not my life I bargained for if I did this thing; it was the lives of those about me, together with what might well be the future of this land. So I slipped from the back of the renthan and I ran out from them, facing that thing we could not see.

As I went I called for help as one might who was lost: "Your banner—I summon—"

Why I framed my plea thus I could not tell. But I was answered by a flash of gold across the sky, seeming to bring with it a measure of the sun's warmth, which had so strangely gone from us. Under it Hilarion stood, not looking back to me, but facing the thing, with no bared sword but a wand in his hand.

He raised the wand as a warrior salutes with his blade before he gives the first stroke in a measured bout. Formal and exact was that salute, and also was it a challenge to that which came behind us.

But of the rest of that battle I saw nothing, for there was an increase of that flickering, vastly hurting to the eyes so I had to shield my sight or go blind. Only, though I could not look upon what chanced there, there was one thing I might do: what Hilarion had demanded of me as Zandur's prisoner, now did I give freely, and not for his asking. I allowed to flow to him all that was in my Power, emptying myself as I had not wanted to do since I regained what I had lost.

I think I fell to my knees, my hands pressed to my breast, but I was not really aware of anything but that draining and the need for giving. So did time pass without reckoning.

Then there was an end! I was empty with an emptiness which was deeper than the wound Dinzil had left in me. And I thought feebly that this was death, what death must be. But I had no fear, only the wish to be at peace forever.

But suddenly there was the warmth of hands on my shoulders and I was drawn up from where I crouched. Through that touch there flowed back into me life, though I did not want it now, knowing what I had done with my summons.

"Not so!"

Thus I was forced to open my eyes, not on the terrible blinding chaos I had thought, but to see who stood by me. And I knew that this was not one of Dinzil's breed, those who do not give, only take. Rather it was true that between *us* there was neither ruler nor ruled, only sharing. There was no need for words, or even thoughts—save a single small wonder quickly gone as to how I could have been so blind as to open the door to needless fear.

We walked together to those who had watched and waited. And the opener of gates so became a defender of life, while I had an ending to my part in the saga of Escore.

We wrought well together, and with our combined Power we rode and fought, and rid the land of the Shadow, driving it back and back. And when it crept away into holes and hiding places we used the Power to seal those. When most of the cleansing was done my parents rode for Estcarp, for it was there their hearts were bound. Yet between us roads would now be opened and our thoughts would also move faster than any messengers could hope to ride.

My brothers and their people came forth from the Valley to take up lands their swords had bought. But I looked out upon a many-walled citadel thrusting boldly into the sea. And out of the dust of years came a new awakening which was very rich and good.

CLASSICS OF GREAT SCIENCE-FICTION
from ACE BOOKS